Mercy
of the Moon

by

Jennifer Taylor

Rhythm of the Moon Series

Mercy of the Moon

Cover Art by *Angela Anderson*

The Wild Rose Press, Inc.
PO Box 708
Adams Basin, NY 14410-0708
Visit us at www.thewildrosepress.com

Publishing History
First English Tea Rose Edition, 2014
Print ISBN 978-1-62830-503-6
Digital ISBN 978-1-62830-504-3

Rhythm of the Moon Series

The door swung open,

and Mr. Pierce, the singer from the kirkyard, thrust himself into the room. He carried a body in his arms, covered in a cloak. Blue-tinged, slender feet dangled from the tattered, mud-soaked hem.

Samuel stared in slack-jawed shock and backed away. "Why have you brought this body here?"

To Maggie's astonishment, the body began convulsing in great spasms, and the singer struggled to hold it. The cloak fell off, revealing a shroud-wrapped body, only the face exposed. The eyes, ice blue, stared wide and unblinking and blank with terror.

Sarah's eyes. Her lips blue, dirt-encrusted eyelashes, cleft chin. "It cannot be," Maggie whispered, and shrank back. Coldness enveloped her, as if she had slipped into a frozen lake, cold water surrounding her, and could hear only muffled voices, echoing urgent and sharp. She saw only shapes above the icy water.

"Miss Maggie."

A voice, masculine and hoarse, broke through the ice, and she stared into the singer's eyes. They steadied and warmed, pulled her out of her daze.

"We must move her by the fire and rid her of this shroud," Ian urged.

She took a deep, shaky breath. Yes. It was Sarah, yet the eyes stared unseeing in a blue-mottled face covered in dirt.

Samuel's voice escalated in panic. "She was buried, she was dead. I saw her. How can this be?" He turned his head away.

Maggie grabbed him by the shoulders. "Samuel, you must look at her. Somehow it is our Sarah."

MERCY OF THE MOON
was
2nd place winner
in the
Historical Category
of the
2013 Lone Star Writing Competition.

Dedications

To Wayne, for his endless devotion and understanding.

~*~

To my beloved mother Gloria, who lets me be myself.

~*~

To Geoffrey, Leslie, and Emily,
who have shown me the fullness of life.

Acknowledgements

In the fourteenth century, nun and Christian mystic Julian of Norwich spoke these words in her work, *Revelations of Divine Love:* "All shall be well, and all shall be well, and all manner of things shall be well." I have respectfully borrowed variations of those words throughout my story. They have often been a source of comfort to me, and I thought they would do the same for my heroine, Maggie. I sincerely hope I have honored her by repeating her timeless words.

My profound thanks to Allison Byers for giving me the opportunity to tell my story, and editing it with calm expertise and kindness. I couldn't have asked for a better experience.

To the members of Romance Writers of America chapter, Sunshine State Romance Authors, for their support and guidance.

And finally, in gratitude for Inspiration across the Atlantic:

To Jo Kirkham for a bounty of endless knowledge, kindness, and patience, and to the Rye Castle Museum for a wealth of information.

To Judith Blincow, Proprietress of the Mermaid Inn, for her grace and generosity.

Chapter One

King's Harbour
England 1734

The sun sulked low in the sky as Maggie Wilson stood over her sister's grave in the kirkyard of St. Agnes the Virgin, the ancient church towering over her in judgment. Perhaps if she had not been away when Sarah had borne her child, she could have saved her. The midwife of the town of King's Harbour knew well that death all too often triumphed over valor. But must it be Sarah?

She endeavored to picture her lying under the dark earth, lifeless and cold, to face the reality she was gone, but could not fathom it. Yesterday her sister had been full of cheer as always, and yet only hours ago she had died and was buried hastily, and Maggie did not know why. But her grief did not matter just now, for Sarah's husband Samuel, daughter Ruthie, and their sickly newborn babe depended on her.

A gust of wind sent a shower of water from the trees overhead, splattering the top of her head. Wind picked up the edges of her cloak and whipped it around her legs. Sarah was gone. She must mourn alone and carry on.

At first she thought the wind cried. But a man's voice, singing of loss and sorrow, a plaintive cry knife-edged with rust, cut into her with cold desolation. She clenched her jaw and willed herself not to feel it. Searching into the twilight for the singer, she saw a figure shrouded in shadows, standing at the far end of the kirkyard, face turned to the clouds.

He sang on, silver notes of sorrow, otherworldly and heart-stopping. Against her will, the music seeped bone-deep, cold covering her like a winding sheet. She sank onto the grave, trying to gather Sarah to her to keep her safe. But she could not save her—she was gone. Harsh sobs racked Maggie's body. The control kept throughout the day broke apart like clods of newly dug earth.

She did not know how long she lay upon her sister's grave. She felt a hand on her shoulder and looked up into a man's face. It must be the singer, for no one else was about. He stood quite tall. His eyes, green like spring leaves dappled with sunlight, gleamed against the grey sky.

"Madam, I fear for your health. Are you able to rise?"

"I heard singing," she said. "And then..." She began to sob again, cursing her weakness.

The stranger helped her to her feet. As he bent down, the scent of cloves and oranges wafted from his cloak. The long fingers gripped her arm, warming the wet wool. Maggie gulped and struggled to control her sobs, standing and swaying, focusing on his face, his high, sunburnt forehead, slightly sunken cheeks with brown stubble visible in the muted light of dusk. Hair blew around his shoulders in tangled curls. He regarded the midwife with concern.

Between gasps of air she said, "I am quite all

right." Nothing could have prevented her from asking, "Why were you singing?"

"I was mourning my older brother, in my fashion. He was the town apothecary. I have come to King's Harbour to open the shop in his stead. My given name is Ian," he added without invitation.

She began to feel like herself again. "Daniel Pierce? He died from smallpox six months ago, and you are only mourning him now?"

He flinched. "I have just returned from the Orient. I was searching for herbs and medicines. And other things," he added, an odd, pained look passing over his face.

She glared at his fingers still gripping her arm. The warmth of them was a reminder her reputation would be in jeopardy if seen alone with him, yet they stood still as tombstones while the sky darkened with the coming of night. A red, jagged scar on the left side of his jaw curled toward his earlobe. As they stood there, he began to sing under his breath, the words unrecognizable. He gazed at her intently, Adam's apple moving in his muscular neck.

She jerked her arm from his grasp. "Why must you sing? There is no need for it. If it weren't for your damnable singing, I would not be losing my composure. And that is something I cannot afford to do." The tears came again against her will.

His eyes widened. "I am sorry for your grief. Was it your husband?"

"No, she was my sister and midwife partner."

He searched her face and smiled wanly. "I am sorry to have disturbed you."

"I must go and attend to the living." Maggie turned

away from him. The need to return to Sarah's family compelled her to hurry toward Church Square. What if the wet nurse had not yet arrived?

He followed her. "Then I will get you home as quickly as I can. It is nearly dark, and the Hawkhurst Gang might be lurking about even now. What kind of a man would I be to leave you to the smugglers' devices?" He took her arm, murmuring, "It's a shame there are no rickshaws—'twould be faster."

"I beg your pardon?"

He shook his head and smiled, a dimple appearing below his right eye. "Forgive me, I was just remembering."

What a peculiar man. "Your company is not necessary. I travel these streets day and night to deliver babies, and I've not been harmed yet," she said. "They leave Maggie Wilson, the work horse alone."

He halted. "Work horse?"

"Oh yes, so named by the men of the town, and it matters not. 'That Maggie,' they say, 'crippled and old at five and twenty, and if you marry her, your children will likely limp. But she works so hard you'll never have to.'"

He paused again, laughed and then coughed. "Work horse? Miss, I assure you—when I look at you, I do not see a horse. Oh, no indeed. Not with those eyes, grey like early dawn."

His long fingers warmed her arm against the wind.

"What I am does not matter," she said.

"Does it not?" Rain glistened upon his unbound hair. How careless of him to venture out in this weather without a hat.

"No," Maggie said. "My family is my only

concern."

She quickened her pace and pulled her cloak against the blast of wind from the English Channel. What had possessed her, to confess to this stranger what she had told no one else except for dear Sarah, engaging in idle conversation as if there was not a cottage full of grief and two motherless children to care for? Keeping them alive was the only thing she could do for Sarah now.

The trip home seemed interminable as they walked against the bitter sea wind.

"If I might ask, what happened to your sister?"

Must she be forced to say it aloud? "I do not know what happened, other than she died in childbirth while I delivered a babe in Winchelsea. Having been forced to spend the night there, I had only just disembarked on the ferry this afternoon to learn Sarah had already been buried."

His pressure increased upon her arm in comfort. "Had she been ill?"

"Other than a slight headache and swollen ankles, she had been in the best of spirits. I do not know why she was buried without the traditional mourning period."

"And you must find out what transpired," he added.

"Yes. I do not even know who delivered the baby."

As they turned onto Market Street, she slipped on a patch of grass that grew amidst the cobbles, the result of centuries' worth of grain-laden wagons on the way to market.

His hands steadied her at the waist. The heat of them braced her against the salt-tainted wind from the sea. Clove wafted from his cloak, and he stood, not letting go, and hummed a minor melody foreign to her ears.

She pulled away. "Thank you."

He nodded and sniffed. "I smell herring."

"Yes, yes. Of course you do." The wind from the Channel pummeled and forced her to raise her voice. "The rippiers selling fish are gone for the day, but the smell never leaves. We must give King George his fish." Why was she babbling about fish?

Conversation had shortened the distance. It would not be long now before she arrived at the cottage shared with sister and family. Maggie walked as rapidly as possible, her foot growing numb as it often did after a long stint of birthing; breech births were fraught with difficulty. She said a quick prayer of thanksgiving for the child delivered this morning.

She carried a daily reminder of her own breech birth, thanks to an incompetent midwife. According to her late grandmother, the midwife in her impatience pulled her out of the birth canal by the right foot, leaving her with a permanent limp and a tendency to stumble, especially when fatigued. But she got to where she needed to go and needed to get home quickly. Was Sarah's newborn still alive?

Lost in her own urgency and thoughts, she did not at first notice the man was humming again. She did not recognize the tune, but something about his voice warmed her like a foreign sun—how tired she must be to be so fanciful. Sarah was the fanciful one in the family.

They passed the Siren Inn, a favorite meeting place for the Hawkhurst Gang, a group of smugglers who terrorized the area. The roar of revelers overpowered the wind. A few sailors and townsmen hung about outside. Mr. Pierce exchanged sides to put himself between Maggie and the inn, encircling his arm around her shoulders protectively. She sidled away from him.

He cleared his throat. "I heard the smugglers killed again last eve."

"No, I did not know. Who was the unfortunate victim?"

"Jacob Morris. He was seen leaving the Siren Inn and found hours later with a knife in his back."

"He must have seen something he shouldn't have. Remaining invisible is the best way to survive. Even a child learns to keep a cautious eye out." She quickened her pace, listening for the owl hoots that the Hawkhurst Gang used as a way of communicating with one another.

They turned north at the docks. The frantic lapping of the ocean against the pilings echoed her anxiety at what might have transpired at home. She set her shoulders against the weight of all that needed to be done.

Finally, she stopped in front of Samuel's blacksmith shop. "Thank you for accompanying me."

"I am at your service. And once again, I am sorry for your loss."

"And I am sorry for yours as well," she said.

The leaf glow of his eyes carried a warm breath of spring toward her. He bowed and turned away.

Maggie passed through the entryway to Samuel's blacksmith shop and inhaled the acrid odor of smoke and horses' hooves. She felt her way across the length of the dim barn, dodging wagon wheels and bits of metal, and shuffling to alert the rats that burrowed in the straw-coated ground.

The cottage lay at the end of a well-worn path. She opened the heavy oak door to find a hearth fire roaring and illuminating Ruthie in a rocking chair, curled around the bundle in her arms. Setting her coat on the scarred trestle table beside the front window, Maggie removed her apron and cap and peered over Ruthie's shoulder.

"How is the baby?" She pulled down the top of the swaddling blanket.

"She is breathing dreadfully fast, Aunt Maggie, and holds her breath at times." Ruthie's pale blue eyes so like her mother's turned cloudy with worry, her plump cheeks flushed from the fire.

The midwife had seen this trouble before with the early babes, and despite the urgency of the situation, could not resist assessing Ruthie's innate and precocious skill. "And what do you do when she holds her breath?"

She folded her arms around the bundle, eyes alight. "I joggle her just a tiny bit, and she does…like so…" She took a breath, held it, and then blew it out.

She leaned down to kiss the little head, a slight smile upon her face. Her aunt marveled she had known instinctively what to do.

"You make a fine nurse for a mere lass of eight, my sweet," she crooned. "Your mother would be proud." She stroked Ruthie's dark curls.

The little lips quivered, and Maggie cursed herself. Could she not learn to think before speaking?

She blinked repeatedly. "It's windy out tonight. Is Mama cold, Aunt Maggie?"

Maggie lifted her and the baby and sat them on her lap in the rocking chair. "No, Ruthie. Your mother is with the angels now. She is warm and safe."

At that, the little girl fell apart, sobbing in her arms, bony shoulders shaking.

Maggie wiped her tears with the blanket her mother had spun for her and longed to join her in weeping, but it was up to her to remain strong. Besides, at the kirkyard, she had opened up the floodgates only to leave herself vulnerable to the familiarities of a stranger, allowing him to put his hands upon her, more than once.

Despite herself, Maggie sniffed her forearm, where a hint of clove and oranges lingered, warm like the stroke of his long fingers. She bolted upright, appalled.

Ruthie eventually ceased her crying and met the baby nose to nose, humming softly. She glanced up, eyes bright. "Oh! I coaxed Sissy to suck a bit from the bubby pot."

After Maggie had arrived from Winchelsea, before going to the kirkyard, she mashed together a mixture of bread soaked in ale as a substitute for mother's milk until the wet nurse could arrive. She then scooped the mixture into a bubby pot, which resembled a shallow gravy boat, covered with a piece of linen fastened on the narrow end acting as a nipple for the suckling baby. While far from ideal, this concoction saves many a babe from starvation.

"Oh, well done," Maggie exclaimed. "Hand over your sister now and have a bit of bread before you rest."

With exquisite gentleness, Ruthie placed the baby in her arms and slid off the chair. She sat at the table, poured herself a mug of milk from the pitcher, and then smeared blackberry preserves on a hunk of dark bread.

Maggie removed the swaddling in order to properly acquaint herself with Sarah's babe, who had yet to be named. The wee thing's body measured no longer than her forearm and the little bottom fit into her palm. She had the fine downy covering of hair she had seen before on babies born early. Truly, there was no earthly reason why she still drew breath. They could only attempt to feed her, keep her warm, and perhaps she would thrive. It all lay in the hands of God. And perhaps, Maggie mused, the new apothecary might have some exotic herbs to strengthen her.

The door slammed with the arrival of the wet nurse, Joannie O'Neal. She set a cloth-wrapped bundle on the table and swooped down on Ruthie.

"Hallo, sweet Ruthie. Me mum made you a mutton pie, fresh out of the oven."

Ruthie grunted as Joannie hugged her hard but followed her over to the hearth.

Joannie's joyous bellow jolted Maggie out of her stupor, and her heart eased a bit with the appearance of this buxom young mother of six. The midwife rose and stamped the numbness out of her foot.

"Joannie," she greeted. "You look healthy and robust."

Joannie rushed over, skirts bustling over ample hips, her broad face shiny and kind. "Aw, Miss Maggie, let's see the babe."

A fortnight ago, she had delivered her of healthy twins, and Providence had blessed her with an overabundance of milk. This had been one of the last deliveries Sarah and Maggie had attended together.

The baby's open eyes lay dark and small like

raisins in her tiny face.

"She's a wee thing, smaller than my Bertram," Joannie whispered. She took her, settled into the chair like a hen, and plopped a mammoth breast out of her dress. Ruthie leaned over the back of the chair, eyes wide as moons, mouth open.

"Don't fret," Joannie murmured. "I'll get the wee sweeting to suckle."

First she squeezed a bit of milk onto the baby's lips, which caused the little mite to smack them delicately. And then she positioned her nipple against the child's mouth. The babe instinctively turned toward it, tried mightily to latch on, but could not take hold. She screwed her tiny face up and creaked softly like a rusty hinge.

"Never fear," said Joannie. "The babe needs only to practice."

At that moment, Samuel trudged down the stairs from the bedchamber. He had the powerful chest of a blacksmith, muscular and broad. Oftentimes prone to her fanciful notions, Sarah used to say he looked as if he sprang from the earth like a tree trunk, all earthy browns and chestnut-colored eyes. Maggie had always laughed at her foolishness but could not help thinking that Sarah was more like the leaves, delicate and full of light.

But this evening he drooped as if his roots had died. She did not bother asking him if he had rested; the bloodshot eyes and grey shadows underneath bespoke volumes.

Ruthie said, "Father, are you well?"

He stopped, took a deep, ragged breath, and looked up. "Yes, my dear." He moved toward the baby and then recoiled at Joannie's bare bosom. "Erk," he muttered.

With no awareness of his discomfort, Joannie turned toward him. "Aw, Mr. Ackerson, 'tis a beautiful wee daughter you have here."

He backed away, a blush blooming under his two-day beard. "Er, thank you," he croaked.

Maggie mercifully draped a spare apron over her shoulder, hiding a smile. Men are puzzling animals, more than willing to peek at a woman's breast if given the opportunity. But confront them with a woman using her teat as nature intended, and they became as squeamish as a young maiden. To make matters worse, Samuel had just been reminded his child was being nursed by a woman not her mother.

She served the pie and poured Samuel and herself some ale, bringing a mug to Joannie. Samuel chewed absently, stone-faced, and eyes glazed.

To Maggie's great relief, a wet slurping sound issued from the little one. She was strong enough to nurse.

"Aw, that's the way of it, sweeting."

Samuel hung his head in his hands. After Joannie had left, they sat at the table, eating without tasting, lost in remembrances of Sarah.

Suddenly, a pounding on the door shattered the silence. They bolted from the table and rushed to the door. Maggie opened it cautiously. Who would disturb them on the eve of Sarah's death?

Jonas, the town's gravedigger, stepped over the threshold, wringing his hands, opening and closing his mouth convulsively. Rain dripped off his red, wizened face. "Miss Maggie," he gasped, "I was about my rounds...in the graveyard...the dogs..."

"Jonas," her voice rang out sharp above the din. "Jonas, speak sense."

"The dogs found her...that she had..."

"Found who?" She shut the door hurriedly lest the neighbors hear his caterwauling.

"Mistress Sarah," he screamed. "She has risen from the dead!"

Chapter Two

Samuel grabbed Jonas by the neck. "My Sarah is gone, God rest her soul. How dare you say such things in this house of mourning?"

"Samuel," Maggie said. "Release him."

Jonas howled, holding his throat. Samuel backed away, panting, hands fisted at his sides.

She slammed the door against the icy wind. "Jonas, have you lost your senses? Be still," she yelled above the cacophony of Jonas' wailing and Ruthie's sobbing.

The sexton pointed to the door. "She is coming. The apothecary, he brings her. I swear to you, she lives!"

Samuel surged forward. "Get out."

"I swear to you." Jonas squeaked, backing away from Samuel. "It is true."

The door swung open, and Mr. Pierce, the singer from the kirkyard, thrust himself into the room. He carried a body in his arms, covered in a cloak. Blue-tinged, slender feet dangled from the tattered, mud-soaked hem.

Samuel stared in slack-jawed shock and backed away. "Why have you brought this body here?"

To Maggie's astonishment, the body began convulsing in great spasms, and the singer struggled to hold it. The cloak fell off, revealing a shroud-wrapped body, only the face exposed. The eyes, ice blue, stared wide and unblinking and blank with terror.

Sarah's eyes. Her lips blue, dirt-encrusted eyelashes, cleft chin. "It cannot be," Maggie whispered, and shrank back. Coldness enveloped her, as if she had slipped into a frozen lake, cold water surrounding her, and could hear only muffled voices, echoing urgent and sharp. She saw only shapes above the icy water.

"Miss Maggie."

A voice, masculine and hoarse, broke through the ice, and she stared into the singer's eyes. They steadied and warmed, pulled her out of her daze.

"We must move her by the fire and rid her of this shroud," Ian urged.

She took a deep, shaky breath. Yes. It was Sarah, yet the eyes stared unseeing in a blue-mottled face covered in dirt.

Samuel's voice escalated in panic. "She was buried, she was dead. I saw her. How can this be?" He turned his head away.

Maggie grabbed him by the shoulders. "Samuel, you must look at her. Somehow it is our Sarah."

He stared. "Sweet Jesus." He reached a trembling hand out to touch her face. "Sarah?"

Eyes flat, no recognition.

"She does not know me." He thrust his arms out. "Give her to me."

Ian Pierce handed the writhing body over to Samuel and hurried to stoke the fire; Maggie made a pallet in front of the hearth. Jonas cowered at the door.

"Go away, Jonas. And tell no one," Maggie cautioned. "Samuel," she ordered. "Put Sarah on the pallet and fetch the scissors. We must rid her of the shroud—quickly. Good, now hold her steady."

Samuel held Sarah by the shoulders, his knuckles white. Ian grasped her legs as she thrashed from side to side. The winding sheet was caked with dirt, bits of gravel, dead leaves. Maggie's hands shook as she grasped the scissors, lifted the sheet away from her body at the neck and began to cut, quickly and carefully. A dank, earthy smell rose up from her body. Maggie fought to hold her bile down.

She grabbed both sides of the shroud and tore it to her waist down to her feet. As one, the men lifted her up, and she pulled the shroud out from under her, rolled it into a bundle and flung it into the fire.

Sarah wore a linen shift, sodden and bloodied where her legs met. Maggie covered her with a sheet, leaving only her face exposed to the air. Ian placed warm bricks wrapped in flannel around her body, tucking them by her feet and at her side.

She resisted the urge to pluck the soil and pebbles out of Sarah's blonde hair and instead wrapped it up in a cloth to be dealt with later. First they must bathe the stench of death from her. As she filled a basin with hot water from the blackened kettle by the fire, she spied Ruthie whimpering in the corner, poor lamb.

"Ruthie, bring me the French-milled soap. We must wash your mother."

Perhaps the child would cope with this crisis better if she could help. Samuel stared blankly into the fire, his grip on Sarah loosening. She realized with a sinking feeling he was too overwhelmed to be of any use.

Ian released his grip on Sarah and placed a hand on Samuel's shoulder. "My good man, I assure you that your wife will recover."

He cannot know that for sure, Maggie thought, but

something in the tone of his voice brought Samuel back to awareness, and he noticed Ian for the first time.

"Who are you? How did you come upon Sarah, there in the graveyard?"

"I am Ian Pierce, Daniel's brother and your new apothecary. I had returned to the graveyard tonight to mourn him and came upon Jonas. He had somehow discovered your wife was alive. And I brought her here."

Samuel nodded.

She handed him the warm rag. "Wash her."

With great tenderness Samuel washed his wife and upon feeling the warm, scented water, her agitation eased a bit. Still, her bloodshot eyes gazed wide and unseeing, and she did not know him. Bits of dirt swam in the pale blue orbs; her lashes were encrusted with dirt. Soil was caked in every orifice: her nostrils, her delicate ears, in the cleft of her chin. Maggie leaned over her chest to watch it rise and fall. Her breath issued in ragged gasps, hissing against her cheek and so foul it took every effort not to recoil. It smelled sour, with the metallic scent of old blood and an unidentifiable bitter odor.

Dirt smeared Sarah's teeth. The space between Maggie's eyes grew cold.

Dirt from the grave is in her mouth. How could this have happened?

"We must get the dirt out," she said.

"Yes," Ian said. "Turn her onto her side." He bent over her, quickly reaching his index finger into her mouth and removing the dirt. His finger emerged bloody. He lifted up her lip with great care. "She is missing a tooth."

17

"What? Sarah had all of her teeth." And a lovely smile she used often.

"It has been recently pulled, and badly executed."

"We must find out who has done this to her, but not now," Maggie said.

Ian resumed cleaning her mouth, dirt gathering on the pillow. After he finished, she seemed to breathe a bit easier. Had she swallowed the burial dirt? Once the dirt had been cleaned from her face, the webbing of veins stood stark against the pale blue pallor.

"She needs nourishment. Samuel, help me sit her up. Brace her from behind. Ruthie, fetch a cup of broth."

Ruthie skirted around her mother like a frightened horse, handing the broth to her, and retreating into a dark corner.

Maggie lifted a spoonful of broth to Sarah's mouth. It dribbled out of the side as her sightless eyes bore into hers.

She searched Ian's eyes. "How can my sister survive if she cannot take sustenance?"

"She must be more alert to eat, I think. I will bring some herbs over in the morning that will help to strengthen and calm her."

They lay her back down. Ian emptied and filled the basin with fresh water, while Maggie pulled the blanket down to her collarbones and resumed her examination and cleaning. Veins like snakes bulged and pounded in her white neck. Maggie cautioned Ian to look away as she cut the shift down the middle. She and Samuel removed it.

"Samuel, I know this is most improper. But I need Mr. Pierce's help." She looked to her brother-in-law for his permission, and he nodded. She covered her up again and threw the bloody shift into the fire.

The cold that rose from Sarah's body as Maggie cleaned sank into the midwife's bones despite the roaring fire. Skin mottled with blue stretched tightly over her collarbone, and a deep shuddering coursed through her body. She had stopped writhing, at least. She pulled one limp arm out of the blanket and washed her from shoulder to hand, wanting to immerse her in a full bathtub, but that would have to wait until she regained her senses. Would she?

She cleaned each finger one by one and saw the bits of shroud imbedded in her dusky fingernails. She must have tried to claw her way out of the grave. Maggie's throat pounded.

"It is no wonder she is senseless," Ian murmured, voice hoarse.

She glanced up. His eyes, jade now with flecks of gold, stilled her panic with a bright calm. She reached for Sarah's other tightly fisted hand, pried her fingers open and removed a small clay figurine. Maggie shoved it into her apron pocket. Sarah stirred. Her lower half needed attention, and it was no longer decent for the apothecary to be of assistance.

As if reading her thoughts, he said, "I will leave now and allow you to finish your ministrations." The fire reflected upon his face, accentuating the hollow cheeks and dark circles beneath his eyes. "But first I will stoke up the fire and replace the warming bricks."

Maggie nodded. "Thank you."

Samuel lifted his head. "I can never repay you for saving my wife. You are most welcome here, always."

Ian grasped Samuel's hand. "There is nothing to

repay. I only did what any decent man would do." He glanced at Maggie. "I will return tomorrow with the herbs I mentioned." He left as quietly as he came.

Maggie commissioned Samuel to empty and refill the water basin. She pulled the covers down to Sarah's waist. Would her breasts fill with milk? Of course she had never encountered this situation before and must consult the midwifery book; certainly Sarah could not feed the baby while senseless. Her sister needed sustenance, and soon.

She finished cleaning her top half and put her softest night rail over her head, gathering it at her waist until she was clean below. At least half of her smelled of rose-scented soap and not of the grave. She pulled the covers down to Sarah's feet. Samuel blanched at the dried blood on her inner thighs. She cleansed her privities as thoroughly as possible, checking carefully for any tearing or trauma that would indicate a difficult time during her labor.

It looked as if she'd had a normal birth, and she could not tell how much her sister had bled. Had she delivered the afterbirth? Maggie prayed she had, because if she had not, she would most assuredly die of childbed fever. She sent Samuel for more warm water and pressed Sarah's lower abdomen to feel for the afterbirth.

Without warning, Sarah stiffened and began to jerk spasmodically, torso rising as if pulled by an invisible force. Samuel dropped the basin of water. She tried to calm her, without success. She opened her eyes and hissed. The hair rose on the back of Maggie's neck.

Samuel gathered his wife in his arms, bent his head to her ear, and urged, "You are home, my heart. You are safe." He rocked her back and forth, crooning to the rhythm. "You are home, my heart. You are safe."

She grew quiet.

Maggie stared, open-mouthed. Why had she not thought of it before? Sarah had endured being buried alive, one of man's most primitive fears. She needed to feel safe, to be reminded she resided in the living world. Samuel's chanting seemed to calm her and perhaps made her feel safe.

Samuel continued to croon in his low, rumbling voice. "Do you know, my dear? Do you know? You have a daughter, a beautiful, tiny daughter."

She did not seem to recognize him, but it was enough that she closed her eyes and leaned against him, cheek against his broad chest.

The respite did not last. Sarah soon stiffened and returned to her open-eyed trance. Maggie urged Samuel to lay her back on the pallet so she might finish cleaning. Her legs, always slender, looked emaciated. She swallowed her alarm and soon finished her ministrations, piling every available quilt on her to stop the bone deep shuddering. It was encouraging her fingernails did not look as dusky, and her lips merely colorless instead of blue. Samuel stretched out beside her. He soon fell asleep, turned toward her, one arm under her neck, while she lay stiff, eyes wide and bloodshot.

Maggie shivered, poured herself a portion of whisky and gazed at the fire, thinking about what had transpired. The enormity of their situation assaulted her. Questions drifted in her head like flotsam from a shipwreck. What had happened at the birth? She felt the weight of the clay figure in her apron pocket and reached in to examine it.

How very odd! Although crudely wrought, it looked to be the figure of an old woman with a hawk nose and fierce expression, her back bent with age. A snake coiled on top of her head.

She could swear it hissed and grew warm in her hands. She flung it into the fire and gulped her whisky to quell the chills that skittered up her backbone. Where had this strange object come from?

The whisky soon soothed her, and rational thought returned. Surely it was due to lack of sleep and the traumatic day that it seemed to heat in her hands. Her imagination had gotten the better of her. There were more important questions that needed to be answered: Who had attended Sarah and declared her dead? Why had she been buried so precipitously? Who could have done this to her, and why?

The fire popped and hissed, and the sound of Samuel's steady breathing lulled Maggie into a fitful sleep. She awoke with a start and became aware her clothing stuck uncomfortably to her skin and belatedly realized that earlier, Samuel had soaked her when he dropped the basin in response to Sarah's eerie hissing.

She rose and removed overskirt and then wool stockings, the feel of the fire on her bare, damp legs pleasant and foreign. She glanced at Samuel to ascertain he was still asleep, removed her waistcoat, and stripped to her shift, hanging the clothes on a hook by the fire to dry. The warmth of the fire through the shift on her damp skin raised bumps on her thighs, tingling with a fine thrill of shivers.

She took the pins from her hair and let it cascade down her back. Her legs thrummed with fatigue, and her bad foot throbbed heavily with every heartbeat. She desperately needed more sleep, for she had lost all ability to think coherently, with no comprehension of what to do next.

The impossible had happened. Sarah was alive but seemed to be halfway between death and a dream. It was up to her to return her to the world of the living, but how? She felt alone in her cares. She stretched her arms toward the ceiling and inhaled deeply, trying to breathe in clarity.

Lost in thought, she did not hear the door open but felt a draft of cold air upon her nearly bare back. She turned. Ian stood frozen by the door, one hand holding a bundle of herbs, the other crossed at his chest, long fingers drumming a rhythm. And all the while, he stared at her as if transfixed.

"Whatever are you doing here?" She hissed. "Why have you come in unannounced? How long have you been standing there, watching me?"

He gazed at her, a smile like sun on sea lighting the hollows of his cheeks and raising the corners of his mouth. "I am sorry, Mistress Maggie, but I did knock— softly. I did not want to wake anyone."

She followed the path of his eyes upon her, starting with her eyes, then resting languidly on her mouth. His gaze glided to shoulders, arms, one to the other. She felt his eyes burn through the thin linen cloth of her shift. Her nipples tightened in response. Her heart beat at the base of her throat. A slow trickle of honey spread throughout her center. She could not escape those eyes, that green glow, as they followed the rise and fall of her belly and swept to her bare legs.

"I did say I'd return." He met her gaze and closed

the gap between them, holding out the bundle of herbs tied with raffia.

"Could you not have waited until morning?"

When she did not take the herbs, he put the bundle in her hand, wrapping his fingers round, and covering it with his own. Every bone in her hand felt lit from within.

"Ah, but you see, it is morning."

She raised her eyebrows. "It is still dark out."

He closed the gap between them. "But past midnight." His breath swept over her shoulders like a zephyr.

She stepped backward, faltering. Maggie the workhorse never felt this...alive. He caught her at the waist and steadied her. She smelled the sharp tang of orange and tasted saltwater on her lips. Each of his long fingers pulsed with heat through her thin fabric. Warmth flowed to her secret place as he slid his hands down the curve of her hips, fingers whispering across her thighs, spreading his fingers wide, closing and opening, rhythmic and hypnotic. She could not look away.

She came to her senses upon hearing the frantic rustling on the pallet and Samuel's panicked, "Maggie, something is amiss with Sarah!"

Chapter Three

Maggie and Ian rushed over. Sarah thrashed on the pallet, limbs jerking spasmodically, arms flailing, eyes wide open, bloodshot, and filled with terror. Her mouth opened and from her very center, she hissed, *"Venganza. Venganza."*

Samuel kneeled and grabbed her shoulders. She hit him across the face, the slap echoing through the room. He held her arms to her sides.

"Talk to her, Samuel," Maggie urged, as together she and Ian held her legs. "She must stop this thrashing. It will weaken her and make her womb bleed too much."

"Perhaps," Ian told Samuel, "if you embrace her skin to skin she will recognize and find comfort in the familiar."

She watched as Samuel nodded, stripped down to his drawers, and climbed in beside Sarah, wrapping his muscular arms around her. He scissored her legs with his own to keep them still. Sarah's thrashing abated, but she shook with such force that Samuel's chin knocked against her head with a hollow sound.

Out of the corner of Maggie's eye, she saw Ruthie cringing in the corner, holding the squalling baby in her arms. "What is wrong with Mother? That thing is not my mother!"

Ian went to Ruthie, kneeled, and took the baby out

of her arms. He led the poor girl to the table and put his arm around her. With the other arm he held the babe, jostling her slightly to calm her. "Ruthie, your mother has been through a terrible ordeal. She has had a frightening experience, and it has overwhelmed her. Have you ever had a nightmare?"

"Yes," Ruthie sniffed.

"Your mother is experiencing a nightmare from which she cannot awaken. Do you understand?"

She nodded, her face white and pinched.

He smiled and met her eyes. "It is alarming at present, is it not?"

Again she nodded.

"Do not worry, we will heal her." He joggled the babe. "It will take a bit of time, and you will have to be brave. Do not worry, my sweet. She is still your mother—just very frightened, that is all."

He took his arm from her shoulders to pull an orange out of his pocket. He gave it to Ruthie. Her eyes grew round. She held it to her nose, sniffing. Maggie wondered from what exotic place he had procured that orange, a most delectable and rare treat.

Samuel had succeeded in calming Sarah down a bit, murmuring over and over like an incantation. "All is well, my love. You are safe. Rest, all is well."

Sarah leaned against Samuel's chest again, eyes closing to slits, but the deep shuddering continued.

The babe cried in Ian's arms and began to root for a teat. He grinned. Maggie hurried over to retrieve her. As she bent to fetch the baby, Ian leaned forward as well, and she felt his warm breath upon her breast through the thin shift.

Samuel's voice slapped her. "Maggie, for God's

26

sake, clothe yourself!"

A blush crept up her body, but she could not look away from Ian's eyes. Her world became his gaze on her. Never had she exposed herself so to a man, yet it felt as natural as breathing to have Ian look upon her body.

With the next breath, she roused herself from her fancy and backed away, setting the baby in her cradle and grabbing her cloak off the hook by the fire. There was not a man alive who could entice her to undergo the rigors and mortality of childbirth, not after what Mother had endured at the hands of Father and all she had seen in her daily life as a midwife. What could she be thinking, letting him ogle her?

Perhaps the tone of Samuel's voice had disturbed Sarah, for she began to thrash again. Samuel lay down with her as before. Maggie could not help echoing Ruthie's words in her mind. This was not Sarah—the blank blue eyes darkened with terror, fighting against—what? Did she still think she was buried? Had she plunged into madness from the horror of it? She must heal her sister and find out who had done this to her.

She racked her brain for the answers, but her thoughts misted around her murky as the morning fog. She fixed a pot of tea and set bread and preserves out for a repast. It seemed this odd apothecary was making himself at home here and would require feeding. He certainly was thin, except for those wide shoulders and upper arms, muscled and straining against his coat.

Ruthie sat at the table, peeling the orange with painstaking care. Ian grinned at her, receiving a gap-toothed smile in reply. The tang of the orange wafted over from where she stood by the fire.

He rose and pulled a wooden flute out of his coat. "Might I play, softly? It may soothe your sister."

She nodded. He played a slow, rhythmic tune, eyes closed, body slightly swaying. She watched his fingers covering and uncovering the holes on the thin pipe. He could not seem to hold still, this musical apothecary, and she could not seem to look away.

Before long, Ruthie fell asleep, her head on the table. Sarah rested quietly, nestled in Samuel's arms. The music seemed to calm her and indeed, a feeling of peace enveloped the room. The tea grew cold. After a time, Ian put down the pipe and stretched, his gaze alive on her, always on her. Did he never fatigue?

"I'd wager a guess you have not eaten," he said. He went to the table and lathered a piece of bread with butter and preserves. He put it on a plate in front of her.

She choked back a retort. Why would this man show such concern for her, Maggie the workhorse, black hair, sturdy body, nothing remarkable? He was fair taking over.

He warmed up her tea and sat down again, nibbling on a piece of bread. "The word that your sister hissed, '*venganza*.'"

She shivered at the memory. "Yes?"

"It means 'vengeance.' I learned some of the language of New Spain in my travels."

"Vengeance? Why would Sarah say that, and in a voice not her own? What does this mean?" Her head ached with confusion. "Who delivered Sarah? Who is responsible for burying her alive?" She set her cup down on the table hard, making Ruthie startle in her sleep. "What do you think? Do you believe she was resurrected from the dead?"

"I have been trained as a physician, although I do not practice as such, and I confess I do not know what to do for your poor sister, other than keep her warm and dose her with herbs."

Maggie gaped at him.

"Although I have seen many strange things in my travels, I have never seen anyone buried alive. I had thought about bleeding her, but my instincts tell me it would only be detrimental." He gave her a pleading look, as if he asked for forgiveness.

"I promise you I will do everything in my power to help awaken your sister," he murmured. "I'll begin immediately." He smiled, showing the dimple under his right eye, and took his leave.

Soon after he left, the baby began to squall. Maggie quickly changed her clout and picked her up. Sarah suddenly grew more agitated, her glazed eyes open and hands grasping the air. Had she possibly heard the baby cry? Ideally, she could give her sister the child, and she would feed her, but that was impossible while she was in this state.

Luckily, Joannie the wet nurse arrived, and she soon had the baby sucking greedily. A similar sound emanated from the pallet. Maggie turned to see Sarah, eyes open, sucking noisily on two fingers. A chill skittered over her. She had thought nothing else could shock her, but she was wrong.

Chapter Four

He returned to his apothecary shop in a sea mist as grey as Maggie's eyes, skin tingling from the sight of white arms, strongly muscled, stretching upward in supplication, black hair with chestnut sheen flowing to the cleft of her bottom. Firelight illuminated her wide hips in the worn linen shift, drawing him like no Eastern temptress ever could, wide hips innocent of his hunger, the sweat upon her full upper lip, the taste he longed to have salty upon his tongue. And then to touch her softness, fingers' journey on generous hips...he could no more help himself from touching her than keep a song from rising up within, but swallowed it down for her sake.

The dust motes appeared as dawn lightened the shop room. A heavy coat of dust covered the vials, bottles, jars of remedies, and herbs. He studied the shelves, unfamiliar with brother Daniel's organization of the materials. The crates and supplies gathered on his journeys would have to be catalogued and assembled today. Work would still the music in his mind for a time if he applied himself.

Daniel lingered everywhere, in the minute details of his efficiency, in the broad, legible script on the jars, so much so that Ian could not resist speaking aloud. His voice echoed in the empty room.

"You were always here when I returned, Brother.

No matter where, the Far Seas—a year or London for a day, you showed no surprise at my sudden appearance, only acceptance."

It would not do for someone to find him talking to himself like a lunatic. Poor choice of words, that. He grabbed a rag and wiped the counter down. He would wipe the memories of Bedlam clean, the chains biting into his bare wrists, stone walls dripping with cold, the reek of unwashed bodies discordant with the perfume of weekday visitors, and the cries of fellow Bedlamites.

He would sing now, to silence the rattle of chains like cymbals crashing in his head, the echoes of laughter down the long gallery as tourists and society came for their entertainment, the keepers happy to show the lunatics off for profit.

His turn. Throw a few buckets of cold water on him, and he would comply with a song and perhaps a dance, bones rubbing against each other resounding in his head: phalanges, talus, and tibia screeching with fellow unfortunates, made a melody and vied to emerge. Fellow inmates beating on the bars in sympathy provided rhythm for the song gushing out of him like blood from a slit artery. Visitors pelted apples, nuts to spur him on. The perfection of the music in his head pulsed within him. He tried to share it with the guests, but they only pointed, laughed. The stench of his humiliation overcame him.

Ian dropped the rag, and as he had been taught, took the air into his lungs, slowly and steadily, listening to his breathing. He let the memory pass by until the memory of rescue took its place, recalling the feel of Daniel's arms wrapping the blanket around him, his strength and calm encircling his emaciated body. His brother had saved him, and he had failed his brother.

A jar of Rauwolfia fell to the floor, and the lid rattled off. Indian Snakeroot, obtained in the holy and most ancient kingdom of Varanasi where he had hoped the most learned doctors could help him. The good Hindu doctors in Ramnagar did dose him with it there. The bitter smell assaulted his nostrils, and so too did his stomach cramp up reflexively at the body's memory of the medicine and the bitterness of yet another treatment failing. But perhaps a smaller dose, mixed with something yet unknown would save him and keep him here, close to Maggie.

He took a candle into the living area behind the shop and lit a fire in the sitting room. There was no portrait of Daniel, only the memory of his lanky frame and the way he made him laugh with dry asides. What would he have thought of Sarah's return from the dead? Ian's heart raced as he relived the horror at the kirkyard, feeling the import of all he had seen.

After his first encounter with Maggie, he returned home. But there were things he needed to say to Daniel at the grave, with a melody. So later, he ventured out again to sing his grief. But he was not alone.

He heard the dogs howling before he arrived. Surrounded by piles of dirt, a man crouched over a grave. He stumbled backward and screamed, staccato and high-pitched. The whites of his eyes gleamed in his lantern light. Ian approached and beat the dogs away. A figure, wrapped in a shroud, writhed upon the ground.

He grabbed the gravedigger by the shoulders. "What has happened?"

The old man covered his eyes, gasping between screams. "It was the dogs—they dug her up—Mistress

Sarah, moving. I cannot touch her, I cannot."

Blood gleamed on the sleeve of his cloak, but no time to tend to him. Ian bent over the shrouded figure on the ground, medical training coming to the fore.

"What is your name, man?" He removed his cloak to cover up the writhing figure.

"Jonas."

"Jonas, you must be quiet and tell no one what has transpired. Do you hear?"

He stared with abject fear. Ian gathered Maggie's sister in his arms and tore the linen shroud off her face to reveal ice-blue eyes, blank and wide with terror.

He spoke above Jonas' screams and the howling of the dogs. "Mistress Sarah. All is well."

She thrashed so violently it took all of his strength to hold her. "Mistress Sarah, you are among the living, do you hear me? You are alive and safe."

Her blue lips opened in a silent scream.

"I am taking you home. Home."

Thank God he knew where she lived, for there would be no help from Jonas. "Be still, man, and tell no one what has transpired tonight. You need not accompany me. Do you understand?"

He covered her face with the cloak to keep out the rain and fought against the wind to her cottage.

Jonas followed behind him, moaning.

"If you must follow me," Ian yelled, "then be silent or be gone."

They sped through the dark streets of town, down alleyways, heading north. By the time they had turned toward the docks and around to the blacksmith's shop, he had to caution Jonas again to keep still. The townspeople should not see her in this shrouded state.

Ian had seen what superstition could do to a town and would not have it happen to Maggie's sister.

Jonas reached the door before he did and pounded, but he shoved his way into the warm, smoky air, standing in front of Maggie, her sister's body in his arms. Maggie froze, face white, pupils huge in shock. Then, as she recognized her sister Sarah, she sparked alive and sprang into action. She took control without flinching, hands and mind capable and strong in the midst of her terror.

How would it be to command the focus of Maggie's attention, to have those eyes and heavy brows survey *him* with such intensity, to be the recipient of her good intent? She looked as if she could withstand anything that befell her. Could she withstand his affliction?

His mind spun in revolutions, like a carriage wheel beset by the wind. His blood sang with all his senses had taken in—the memory of her sweet skin and the sight of her welcoming hips in the firelight inviting him to the peace and comfort of her body. If he could but silence the cries, clean the filth of nightmares from his soul, so she need never know where he had been, perhaps then he would be worthy of her. Somewhere, in the storehouse of Mother Nature, was an herb, mineral, concoction that would cure him.

Chapter Five

After Ian's departure, Maggie had fallen asleep with her head on the table, sleeping deeply for a few hours. Joannie the wet nurse had just slipped in and stoked up the fire.

As Joannie filled the kettle for tea, she whispered, "Mistress Maggie, ye must be done in."

She shrugged her tight shoulder muscles. "Oh, midwives aren't allowed to be tired, you know that, Joannie."

She glanced at Sarah and pressed her lips together. "Mistress Maggie—"

Just then, the babe began fussing.

"Looks like the little mite smelled breakfast," Maggie said, gratified to see the babe latching hold in no time. She and Joannie shared a smile.

Joannie deserved credit for her calm reaction to Sarah's eerie condition. Sarah breathed evenly and deeply, her coloring pale like parchment with only a trace of blue around the lips. Good. She had improved, but the sight of those light blue eyes and their sightless stare chilled her. What was she to do?

Samuel rose from the pallet and tucked the covers around Sarah. He lumbered over to the table, resembling the baited bear they'd seen at the county fair. Poor man, who could blame him, for all he'd been through?

"I have repairs to do this morn," he mumbled, rubbing his eyes.

She handed him some bread and a cup of tea. "I must go to the Siren Inn."

He narrowed his eyes, his broad face dark with stubble. "You know how I feel about that, Maggie. No place for a lady."

"I'm not a lady, I'm a midwife," she quipped and was rewarded with a dark scowl from Samuel and a muffled giggle from Joannie. The sound of laughter helped to lessen her strong sense of unease about the strange word Sarah had uttered—"vengeance"—and the figurine that seemed to burn in Maggie's hand. Surely she had imagined this, due to her profound fatigue!

"A foreign girl staying there is due to deliver in a fortnight or so," she said. "Sarah had checked on her and did not like the looks of her. She said she was very thin and sporting bruises." How odd to be talking about Sarah as if she wasn't in the same room. But was she really with them? Yes, it was her body, but so far no sign or recognition of the woman they once knew. No time for these answerless questions; there were too many people to care for.

"Mind you don't call attention to yourself," Samuel said. "Do your business and get out. That includes Lena."

She held her tongue, well accustomed to Samuel's protective efforts. But she intended on doing as she pleased. "Samuel, you know Lena has been a good and tender friend."

He considered Lena to be a bad influence because of her tough and outspoken ways. It was good Lena was tough—as alewife at the Siren Inn, she served the roughest of sailors and the Hawkhurst Gang to boot—she had better be tough. Two years ago, Maggie delivered Lena of a stillborn son and sat with her often in comfort. God had not blessed the alewife with the children she so dearly wanted. The women's friendship grew, and she in turn mothered Maggie as she had never been mothered.

On the subject of mothering, little Ruthie had been neglected long enough. Maggie found her upstairs wrapped in a blanket. She lay down and curled her arms around the child's shaking body.

"Ruthie, everything will be okay, I promise you."

"She frightens me. Why does she not know me?" She rubbed her eyes with her fists.

"Ruthie, do you remember what Ian—Mr. Pierce said last night? Think of your mother as being in the middle of a very bad dream right now." Maggie took her hands away from her face and covered them with her own. "I promise that I will set your mother to rights. Have I not always done what I promised?"

She nodded.

"Come downstairs with me, child. You must practice your stitches. With the new baby here, your mother will need your help with the mending."

A few minutes later, as she watched the little girl's progress, she wondered how would she accomplish what she'd promised Ruthie. First, she would take advantage of the quiet to question Samuel about Sarah's delivery and hasty burial. He sat by the bed holding Sarah's hand.

"Samuel, tell me what happened yesterday."

"I don't know, Maggie. I was working in the shop and heard a ruckus. Mr. Smyth brought Sarah home in his wagon. Sarah had been looking in on his wife and their newborn and went into labor. His son was fetching the new doctor, and he would meet us here."

"New doctor? Oh yes, the one who set up shop a week ago? I have been so busy with deliveries that I have not crossed paths with him. What is his name again?"

"Edward Carter," he said. "Come from Hastings. So the doctor came, and we had to put her upon the table. She screamed that her head hurt to bursting. The doctor sent me outside. I did as I was bidden. He said it was happening fast, and he would take care of her."

He released Sarah's hand, stood, and paced the floor. "I wanted to fetch the gossips so she would not be alone, but there was no time for the women to come. I sent Ruthie in, but he sent her out. Minutes later he came out holding the babe. He said Sarah had died of brain fever, and he scarcely had time to deliver the babe before she died. He said she must be buried quickly before it spread."

Brain fever? She'd not heard of a case in the area for quite some time. There had been a smallpox outbreak several months ago. She and Sarah had nursed a goodly number of townspeople back to health. But a case of brain fever was certainly a cause for alarm.

At the sound of his agitated voice, Sarah stirred and mimicked his distress by tossing and turning upon the pallet. Maggie tucked the blankets up to her chin again and felt her forehead. Good, no fever, but she was still so cold, despite the roaring fire that filled the length of the unusually long hearth.

"Samuel, you are upsetting her, I think. Comfort her and tell me the rest of what you know."

He nodded and crooned to Sarah for a time, and she soon quietened. He straightened again. "It happened so fast. Before I knew it, I was standing over her grave. Oh God, Maggie. I saw her. She was dead, I swear. This is my fault. I should have seen that she was not dead."

She touched his hand. "Samuel, no. It is not your fault." No, it was hers. She should have been there. "There must be a logical explanation for this, and I ask you these painful questions so we can find out what really happened."

He spoke so softly she scarcely heard him. "Mayhap the Lord knew how good she was and that I could not have lived without her, no matter if she is never the same as she was."

"Oh Samuel, the Lord does not bring people back from the dead. If He did, my mother would not have died in childbirth, and he would have saved my brothers and sisters from smallpox."

Sarah was all she had left. She must help her recover from this strange state, and somehow her sister must nurse the child. But her milk had not come down yet—would it? The midwife's manual might shed some light on Sarah's condition. What did it mean when a delivering woman had a headache? What might the book say of Sarah's humours, and what could be done to remedy her imbalance? Her feet and ankles *had* been swollen. As to her condition now, Ian had promised he would work on a remedy.

Maggie suddenly became aware of a most foul odor and realized she had not emptied the chamber pot in a good long while. As she donned her cloak, she heard the night soil man and his son making the rounds to empty the town's cesspits: the creak of the wagon wheels, the tuneless whistling of Henry, the father. Normally, Henry came in the dead of night with his simple son, George. Due to the unpredictability of women's wombs, she was often about town at that time and had occasion to converse with them frequently. It was nearing daylight. He would catch hell from Constable Stowe if he wasn't finished soon. Some of the townspeople might complain if he was seen doing his work, for as long as he was invisible, they could all pretend they did not shit.

She wiped her hands on her apron and checked for the peppermint-scented handkerchief tucked in the pocket, in case the stench was more than she could stomach. She ventured out into the fog to say hello. Despite the nature of his job, Henry was quite likeable. He had manners like the royalty for whom he was no doubt named and always charmed her with his sweet, attentive chivalry. Henry had lost his wife during the last smallpox outbreak, despite their best nursing efforts. Sarah had thought he now carried a torch for Maggie. She knew better; it was merely that she didn't ignore him like some folks did.

He doffed his hat and jumped out of the cart to fetch the wood barrel from the back of the wagon. He maneuvered a long pole through the slots at the top of the barrel, which enabled George and Henry to put the pole on their shoulders and carry the shite-filled barrel more easily. George, who ordinarily had a shy smile for her, lumbered out of the wagon. He held his jaw, tears streaking trails on his dirt-sodden face.

"Hi ho, George. How are you this morrow?"

Well accustomed to his slow responses, she waited

patiently, but no response. "George, what ails you?"

He eyed her pitifully, rocking back and forth on his heels, holding a bloody rag to his mouth.

She walked closer, hanky over mouth. Henry approached and put his hand on George's shoulder. "It's his teeth," he said, the muscles in his jaw clenched.

"Do you want me to take a look?" she asked. "Perhaps it's festered."

"Miss Maggie, don't be troubling yourself for us."

"Never mind about that—let me take a look."

Henry pushed George forward. "Open your mouth."

With painful effort, George opened his mouth to reveal a ragged crater where several teeth had been. Blood pooled in the sockets, and the surrounding area looked inflamed. It was a brutal, botched job.

"Who did this to you?" Maggie whispered, rage setting her stomach afire.

He whimpered.

"It's the work of the new doctor in town, Edward Carter," Henry said. "He has set up shop next to the Shipwreck Hotel. Offered us a deal. Since the one tooth had been paining him for ages, I sat him down." Henry's face hardened. "He only had the one bad tooth, but the doctor up and ripped three others, no warning, from the poor lad's mouth. It's a wonder you did not hear him screaming from here. I almost flattened the man, above my station or no. Well, I must have scared the bastard, excuse the language, Mistress Maggie, because he stopped."

"Did you not inform the constable?"

He laughed shortly without humor. "Pete Stowe?

41

Full-pocket Pete? He'd sooner take a bribe than help an honest man."

"Why would this Edward Carter bribe him in the first place?"

Henry shook his head.

She could not resist patting George's head, shite-ridden or not. "Don't you worry, George. The new apothecary in town will ease your pain. His name is Ian Pierce, and he will be receiving customers today."

She turned to Henry. "Take him there and tell him I sent you. Mayhap he will have some oil of clove or willow bark to ease the pain."

She handed George her handkerchief and helped him place it upon his jaw. The peppermint smell might distract him for a while.

"And from now on," she said. "Go to him should you need teeth pulled. He is skilled and has been trained as a doctor."

Henry sketched an elegant bow, so contrary to the nature of his employment that she stifled a chuckle. Father and son set to work emptying her cesspit. She returned to the house.

She had no sooner checked on Sarah and ladled out the porridge when a pounding on the door and a cacophony of voices sharp with alarm shattered the silence. She eased the door open to find a group of townspeople gathered. Ben Sutton, the town magistrate, worked his way into the room, followed by Martha, the baker's wife and her two grown daughters. The owner of the Shipwreck Hotel and some sailors reeking of gin forced their way in before she could slam the door shut.

Samuel stood sentry at the foot of Sarah's bed and glared at the crowd. "Go home, all of you. My wife needs rest."

"It's true, then." Sutton yelled and tried to get closer to Sarah, without success. "Mistress Sarah has come back from the dead."

"Impossible, a miracle, Mistress Sarah brought back to life!" Martha screamed. Her daughters prayed aloud in unison.

This had to stop. "Kindly take your leave," Maggie shouted above the din. "Miss Sarah needs quiet and warmth. I promise to apprise you of her condition on the morrow."

The chaos continued as if she had not spoken.

One of the sailors cried, "Unnatural, evil, this is the work of the devil. Look at her."

"Nonsense," Maggie barked. "There is a credible explanation for this, and we will soon discover what happened."

"Miss Maggie," Martha called. "I will send my husband for the vicar."

"She does not need the vicar. What she needs is warmth, food, and nursing. The vicar can wait."

Martha gasped. "But the vicar must come. Miss Sarah has been resurrected from the dead."

"Yes, yes, it is unnatural, is it of the devil?"

"It is of God," Sutton cried.

"No! Satan has his hand in this," a sailor argued.

"You are Godly people. You know that only our Lord Jesus was resurrected, and there is no evil in this good woman who has served you all." Her voice rose above the babble.

Samuel would not leave his spot beside Sarah. It was a good thing, for she did not like the tone this was taking, and Samuel's fists would not improve the situation. She summoned all the authority she could muster.

"You must leave us, good people. My sister has been a victim of incompetence, not divine intervention *or* the devil. Use your reason, I beg you. Employ yourselves by praying for this good woman. I must tend to her now."

"Get out," Samuel bellowed.

Finally they left. She bolted the door. The confusion and noise had upset Sarah. Her eyes were glazed with fear, and a spasm shook her. Samuel climbed in beside her and enveloped her with his arms, crooning to her. Once again, it seemed to calm her, but they were no closer to reviving her sister than the night before.

Word would spread like smallpox about her "resurrection," and it didn't help that Maggie had dismissed the need for the vicar. Soon they would have everyone coming to the cottage. They must try to keep the villagers away until they could discover and prove what had happened to Sarah.

She had forgotten to draw the curtains. Ed the butcher passed by the window. She let him in.

"My grandbaby is coming," he panted and glanced over at Sarah. To his credit and no doubt also due to his preoccupation with his daughter, Betty, he said not a word about Sarah. "Can you come now, Mistress Maggie?"

"Yes, let me fetch my bag and cloak."

She prayed for the strength and endurance needed to deliver another soul into the world.

Chapter Six

In her lying-in room, Betty, the young mother-to-be, lay in the rickety bed, screaming and shaking her fists. "William Hobson, I swear you'll never touch me again." Her face shone like a wet beet, and sweat poured off her body as another wave of labor pains hit.

Young Will slumped against the wall. "Miss Maggie, is my Betty dying?"

The midwife skirted the rough-hewn bed and patted Will on the back. Despite preoccupation with her own concerns, she laughed inwardly at the shock on the young man's face. He looked as if he'd been slapped with a haddock. He slid down the wall, face in his hands.

She spoke slowly, meeting his eyes. "No, Will. She is not dying. This is what a woman must endure to bear a child."

All laboring women need the comfort of other women during their travail, and in Betty's case it was her family. Betty's sister held a wailing child on one hip, bending over to pat her sister's arm with the other in silent support.

On the other side of the tiny room, Betty's grandmother guffawed. She sat in the room's only chair, jowls shaking with laughter, gnarled finger pointed at Will. "Fear not, Sir Randy," she said to him. "Come spring the girl will be singing a different tune."

Betty's mother, Margaret stood at the foot of the bed. "Mother, must you be so vulgar?"

Maggie helped William up. "Come, take heart. Your young bride is doing well for her first time. She probably doesn't mean what she says. Besides, it's a good sign she has the energy to curse you."

Ed the butcher burst into the room, carefully averting his eyes from the bed. He grabbed Will by the arm. "What are ye doing in here, boy? Can ye not see Mistress Maggie is working? I'll give ye a bit of whisky to calm yer nerves." He winked at her and thrust the protesting lad out of the room.

Will's exit was timely. Betty's screams increased in volume and intensity, and there was no time to coddle the lad. At this stage of delivery, a woman believes she will die and indeed, sometimes she does. She could not think about what Sarah must have gone through, not when she had a child to bring forth. First the laboring mother must be calmed.

In truth she did not excel at comforting, for that was Sarah's gift. It did not help that the child in the room screamed in unison with his aunt. She took a deep breath for patience. Her sister had an abundance of it. She did not but would do her best.

"Eunice," she addressed Betty's sister. "Are you trying to frighten your poor boy back into the womb? Give him to his grandfather for a spell."

Betty's screams continued, and Maggie could not help but think they were a far cry from the screams of ecstasy she might have made in the begetting of the child. She would not know about ecstasy; in light of what she'd seen over and over in her daily work as a midwife, she'd yet to meet any man who could entice her to suffer the rigors and possible mortality of childbirth. But the singer, the apothecary, strange man with eyes the color of spring, his touch warming her like...what possessed her? Now was not the time to think of that man.

She patted Betty's thigh. "It shouldn't be long now. Allow me to examine you to see how you are progressing."

She did so gently and reassured mother and daughter that all would be well. God willing, she'd deliver in the next hour or two and none too soon. Maggie had not slept in two days and likely would not sleep tonight, between the babe's pap feedings (she could not ask Joannie to tend three infants during the night) and Sarah's precarious health. Last year's raucous May Day celebration had yielded an abundance of births this February, and with Sarah incapacitated she was the only midwife in town. She must get some sustenance into her sister somehow or she would perish.

She stood up straight, flexing her shoulders back. All that mattered now was the task at hand. The room echoed with silence. At this time in labor, nothing else exists but the mother and the fight to bring forth her child.

At the next pain, Betty gasped, "I must push!" She lay panting, her immense belly rock hard, eyes glazed.

"Push, then," Maggie urged.

She pushed, gasping for breath between moments of sweat-soaked rest, veins in her neck bulging, eyes wide and staring. And before long, with one last push, the glistening, blood-covered head appeared.

"That's right, sweeting. Just the shoulders now."

Praise God, the babe cried already and only its

head out of the birth passage.

"Do you hear it calling to you, Betty?"

One last guttural groan and the baby slid out and into Maggie's waiting hands. "Oh, well done, Betty. It's a boy." She cleaned him as quickly as possible.

Betty reached for him and soon had the babe settled at her breast. Young Will burst in, held her hand, and kissed it feverishly, eyes upon her beaming face. Maggie soon had Betty regally receiving praise from her family and took Betty's mother aside to remind her to make the babe a comforting posset of butter and sugar. She promised to come over next day to check on mother and baby. Ed said he would bring a nice cut of young lamb over to the house tomorrow.

She headed for the Siren Inn, taking a moment to offer a prayer of thanksgiving for an easy, uncomplicated delivery, a bit of a rare thing for a first time mother. Her own mother had not been so fortunate; she had suffered three stillbirths and countless miscarriages, yet still Father forced himself upon her in the night. One night when Maggie was but twelve, her mother bled to death in childbirth before the midwife could arrive, and she had to help her lifeless brother into the world. Are all men as selfish?

Some of the fog had cleared, and she could hear the ships' bells clang and the hearty shouting of men working on the docks. The incline on Siren Street was steep, and treated her to a clear view of the English Channel, where the white caps folded in on themselves like meringue. The fishing boats had already forged their way to shore, having been out since before dawn.

The Siren Inn was ancient, built in the twelfth century and burned by the French two hundred years later. Rebuilt from ships' timbers in the 1400s, the inn was a haven to weary travelers and sailors and a watering hole for the thirsty residents of King's Harbour. A rusty sign depicting the figure of a sea maiden swung in the wind, and ivy climbed the exposed beams of the white-washed building.

At this early hour, no evidence existed of the revelry that usually met her when she occasionally helped a laboring mother during business hours.

Lena's husband, Josef polished mugs behind the bar. "Hello, Mistress Maggie. Watch your step, now. My wife's not cleaned up yet."

She picked her way carefully over the bottles of ale and snoring sailors that littered the floor. The smell of stale tobacco, spilled ale, and unwashed sailor made her wish briefly she had not given the peppermint-soaked handkerchief away. It was no secret she had the nose of a bloodhound. Nothing smells quite as repugnant as a sailor fresh, or most emphatically *not* fresh, off the boat. Some were so filthy their clothes had been known to crumble off their body.

"Busy last night, eh, Josef?"

He nodded, scowling, and she wondered what had him so out of sorts.

She warmed her hands at the massive fireplace, breathing in the pleasant scent of the fire. The fireplace was big enough to house a family of five, surely the largest fireplace in all of Britain, even Europe, she wagered, with no small amount of pride. In this corner, centuries of history abided. There was even a priest's hole in the chimney breast. When King Henry VIII decreed Roman Catholicism a crime, many a priest had found refuge there.

She had best go up and see the foreign girl. But first, she paused to gather her thoughts and pray for guidance before climbing the stairs to her room. The girl, whose name was Sabine, spoke no English, Sarah had said a few days ago, and they knew not where the girl came from. Sarah had to depend upon the girl's husband or lover, and she said he was less than cooperative. He had probably not even bothered to translate correctly her sister's questions regarding the girl's health. She hoped Sabine had improved and made her way up the stairs.

The "husband" wore a scowl upon his darkly bearded face. His stocky body filled the doorway, meaty arms crossed. "What do you want?" His eyes skewered her.

The mewling of an infant in the background both alarmed and confused her. The girl had given birth? When had this happened and who had delivered it?

"I am Maggie Wilson, the midwife. My partner was here a few days ago to check on the mistress. Now it is I who've come to check on your, er, wife. She has had the baby?"

He sneered. "Name's Gerard Blanc, and the chit's not my wife. She had the pup, ugly little thing it is, too. Come in, then."

She stifled a retort. The huge canopy bed swallowed the tiny, painfully young girl, at best perhaps fifteen or sixteen. She stared, almond-shaped eyes the color of toffee. Her blue-black hair, even in a state of disarray shone like a raven's wing.

"She don't look right," Gerard Blanc grumbled.

"When was the infant born? And who acted as midwife?"

"Born two days hence. A colleague of mine did it," he barked. "What of it?"

A colleague? She shuddered to think what kind of colleague this miscreant had. "What is his name, sir?"

"His name is Edward Carter, and he will drive you out of business with all his fancy instruments, so speedy did he yank the brat out."

Sabine was so pale she all but blended in with the bed linen. She held the baby at her breast.

"Has Sabine eaten?"

"Won't eat. Won't talk."

"You should have fetched me," Maggie said. "She needs to be examined. Leave." Then she remembered too late her medicines were dangerously low. With Ian's brother gone, they'd been bartering and trading with the townspeople for herbs. There was only enough for one dose to ease the poor girl's pain. She would have to make a trip to the apothecary shop on her way home.

He narrowed his eyes. "How long is it going to take her to be at rights again? What good is she if she cannot tend to her business? If you know what I mean." He eyed Maggie speculatively.

The look in his eyes recalled the look of her father as he advanced toward Mother only days after her brothers and sisters were born. He had waited long enough, he said, even as she lay in bed covering her ears against the sounds. She had not understood as a child, but now—her fingers clenched into a fist.

"A woman who has just given birth must rest for at least a month, and it will be a good long while after that before she is able to, er..."

His beetled brows rose in shock at this, and his lip

curled in disgust. "Damn women."

He loomed over her, so close she smelled his filth. Covered in shite, she thought darkly, the night soil man was immaculate compared to this slime, inside his soul and out. She reached behind into her bag and pulled out the small knife she carried for the cutting of cords, and wielded it in front of him with a sure hand, eyeing him with no sign of fear. He left the room, grumbling. She had made her point. Thankfully his desire for drink was stronger than the desire to bedevil.

Sabine had fallen asleep. She gently roused her and put the baby over to the cradle next to the bed. Miraculously the child seemed perfectly healthy. Maggie smiled, introduced herself in English, and used one of the only French words she knew.

"*Belle*," she tried. It was the word for "beautiful."

The girl smiled wanly, but with no sign of understanding. She did not speak French, then? As best as Maggie could, she pantomimed that she would be examining her. She thought the girl understood her intent. At any rate, she was too weak to object.

She was not prepared for the sight of the damage: numerous lacerations from the front to the back of her privities, in danger of festering, bruising everywhere. Clearly the baby had been pulled out before its time. It was nothing short of a miracle Sabine had not bled to death.

Anger rose in Maggie like flames, but she tamped them down as best she could, spoke calmly, and palpated the girl's abdomen to ascertain if the afterbirth had even been delivered.

She winced and moaned, "*Aii, qing ni!*"

Maggie did not know what language she spoke, but

her expression of pain was obvious.

"I am sorry." As quickly as possible, she mixed up the willow bark and applied some ointment to ease the inflammation. The only bright spot in this travesty was she did not bleed excessively. She covered her patient and sat on the bed beside her, holding her hand. She looked toward the door to make certain her "keeper" was not nearby.

"If only we could speak about what has happened," she said. "You may not be able to understand what I am saying, but I promise you that somehow I will make that butcher accountable for your suffering."

She smiled weakly and croaked, "*Xie xie.*"

Was that her name? She patted her chest. "My name is Maggie."

Eyes bright with intelligence, she mimicked her hand motion. "Sabine."

It was most decidedly a French name, but she was not French. Where had she come from?

As Maggie bent to put the empty medicine bottle back into her bag, it slipped from her hand. She cursed her fatigue and squatted to retrieve it. Under the bed hid a man-made beekeeper's hive, called a skep. It was made out of straw, two holes cut out for eyes. The Hawkhurst Gang used the skeps as a disguise to hide their identity while they committed their smuggling crimes.

She fought a rising panic. She had brandished a knife in the face of a Hawkhurst Gang member; getting on the bad side of a gang member was akin to throwing oneself in the path of an oncoming carriage. By the time she heard Gerard Blanc's heavy footsteps on the stairs, Maggie had wiped all traces of alarm off her face.

She made an attempt to smile as he barged into the room. "I am going to the apothecary and will return later to bring more medicine and a tisane for strength. I will speak with the alewife and have her bring up some custard and broth." She looked him in the eye. "If she does not eat, she will die."

Hopefully the girl would be worth more to him alive than dead. He stared dully, grunted, and nodded.

She made a quick exit and stopped downstairs to greet her good friend Lena. She had come from Heidelberg ten years ago. The apple dessert she called strudel would make an angel commit the sin of gluttony.

She was making ale, her arms stirring a fragrant, yeasty mixture with a wooden spoon in a huge bowl. "Maggie!" She put the spoon aside and embraced her. "*Liebchen*, it is most remarkable. Sarah lives! How happy you must be." She held her at arm's length. "You are exhausted, look at you. Rest, have a mug of ale. I have not had a chance to check on the girl upstairs today, so busy have I been."

"I shouldn't," Maggie protested, even as Lena pushed her into a chair in the corner of the kitchen. She had not wanted to take the time after the birth to have a meal and a mug of ale as was customary. She *was* quite parched.

"You must take a care for yourself," the alewife chided. "You are pale."

She nodded, drinking the ale with closed eyes. It slid down her throat, so sweet and rich, so delicious. She let the warm, yeasty air sink into her tired muscles.

Lena stood with her muscular arms folded over her

chest, white blonde hair straggling out of her cap, her apron festooned with bits of wheat and the brown syrupy mixture called wert. Her plump cheeks dimpled with her smile. "How is our Sarah?"

Maggie glanced around, making sure no one could overhear. "I beg of you to honor this confidence. It is as if she is trapped in a nightmare. She lies like a corpse at times, then thrashes violently. She hit Samuel across the face."

"Our Sarah?"

"Yes, she was senseless, but her strength is alarming when she is agitated, as if she is aided by— something. She has not eaten, has not awoken. She is not present."

Her friend nodded. "They say that God has resurrected her, or it's the devil's work."

Maggie sat up. "Oh Lena, surely you cannot believe such talk. You are a sensible woman. You know there must be a logical explanation for this, that she must not have died at all. Who can be resurrected but our Lord Jesus? First of all, I must find out about the birth. What have you heard? What do you know about Edward Carter? He delivered Sarah's babe."

Lena frowned as she refilled her mug. "They say the doctor is from London or Hastings, or both. He comes here often." She grinned. "He is handsome and as smooth as our finest brandy. He has a different *fraulein* on his arm each time he comes in. But in the last week since he's been here, I have already heard talk about him that is not so good, that he charms you into the chair and pulls three teeth when he could pull one, and rough about it, too."

Maggie nodded. "I have just been to see the poor

girl upstairs. He delivered her and most inhumanely."

Lena wiped sweat off her forehead with a corner of her apron. "I was going to fetch you today to see to her. I have seen Edward Carter in the company of that Gerard Blanc often. Constable Stowe has been alerted, but he says it is not his concern, that he does not involve himself in the doctor's affairs. He says we should be thankful we have a real doctor trained in London. It's one thing when you hear one bad thing about someone. But when you hear many—"

This news did not bode well. "He told Samuel my sister had brain fever. Have you heard of any cases, Lena?"

She resumed her stirring. "No, I have not. The flux, yes. The morbid sore throat, yes."

"What if there have not been any cases? Samuel said she had a horrible headache. People stricken with brain fever indeed have a headache most severe. I do not know if she had a fever. What if she did not have brain fever, Lena?"

"I don't understand. Why would he say she had brain fever when she did not?"

"I don't know," Maggie said. "But I am going to find out. It sounds as if his intentions toward his patients bear ill will. Why would a doctor do such things? Will you keep your eyes and ears open for me?"

"You know that I will, *Liebchen*. How is the baby?"

"Oh. God be praised, she is beautiful and thriving, though tiny."

"*Ach, das* is good."

Maggie could not help but see the dreamy look in her eyes and asked her if she could check on the girl and administer the medicines she would bring over later.

Then she staggered to her feet, her head spinning a bit as she straightened. "Lands, Lena, what did you put in this batch?"

She smiled. "Das is called the baby maker."

She laughed and embraced her. "Thank you, my good friend."

She opened the heavy oak doors, comforted but a little inebriated.

Chapter Seven

Maggie emerged from the inn to find the fog had dissipated into wisps that parted like lace curtains. A weak sun hinted at warmth. There seemed to be an unusual amount of noise at this time of the morning, and she belatedly recalled it was market day. She hastened down Market Street, intent on finding Ian, who surely must be there, to procure the herbs and simples needed for her mothers, particularly poor Sabine. Now it would be impossible to complete the task without rubbing elbows with the townspeople. She had not the energy or the desire to socialize.

Her limbs felt numb from lack of sleep or perhaps the ale. Tendrils of anxiety wound their way into her stomach at being gone from Sarah, and most of all, not knowing how to help her. She could be fevered right now—and tomorrow her milk would likely be coming in, and Joannie could not feed her babe forever. And Samuel had not named the babe. He must name her, for Sarah could not. How to help Ruthie? Never before had she so desperately needed sleep, to just, for a few hours, escape the heavy burden of responsibilities. But how to do so?

The closer she got to the market, the more difficult it was to walk properly. What had Lena put in that ale? It would not do to be less than alert when she would be barraged with questions. She eyed the uneven cobblestones at the end of the street, taking care for her numb foot, a sure sign of exhaustion. She soldiered on.

Soon the racket of a well-attended event surrounded her: the cry of the rippiers selling herring, yelling and cajoling; the slap of the fish on their counter and the smell of meat roasting on the spit; the yeasty aroma of freshly baked bread and the spice of gingerbread from the baker. Weekly market day was a celebration of sorts, a break from day-to-day labors, an opportunity to exchange new recipes, and a chance to catch up on gossip. She knew what the gossip would be today and steeled herself against questions about Sarah.

It seemed something else captured their attention at the moment. A voice drifted over the marketplace, Ian's rusty tenor calling out, the cultured tones gone and replaced with a rich exotic accent. She combed the square and found him wedged between the beekeeper selling honey and the farmer's wife with her hens in cages. The hens, to Maggie's muffled ears, seemed to cluck in harmony to his dulcet tones.

He had tied his nutmeg-colored hair back, the curls escaping onto his tanned and muscled neck. A gaggle of women surrounded his stall, faces upraised to him, as if to the sun. He vibrated with energy and good cheer, and appeared taller, more powerful than she had last seen him. He wore a dove grey suit that shone like silk and emphasized his wide shoulders. A vest underneath the coat met in two sharp points in the center, and peacock blue embroidery bordered both the vest and coat.

For the life of her, she did not know how he could be so lively. Had he not been awake standing sentinel with her last eve? His vitality was most unnatural, she fumed. Despite the dark circles under his eyes, he gave every impression of having slept from sundown to sunup.

He held a bottle in his long fingers. "My ladies, as beauteous as indeed thou art, I have in my hand"—he displayed it with a flourish—"Argan oil from Arabia, used by women in the harem of the sultan himself."

Gasps echoed round the group.

"Yes." He grinned. "Wicked infidels indeed, but with the most luxuriant, silky hair."

Putting his hand to his heart, he intoned, "I, myself, risked life and limb invading the sheik's harem to bring to you this special elixir that will only enhance your already breathtaking beauty."

The women tittered. He reached down, cupped the face of old Widow Jenkins, and she sighed. He took her hand and rubbed a bit of the oil on it, eyes alight on her face.

"I promise thee, for three pence, a mere pittance, your hair will shine like the sun and glow like the moon." The purses opened, and the coins came out.

She stood at the edge of the square, swaying slightly, incredulous. What was he about?

"My ladies," he announced, "and gentlemen," and bowed to the disgruntled husbands and fathers standing with their arms folded. "I am your new apothecary, ready to serve you. I will pull teeth, I will supply you with the medicines you require, and last but not least, I will make you tonics that are famous the world over."

He bent down and picked a lute off the ground, played a few measures, and began to sing.

Is your cup of love half full?
Desire your man to love like a bull?
My tonic with his morning ale

Will make your love life hearty and hale.
Hearty and hale, ladies, hearty and hale
Hearty and hale with his morning ale."

She was astounded to hear "huzzahs" from the men, and the "ladies," young and old, tittering and preening and opening their purses. The chandler's wife grabbed his sleeve and chattered away. Maggie hadn't seen her so animated in years.

Ian raised his eyebrows in amusement and busied himself taking their coins as they grasped their bottles. In a matter of minutes, his neat row of tonics disappeared.

Suddenly, as if she had called out to him, he glanced up, and their gazes met and held. In his green eyes, a distant tide pounded toward her, pulsing with life, the warm current carrying her forward, his smile lifting her into the morning air.

And at that moment, in the presence of the whole town, she stumbled on her numb foot and fell, the wet cobblestones and the slime of fish slapping her cheek. She cursed herself.

Then there he was, crouching down beside her, face close, those sea eyes framed by dark lashes, brows knitted in concern. "Miss Maggie, have you hurt yourself?"

She shook her head, waves of dizziness washing over her.

He scooped her up and set her on her feet, as if she weighed no more than sea foam, and took a clean handkerchief out of his pocket, wiping her face, fingertips skimming off pebbles, dirt, and the odorous fish entrails. "You have scraped yourself," he murmured. "Are you able to walk?"

She fell against him into the warm, hard plain of his chest and the muscles of his thighs. The spice of a far-off island wrapped around her and warmed her center like a foreign sun.

He steadied her with hands on waist, warm breath ruffling her hair. She stared at the muscular column of his throat, and her fingers crept up of their own volition to feel the life pulsing in his veins. If she could only sink into the warmth and mystery of his body, where she might feel safe and free of worldly concerns and the endless toil that awaited! For one brief moment they stood, all else forgotten, the weight on her shoulders carried away by the ocean tide in his eyes.

Widow Jenkins gasped. "Shameful conduct!"

Ian rumbled into Maggie's ear, his warm breath tickling the tiny hairs on her neck. "Well, you must give me credit. My intentions to distract the townspeople from your family's trials worked for a while. I'd heard about your visitors this morning."

She stepped back abruptly. Ah, so that explained his performance. Why would he do that for her, make a fool of himself singing and the like? But he hadn't—both the ladies and men had enjoyed his display thoroughly. It was her he'd made a fool of, causing her to forget herself so close to him.

"Such a shameful display of lust," Widow Jenkins crowed. "So unbecoming of a midwife."

"We seem always to be colliding, Mistress Maggie." He lifted her hands up and examined them closely, pulling yet another clean handkerchief out of his pocket. "You are bleeding—a sharp stone, no doubt."

She could only gawp at him.

He sniffed close to her mouth. "Why, you are fox'd," he whispered. The corners of his mouth twitched. "A newly discovered side to my Maggie." He tilted his head. "One might say you've had a thump on the head with Sampson's jawbone." He took his handkerchief and very slowly brushed something off her cheek.

She glared at him.

"You're dizzy as a goose." He chortled softly.

She swatted at him and missed. Like a douse of cold water, she became aware of their audience. The men guffawed and pointed, and from the women came hisses of "unseemly, how *very* unseemly," and "is this how our midwives behave these days?"

A flush of embarrassment crawled over her. What had she been thinking? She broke Ian's grip on her hands and ventured over to the vegetable stall to purchase turnips and potatoes. Mr. Simmonds wriggled his eyebrows. She glared at him and slapped the coins into his hand, felt a tap on her shoulder, and there was Ian again.

"Mulled cider and gingerbread." He placed it into her hands and steered her to the bench under the trees that lay just behind his stall. He spread his cloak on it before she sat down. "You need taking care of, Maggie."

Gingerbread! She could never resist the spicy treat. "You caused a scene back there and single-handedly tarnished my reputation," she said with mouth full and took a sip of the cider to wash it down. It was hard to be angry while eating gingerbread.

He sat at a respectable distance and looked comically askance at her comment. "Forgive me, madam, but it was you who toppled over and displayed your toothsome legs." His long mouth quirked at the corners, and the dimple under his eye appeared. "I will cherish the memory."

She sighed in anticipation of the shame Samuel would be heaping on her. Her conduct had always been above reproach. What was it about this man that made her forget herself and all she'd worked for in this town? He made her want to feel, feel her body, feel him. It must not continue.

She handed him her cup. "Master Go-Lively. How can you not be tired after such a night?"

He smiled wryly. "I do not need much sleep. Sometimes it is not such a blessing." He smacked his head. "Zounds! I have left my booth unmanned long enough. I must return."

"Mr. Pierce. I must give you a list of medicines to fill. I am dangerously low on supplies, and I need them today. There is a girl in need of them at the Siren Inn."

He regarded her for a moment. "I will be delighted to bring it to you later this afternoon. Will that do?" His eyes glinted and set off that spark in her center again, which would not do.

No, it would not do at all. "By all means, your adoring public awaits you. Do you not have more songs to sing?"

"Have I more songs? My sweet lady, I think in songs. I dream in songs." He bowed like a courtier. A chorus of titters echoed through the crowd, and she followed him with her eyes despite herself.

He was the strangest man she'd ever met, making a fool of himself in the market square without a care to what anyone thought, charming all the women without angering the men. What was it about him that caused her to allow the liberties he took?

There was only one kind of man, surely like every other—looking after what he needed with no thought of anyone else's welfare. What could he want from her, the workhorse? Only due to fatigue and shameful inebriation had she allowed him to treat her thus. He would not have that effect on her again. She lowered her head and took the shortest route to the cottage.

****

The overpowering smell of the baby's urine-soaked clouts assaulted Maggie's nostrils as she entered the cottage. Ruthie stood swaying by the fire with the baby in her arms. Maggie took off her cloak and opened the curtains, letting a weak light into the room. Samuel had certainly been busy this morning. During her absence, he had built a rough-hewn frame for a bed for Sarah, with leather lacings on the bottom and a mattress of straw.

"I helped Father build it," Ruthie said vaguely.

"Ruthie, where is Joannie? She was to stay for the day."

She clutched the baby closer to her chest. "Her husband came to fetch her this morning. Jimmy fell and cut open his head."

She sensed an undercurrent of fear in her voice. "Did you think to tell her to fetch Mr. Ian?"

"Mistress Joannie sent her husband for Mr. Ian and ran home." She glanced at her mother, opened her mouth, and then as quickly compressed her lips.

She followed Ruthie's gaze. Sarah lay inert as a corpse, eyes wide open, and unseeing. She felt bone deep unease without knowing why. "What is it?"

"I am afraid, Aunt Maggie. Please do not leave me alone. There is someone here with us. I can feel it."

It was too much to ask of such a young girl to be left alone in this situation. She enfolded her niece in an embrace and laid her head against her bosom, the infant in her arms squirming between them.

What had she been thinking, letting Lena ply her with ale, cavorting about in the market square as if she'd not a care in the world? Granted, she didn't know Ruthie was there alone, but she shouldn't have tarried so.

"Where is your father?"

"In the shop," she murmured. "Remember? He said he had much to do today. He stopped in while Joannie was still here, feeding my sister. I did not want to disturb him."

Such a sense of duty in a young girl! "Ruthie, why are you afraid?"

She shook her head. "I told you. There is someone here with us, Aunt Maggie, and Mother is not Mother anymore."

"You are tired, Ruthie, that is all. It plays tricks on us sometimes."

Ruthie shivered. "No, something happened. I had just put Sissy to bed. The fire had gone down, and I climbed upstairs to fetch an extra blanket for Mother." She paused and held onto her tighter. "When I returned, the fire was roaring. You must believe me, Aunt Maggie!"

"Ruthie, surely your father had slipped in and stoked the fire whilst you were upstairs."

"No. I was only gone a minute."

"What you are saying makes no sense, dear.

Perhaps you just lost track of time."

"The fire lit up the whole room, and I looked at Mother and she was whispering—no, hissing— something I could not understand, and her eyes looked like a cat's in the dark, but red."

"My sweet girl. Lay the babe down and come sit with me by the fire." Maggie gathered Ruthie and held her against her breast as they rocked. "Do not worry, child. This will all pass, and you will have your mother back."

How could she have been so thoughtless? While she'd been touching a man's neck in front of the whole town, this poor child had been beside herself with fear. The best thing for Ruthie was to send her outside to enjoy the remainder of market day. She had spent too much time alone. Who wouldn't be anxious seeing their mother in this state? Even she, a level-headed woman, felt unsettled in Sarah's presence.

"Ruthie," she repeated. "Do not worry. Everything will be okay." She wiped her tears. "You have worked hard and deserve some time at the market. Let me plait your hair, then go and get yourself a treat and bring something home later for your father as well. Play a while with Ellen. Perhaps you can help her mother with the chickens."

She jumped up and was ready to go before Maggie could remove her boots to rub her foot. The baby mewled in her cradle. She fetched the pap Ruthie had prepared, spooned it into the bubby-pot, and began to feed her. She was a mighty little babe. She seemed to be thriving, against all odds, and most of this was due to her sister's loving care. What could she do for her own sister? She must try to feed Sarah after putting the babe down. She mulled over Ruthie's story about the fire. Of course it was a story; a fire could not start by itself. Lack of sleep and trauma must have wreaked mischief on Ruthie's mind.

She put the babe in her cradle and approached Sarah. She appeared to be sleeping. Her eyes shot back and forth underneath her lids as if she dreamt. The pallor of her face matched the pillow but for two red spots upon her cheekbones. Her lips were dry and chapped, forehead warm and dry. She must have fluids and food. The cloth that held her hair had become loose. As Maggie leaned down to fix it, she saw the dirt in her ear. She badly needed a bath; being immersed in the warm water might be comforting. She examined her sister's privities and noted her bleeding was average for a woman who had recently delivered.

Next, she ladled out a cup of the beef broth she'd put on the fire to cook that morning. If she would take just a little of this...she propped her head up and held a spoonful of the rich liquid to Sarah's lips, but she tossed her head and a great tremor ran through her, from head to feet.

She opened her eyes and grew very still. Her eyes changed from blue to the color of red clay, and they stared into Maggie's very soul. As surely as her heart pounded, so too did she feel the being in the room and a heat that roared beyond the fire.

A voice echoed from Sarah's lips, "Avenge them. We have saved her. You must avenge the women. *Venganza.*"

Sarah's arms rose stiffly into the air, fists clenched.

She struggled to hold her down. "Sarah, all is well. Be still. You are safe."

Then, as quickly as it had come the presence disappeared, leaving Maggie's skin chilled to the marrow.

Sarah's eyes had returned to their normal ice blue, and her arms rested at her sides. Her fists uncurled. The figurine of the old woman with the snake on her head, the one that Maggie had thrown into the fire, rolled out of her hand.

Chapter Eight

Cold sweat trickled down Maggie's back as she grasped the figurine. She had thrown this into the heart of the fire last night. How could it have returned to Sarah's hand? Ruthie would never have given it to her, afraid of her mother as she was now. She was not the only one who was afraid.

The room had returned to normal, and Sarah lay in her usual state, her eyes once again sightless and blank, not like a moment ago, when they looked into her as if they could see into her soul. She felt the echoes of the admonition—avenge them? Were there more women who had suffered as Sarah had? And now this spirit possessed her. Maggie could no longer deny it or the current of fear that ran through her.

She examined the figure again, the fierce hawk nose, a back bent like all old women, from a lifetime spent in labor for others. Was she evil, this woman? Surely she must be, with a snake coiled atop her head. Maggie felt its power. How had this object come to be in Sarah's hand? Tremors ran through her body and all rational thought vanished.

Sarah moaned and put her thumb in her mouth, sucking noisily. She had an instinctive need to suck, a need for that primitive comfort. Had fear so overcome her she must again become a babe in the womb? Maggie settled her child back in the crook of her arm;

she sucked on the mixture as if her life depended on it and indeed it did.

And then it came to her. She wondered why she had not thought of it before. If Sarah had in essence become a babe again, then she must be fed like a babe with the pap boat, immediately. A surge of hope quickened the midwife's pulse.

A shadow blocked out the weak sun shining through the window. A man stood outside, stock still. Upon seeing that he'd been observed, he disappeared. She sighed and answered the knock. How long had Vicar Andrews been standing in front of the window, staring?

"Good afternoon, Vicar."

Vicar Andrews bowed awkwardly, hat in hand, revealing a poorly powdered wig. He had taken over for Vicar Simmons a few months ago while he took the waters in Bath for a lung infection. Young Vicar Andrews reminded her of an adolescent boy who'd woken up and found himself a foot taller, not yet accustomed to his new body and still learning how to operate it. She ushered him in and hoped against hope his visit would be brief.

Warm hazel eyes searched her face. "Miss Maggie, I have come to pay you a visit, to see the new little angel, and to inquire after Mistress Sarah." He bent over her and murmured, "My, she is so very small."

Without warning he boomed, "Look at you, a tiny servant of God, ready to do His bidding." The baby flung its arms and legs out in alarm. "Oh my goodness—my pardon."

She jiggled her niece a little, and she soon calmed down again. Will he not just leave so she could feed

Sarah with the bubby pot? Vicar Andrews continued to gape, a beatific smile upon his face. As the moment dragged on, Maggie realized the object of his perusal had become the shape of her bosom under her apron.

She cleared her throat. His head flew up. Two spots of red stained his wide cheekbones. Poor boy, he clearly had not meant to gape. The innocent look on his face made it hard for her not to like him. He was painfully young. She imagined what her younger brother would have been like at that age had he not died of smallpox.

He reddened further. "Indeed, nothing is more pleasing in the sight of God than a woman and a babe." He straightened his wig and smiled meaningfully. "I would love to have children of my own someday."

Oh dear. Did he imagine her as the future vessel for those children?

"Please, Vicar." She motioned to the rocking chair. "Won't you sit and have a cup of tea?"

He shook his head, upsetting his wig again. "No, thank you. I can't tarry long. Widow Saunders is in need of comfort. Have you heard about her husband's tragedy?"

"Yes, he went down with his fishing boat, did he not? I am most sorry for it."

The vicar nodded and wandered over to where Sarah lay. "Is she sleeping?

"Well," Maggie said. "Yes, I think so."

He stepped back. "She is sucking her thumb. It is most unnatural," he whispered.

"Yes."

"Why does she do it?"

"I do not know, Vicar, except that I think it gives

her comfort."

He nodded and cleared his throat. "Miss Maggie, I would be remiss if I did not tell you the people of the town are afraid and confused by Mistress Sarah's— return. Already they have come to me with their concerns. They say either Satan has had his hand in this or God has wrought this miracle."

He suddenly looked years older. "I have read accounts of the Inquisition, and my heart aches for the innocent souls that suffered in the hands of ambitious men who created a climate of fear so horrible that neighbors would send neighbors to the dungeon. I strive to be a man of reason."

He paused for breath. "In the two months since I have been in King's Harbour, I have heard story after story of how you and Miss Sarah nursed the townspeople during the smallpox. And your care and succor of the women in this town as they suffer the sins of Eve is beyond reproach. In truth, I have only seen virtue and goodness in your conduct, and I will do my utmost to calm their fears, but they need reassurance. Can you tell me what happened?"

"I don't know, though I believe she was never dead, but was buried alive."

"You do not mean it," he gasped. "Who would have done this foul thing, and why?"

"I cannot explain it as yet. I am still learning about the circumstances surrounding her death. It is possible the doctor who delivered her whilst I was gone mistook her for dead."

For a moment she felt as if she could unburden herself with this kind man and tell him all.

He nodded. "That is most unsettling."

"I have already heard stories about this man, and they've not been favorable. At any rate, I will find out what happened, for I believe with all my heart that Sarah has a soul as innocent as an angel's, and that only Christ can be resurrected from the dead." She pulled Sarah's covers up around her neck and wiped the saliva from her chin.

"As do I, Mistress Maggie. I will do my utmost to calm their fears and petition for understanding and prayers on your behalf."

"Thank you, Vicar."

As he hurried on his way, she felt a slight sense of relief at having the understanding of this man. Had he come in answer to her prayers? There were more pressing matters. If Sarah did not eat soon, the circumstances of her *premature* burial would not matter, for she would be dead in earnest. She set the kettle above the fire for tea and water to heat the pap.

Upon hearing Ruthie's footsteps on the landing, she tried to steady her breathing to cleanse herself of the feeling of unease that roiled inside. She put roasted lamb from Ed the butcher on the table and set the table for tea.

Color bloomed in Ruthie's cheeks, and her eyes had lost that haunted look. "Aunt Maggie, I received so many treats today! Sweets from Mrs. Robins, a sausage from the butcher, pudding, and I saw Ellen, and we helped her mother with the chickens."

The many kindnesses of her neighbors did much to chase the dread away. Maggie grinned at her niece. "Your young charge slept a fair amount this afternoon. You must have worn her out this morning."

She nodded, eyes bright. "I shall take this pie to

Papa. He will gobble it up, I think."

Maggie opened the windows and let in some fresh air to rid the cottage of the smell of clouts. Unlike Sarah, she believed fresh air was beneficial. It is not harmful when one is outside, so why should it not be brought indoors?

Samuel returned with his arm around Ruthie. He sat at the table, face dark with soot from the forge, and his arms were black up to the elbows. She dared not remind him to wash, for he glared at her. "Ruthie," he said, his tone belying the ferocity of his stare, "would you run back to the market and fetch another eel pie, and one for yourself, my pet?"

After the child had left, she said, "Samuel, you have burnt yourself. Let me fetch the ointment."

"Never mind that," he barked, his eyes in slits. "How could you have forgotten yourself so, Maggie? Five people came into the shop just to report your indecent behavior at the market today. I could scarce get a thing done."

He looked her up and down in disgust. "They said you had your hands on the apothecary, and that you displayed yourself like a trollop. I am shocked." He had never spoken to her so harshly before.

"I fell, Samuel! It is not as if I did a jig with my knickers on display. I tripped over my lame foot. He helped me up." She blushed and realized the full consequences of her behavior and how ridiculous she sounded. "I don't know. I merely—he picked me up and I..." she finished, a blush heating her bosom.

Against her will she thought back on those moments, how those long fingers made her skin hum with warmth and light, as if his skin called to hers and she could not help but answer back.

He nodded. "Ah."

"What do you mean, 'ah'?"

"Perhaps it is time you marry," he said, fighting a grin.

"What?"

"Have a husband, children of your own."

"I have no need of a husband."

He chuckled, the warm light reaching his eyes again. "I think you do, or you would not be blushing."

So like Samuel the smithy to hit the nail on the head.

To cover her embarrassment, she spoke. "Samuel, have I ever given you reason to be ashamed of me in the five years I have lived here?"

Samuel glanced at Sarah. "This Ian Pierce, he saved her."

Sarah had begun to stir restlessly.

"But I will not have him ruin your reputation. Midwives must be beyond reproach."

"Think you I am not aware of that?" She sputtered. "Do you think it fitting that you talk to me as if I am a harbor harlot when all I have done is toil my whole life in the service of others?"

"Enough talk," he said. "Just know I will take matters into my own hands if the impropriety continues."

She touched his forearm. "Samuel, we have more crucial matters to discuss. Sarah weakens. She must eat and drink, or she will die. I will prepare the bubby pot for her."

His mouth fell open. He walked over to Sarah and pulled up the covers that had fallen during her restless period and made no attempt to hide his revulsion. "She suckles her fingers like a babe." He went over to the basin and scrubbed his face and arms.

"Yes, exactly. It made me think that if she can suck her thumb she could suck from a nipple."

His mouth gaped open. "But why does she do this thing?"

"It comforts her," Maggie said. "Perhaps her trial was so frightening she returned to that time of innocence and the comfort of her mother's breast."

She closed the window and curtains and barred the door. No one need be aware of their unusual activities. She readied the nutritious mixture and instructed Samuel to prop Sarah up. She became agitated when Samuel removed her fingers from her mouth. Maggie kneeled on her other side and prayed this would work. If it did not, what were they to do?

She put her hand on her sister's shoulder and held the narrow, nipple-like opening of the vessel to her mouth. "Sarah. You must eat, try it."

Sarah opened her eyes blankly. Maggie dipped her finger in the container and put a dab on her sister's tongue. Instinct demanded she swallow, and once again she opened her mouth. She put the lip of the pap boat in Sarah's mouth again, and her lips closed around it. She began to suck. Maggie let out the breath she'd been holding.

After a few swallows, Sarah coughed, and the gruel-like liquid seeped out of the corners of her mouth. But soon she settled, and as she sucked steadily, her hand grasped a corner of the blanket and caressed it. Maggie and Samuel exchanged smiles. Sarah could take sustenance—perhaps there was hope she might recover and return to the living.

Samuel caressed his wife's forehead. "Well done, my love."

Before long, she had consumed the entire contents of the pap boat, and when Maggie removed it from her mouth, her sister whimpered.

She quickly refilled the mixture from the pot by the fire and gave it to Samuel to continue feeding his wife. As she regarded them, she felt a slender hand upon her shoulder, but there was no one there.

A voice of infinite gentleness echoed inside of her, "Well done, midwife. We are pleased." A feeling of well-being warmed Maggie, and she sat at the table, legs trembling.

Outside, Ruthie's high, animated voice called out and a lower one answered. She unbolted the door and greeted Ruthie and Ian, and upon meeting his eyes felt a tiny flip, like a fish caught on a hook, in her stomach. She placed her hand upon her middle. How peculiar. A woman with child often describes the first-felt movement of their babe that same way.

Ian's hair had come out of his tie, and his normally tan face looked pale and drawn, emphasizing his lean cheeks and the scar below his ear. It made no difference, though; the air crackled like a bonfire when he entered a room.

He smiled. "How very clever you are, Mistress Maggie, to have found a way to feed your sister. I had not thought of that."

"Nor had I, until this afternoon," she murmured.

He beamed at her, and she realized with another flip in her gut that what she saw on his face was pride. Why he should be proud of her she did not know, but could not stop from smiling back.

Ruthie ran to her mother and watched her father as Samuel fed her. "Like my sister," she whispered.

Samuel paused in his feeding. "Mr. Pierce," he growled. "You put Maggie in a compromising position today."

He bowed. "I apologize most heartily. It was not my intention, and the good people of King's Harbour have let me know how untoward I was." Ian held a cloth bundle in one hand and held his other arm crossed at his chest, fingers drumming a rhythm on his upper arm.

Samuel narrowed his eyes. "Risk her reputation again and you will regret it."

The drumming stopped. Ian nodded. "My intentions toward Maggie are honorable, I assure you. It is my energy, you see. I am teeming with it. Sometimes I act without thinking." His tapping resumed. "That is not to excuse my behavior in any way."

"I don't care about your energy. Promise me it won't happen again."

Why did the man not just promise Samuel and be done with it? But he merely nodded and said, "I hold Maggie in the highest regard."

She snorted. "Oh indeed, along with all the ladies in the marketplace."

Samuel gave Ian a look that could sharpen a scythe.

Chapter Nine

"What?" Samuel snapped. "All the ladies of the marketplace?"

Maggie's brother-in-law was quite formidable. He would not want to be at the receiving end of those bandy forearms.

His lady had a clever tongue behind that practical midwife demeanor. She could hold her own with any courtier in King George's court. Indeed, Ian would stand on his head and read Shakespeare in Arabic to bring a smile to her face again as he'd done in the market square.

"Oh, surely you heard about his snake charmer program. He had the ladies eating out of his hand like little tame wrens," Maggie quipped.

"Wait now!" Ian cried. "In all fairness, I only thought to sell them some fripperies and beauty aids so I might get to know them. And then they would come to me for their medicinal needs."

"He also thought to deflect attention from Sarah's condition by making a jackass out of himself," she said, her eyes softening, ever so slightly.

Oh, the soft look he liked very much. Surely she is soft all over.

"He made a fool of you." Yon Samuel looked as if he could throttle him with no effort.

Ian felt the buzz of blood in his veins, tried to still

his trembling hands as he set the carrying case full of medicines upon the table.

"You have my medicines, then?" She cocked her head and drew her heavy brows together.

Ian unrolled the packet of medicines upon the table. "I have grouped them according to ailments: for morbid sore throat-licorice root, here; for the stomach-ginger; for pain and swelling-white willow bark and meadowsweet..."

He made a big show out of unveiling the neatly wrapped packets for her benefit, as if they were rubies or diamonds. Not impressed, she waited for the next packet to appear. He withdrew some calendula, for swelling, felt Samuel's gimlet eye upon him and grappled with the melody that rose out of his chest, doing his utmost to wrestle it down. But the melody won, a sea shanty, "the Dockside Doxy," he believed. Sometimes humming slowed the flow of words and melodies, but that antidote proved useless now. He could only open his mouth and release the song.

"I love my dockside doxy,
She is very sweet indeed.
And she supplies the local lads
With everything they need."

He slid a look toward her, simpering like a girl, to see if he could bring a smile to her face, but alas, only a twitch on one side of that stern mouth. Her lips, so full, invited perusal.

Samuel sat in the rocking chair, leaned over his pipe, and upon hearing the song, made an exasperated sound as if Ian was a fly in need of swatting.

He continued, sorely wishing he could stop.

"She's buxom, gay, and sassy.

She's a lady through and through.
She says that I'm the only one
So surely she is true."
A hint of a smile cast light on Maggie's grey eyes.
It was enough to bring him to his knees.

Dawn to twilight eyes, I cannot conceal my lust. I long to see them twilight to dawn, all I long for...need...I must. Her melody surged within him.

In his eastern travels, he'd heard music so strange and mesmerizing it echoed within him like a gong even now. In his mind he put the flat of his hands on each side of the gong to silence it, but still it resonated back to him, like all the other music.

His Maggie suffered from no such weakness; pray God she could not see inside him, for it would repel her. Her impatient glare burned his skin.

She pressed her lips together. "I said, do you have the womanly herbs I requested?"

"Yes, yes, chamomile for monthly pains, lemon balm for expelling the afterbirth; sage-salvia—for strength, as you know. And I dropped by the Siren Inn to leave some with Lena for the young girl."

She kneeled on the bench across from him, leaned forward with her elbows on the table. Samuel had lit his pipe and turned the rocking chair around so he could keep his eye on them, he guessed. He knew he would be observed if he placed his hands upon hers, so he merely leaned into her scent, like rose petals stroked by the sun.

"I am doing my utmost to concoct something that will calm your sister, but I have not come upon the right formula yet. It will not be long, I promise," he said.

The air around them grew expectant like the air

before a lightning strike. He imagined bringing her hands to his lips, kissing their warm softness, and sliding his lips to her shoulders. Would that his fingers could play about her neck and trace the silky thoroughfare of her clavicle down to the rise of her breasts. He longed to run his fingers under the edge of her bodice to see a pink blush stain her creamy skin. What would he not give up to have her secrets revealed to him?

"Do you have anything else?"

He nodded, stifling a sigh. "For when there is nothing else..." He lowered his voice. "Something from the Orient."

"What is it?" Maggie's eyes turned falcon fierce with interest.

He passed her the vial. "It is opium. Pray God you never need to use it."

"You brought this from the Orient?"

"I have sailed to China and trekked from one end to the other, gathering medicines and learning from the masters of medicine more advanced than my mind could comprehend, from the Forbidden City to Mongolia." Perhaps that little speech would hide his agitation.

Her eyes widened.

"I am sure you know," he added, "that laudanum—opium must be used sparingly and is by no means a cure." No one knew that better than he.

"You have been to the Orient? How could you afford such a venture?" She sat at the table and leaned back, arms folded across her breast.

He grinned. "Many times I sang for my supper. I did whatever was necessary."

She studied him with calm expectancy, solemn as an emperor; if only she would wrap him in that strength and calm the storms that plagued him. He rewrapped the herbs with the embroidered silk cloth he had purchased in a village along the Yangtze River, and pushed it across the table to her.

"Thank you," she said, and unwrapped the cloth. He put his hands on hers when she tried to return it.

"You must keep it."

"No."

He could tell she loved it from the way her fingers caressed the tree branch and circled the pink blossoms. "The embroidery is so fine. The birds look almost real. But I cannot accept it." His hands still on hers prevented her returning it.

"Yes, it comes with the medicine. It is medicine for your eyes."

"Of course you give these to all of your customers."

"Only midwives who are as lovely as they are clever."

She snorted.

He turned her palms up. She tried to pull her hands away, glancing at Samuel, who had fallen asleep.

She lowered her eyes. "I am not in the habit of wearing gloves, for they hinder me. My hands are not soft."

"They are lovely hands, priceless hands, for they tell a story. Of their devotion and labor on behalf of everyone but herself. They are strong, competent hands, and there is beauty in every finger, every joint."

He felt the lifeblood hum in her hands; every pore sang with the rhythm of the tide, a pulse that became his own.

Samuel awoke with a start, and she yanked her hands away.

"How much is the medicine?"

"I told you. My compliments."

"If this is your practice with every woman in town, you will soon be in the poorhouse."

"Oh no, only you, my..."

Samuel grunted and sat down at the table across from him.

Maggie rose and soon busied herself at the hearth. "Mr. Pierce, would you like some tea?"

"Please do not trouble yourself on my account," he said.

"Trouble yourself on mine, then." Samuel muttered. "Is there something to eat?"

Maggie put the medicines away, lit the candles against the dark. She prepared the tea, with a quiet efficiency and grace that did much to calm and comfort Ian.

After the meal, Ruthie went to bed, and Samuel returned to his post at the rocking chair, gimlet eye upon him. Sarah's eyes were closed, and her coloring had improved since the feeding.

A spasm—of pain?—crossed Maggie's face. She bent down and unlaced her boot.

"Go upstairs and rest," Ian said. "I can take charge of things down here for a while."

"That is not necessary."

Why would the woman shoot daggers at him when he only tried to ease her? Had no man ever shown her solicitude, no brother, father, ever expressed simple kindness and consideration? He looked to Samuel for support.

"Maggie. I am sure this lad can manage a wee baby while you rest." Samuel cleared his throat.

He longed to kneel at her feet to remove her boots.

"There are more pressing matters than my rest. This little one needs mother's milk, and I am wondering if Sarah will ever be able to feed her. She must be stronger and calmer before we try it. And what about her milk-what if it is tainted?"

"You cannot help anyone if you do not get your rest."

She ignored him. "We know Edward Carter declared her dead and had her buried quickly because he said she had brain fever. He also pulled poor George's teeth. If this Edward Carter is cruel when pulling teeth, how must he be when delivering a baby? My head spins with it all."

She gazed at Sarah, who had begun to stir.

"He studied medicine in London. Oh—do you perhaps know him? You mentioned that you studied in London."

"No, we've not met; he sounds very unpleasant." He had never heard of Edward Carter, but his particular brand of cruelty was all too familiar.

There was something in her eyes, something plaguing her she would not share with him. He knew those eyes well, already.

"Tell me," he said, "how long has it been since you've lain in your bed?"

At the mention of "bed," Samuel stirred. So he had heard the whole conversation. Ian realized he had grabbed her hands without conscious thought and quickly released them. "Go up and rest, Maggie. I will watch over everyone. Even guardian angels need sleep."

Ignoring him, she continued. "Why would this man want to hurt Sarah? Perhaps he is merely incompetent?"

He would find out who this man was and protect Maggie from him, if need be.

The baby began to cry. Maggie rose.

"Please, allow me," he said. "God knows I have a surplus of energy."

Feeding the babe would still the trembling hands he'd been trying to keep under the table, away from her watchful eyes. She thought him odd enough, he knew; he would not have her knowing just how damaged he was.

She rubbed her eyes with her palms. "Why is that, do you suppose? You are the most annoying of men. Do you never tire?"

"Oh yes," he said. "I tire of myself."

She chuckled shortly. He would do his utmost to hear that sound again, at his own expense or no.

He'd seen where she put the other bubby-pot and soon had the baby sucking mightily. It was good to be occupied, to help still the tremble that spread to his entire body, even organs, the humming inside his skin. He held this new life in his hands, so pure; if he could but return to the time of infancy when he was not plagued by this affliction.

Maggie watched him quietly, arms folded on the table. To feel the strength of her arms surrounding him, anchoring him to this world...how could he ever be worthy of her?

Samuel rose and walked over to Sarah, bending to examine her. "She looks better."

"Yes," Maggie mumbled. "Her coloring is much improved, and she breathes easier." And his angel dozed off, head on the table.

"Thanks to our clever girl," Ian said.

Samuel stood before him. "Our girl?"

What had he said? But it was true. Maggie was his. He felt the man's strength, in the hands fisted at his sides, the labored rise and fall of his massive torso.

"You will not take liberties with her, do you understand?"

He met Samuel's eyes. "I will do my utmost to honor her, for she is rare."

"You are good with words, but it is your actions that concern me. Keep your hands off her."

Before Ian left, he draped a shawl over Maggie's shoulders and crept out.

A ship's bell clanged in the fog as he made his way up the Strand. If he climbed aboard that ship, he could escape the memories. The anatomy table with his professors and fellow students. The beauty of the words could not be restrained—latissimus dorsi, salpingopharyngeus- sal-ping-o, phar-in gee-us—over and over, the rhythm pounding through arteries like blood from the heart, the veins back to the chambers of his heart in a song, beating through him, caressing his skin, and he began to sing and knew of nothing else, but someone saying, take him to Bedlam.

Today that ship would sail without him. He must find in nature's storehouse the potion that would heal him, make him whole for her.

Chapter Ten

The next morning she came downstairs blessedly well-rested. Samuel had already gone to the shop, and Ruthie stood by her mother's bed, gazing at her with unease, as if she both dreaded her presence and felt compelled to watch over her. Maggie sipped a cup of strong tea and joined Ruthie at her vigil.

Sarah slept peacefully, her hand curled under her chin. The only sign of abnormality was the frenetic movement of her eyeballs behind the lids. As she puzzled over what that meant, someone rapped on the door.

Martha Wilson, the baker's wife bustled through the doorway carrying a basket heaped with rolls, meat pies, and gingerbread. Maggie had no need to look under the cover; she could smell each and every comestible. The baker's wife put the basket on the table and took off her cloak, peering around avidly. "Is that a pot of tea you've just made?"

It would not do for Martha to be lingering, but she could hardly refuse her friend some simple hospitality. The woman gaped at Sarah, who now shifted restlessly with her thumb in her mouth.

Maggie set another teacup on the table and took the cloth off the basket. "Thank you for the glorious bread, Martha."

"Pardon me?" She tore her eyes from Sarah and

snapped to attention. "You misunderstand, dearie. This basket is intended for Dr. Carter, but do take a slice of gingerbread. I know how much you love it."

Oh. "No, that's quite all right. We have eaten. Wait-Edward Carter?"

"That's right." She sidled over to the bed before she could detain her. "Mistress Sarah seems to be resting well."

"Come have your tea, Martha."

She gaped open-mouthed at Sarah. "Does she speak of her time, er, in the ground?"

"She is tired, of course, like any new mother, but resting peacefully, as you can see."

Martha clasped her hands to her chest. "Holy Father, you have delivered her from the jaws of death, may you be praised. Your servant Sarah nursed my Isadora back to health, and I am forever grateful."

Sarah had nearly worn herself to nothing taking care of the smallpox victims a few months ago. Isadora's case had been severe, and she was left with partial deafness in one ear and unfortunate pock marks. But she was alive, and that was more than could be said for many.

Just then, Sarah opened her ice blue eyes.

"Good morning, Mistress Sarah." Martha waited, but Sarah merely stared, in that vacant, bone-chilling way of hers. Martha backed away from the bed. "Does she speak?"

"No, she doesn't, not just yet. She is a bit altered still."

"Oh my." Martha plopped down at the table, hands shaking as she picked up her tea.

Maggie brought the babe over and hoped that

Joannie would arrive soon to feed her.

"Look at her! She is a beauty," Martha cooed.

She handed her over. "How do your girls fair, Martha?"

She looked up. "My Bess has a sore throat. I sent her and her sister over to Dr. Carter's so he could look at it."

"We must go," Maggie urged. "Now. You do not want Edward Carter touching Bess."

"Why ever not?" her friend scoffed. "He looks like a handsome, competent young lad and charming as a courtier, he is." Her eyes lit with speculation. "And he is unattached."

"Martha, I have heard he is inept and causes pain where there need not be."

"Surely this cannot be true. You must be mistaken. And he says he can do what midwives do, only with instruments that ease the way."

"We must go now to stop him." Maggie snatched her cloak off the hook by the fireplace.

"You want him for yourself, do you?"

She urged the woman on her feet and wrapped her cloak around her. "Please. I will explain on the way." She stopped at the barn to tell Samuel to watch Sarah in the cottage until Joannie arrived.

She grabbed Martha's arm and hurried her along. "I met Henry the night soil man yesterday morning, and he told me how Edward Carter pulled George's teeth, more than were necessary and quite cruelly."

"What? Oh, my sweet girls!" She hastened her speed.

A short time later, they stepped over the prone body of a sailor sprawled in front of the Shipwreck

Hotel and entered the shop next door. Mrs. Wilson gasped like a banked sturgeon, her face alarmingly red.

A painfully thin young man with wispy brown hair hovered in the small waiting room. "C-can I help you?" he stuttered. "D-doctor Carter is busy."

There was a high-pitched giggle in another room and a deeper answering chuckle. A light shone from an open door down a narrow hallway. She ignored the assistant's feeble protests and headed for the sound, Mrs. Wilson in her wake.

A blond man with exceedingly curly hair tied back neatly leaned toward Bess, his hand hovering above her knee. This must be Edward Carter. She gazed up at him from her chair, roses blooming in her cheeks. Isadora sat primly in a corner, shooting daggers at her sister. "Miss Bess," he said, "I find your throat to be raw and red, but minor in its severity. Your ears are free of purulence as well."

Martha barreled into the room and took Bess by the arm and out of the room. "Bess, my lamb. Are you okay?"

Following closely behind, Edward Carter smiled, showing straight, white teeth and dimples in each cheek. "Good morrow, ladies. May I be of service?" He wore a starched white shirt tucked neatly into breeches that displayed his muscular legs to advantage. Although he was not tall, he had a commanding presence and the powerful build of a dockworker. He bowed.

Martha straightened her apron and tucked her hair back into her kerchief, blushing. "Dr. Carter."

"You must be the girls' mother. I see the resemblance immediately. It is indeed a pleasure to meet you, madam."

She handed the basket of food over and curtsied.

"Thank you most kindly," he said. "Your payment far exceeds anything I might have done in service to your beautiful daughters."

The three women glowed with adoration.

Martha tittered. "No, no. It's glad we are that you have come to our town."

He nodded and turned toward Maggie. "Good afternoon, miss. I have not had the pleasure of your acquaintance, for if I had, I would surely remember you."

Martha introduced her and he bowed again, reaching for her hand. She rolled it into a fist and put it behind her back.

His hazel eyes widened. "Oh dear. Have I done something to offend you?"

"You could say that," she mumbled.

He quite ignored her comment and prattled on about how he'd heard of her skill as a midwife and until laying eyes on her had not thought it possible her beauty would outweigh her skill, and so on and so forth. He had a manner of widening his eyes to emphasize a point while spouting his drivel.

She could not help observing he was exceedingly suntanned for someone who spent so much time indoors tending the sick. As she continued to give him the gimlet eye, he began to grow slack. With defeat, perhaps?

"Mistress Wilson, I am relieved to report that Bess will recover, with her mother's loving care." At the word, "loving," Martha fanned herself with her hand.

Edward Carter sighed happily, looking toward the heavens. "Nothing makes me happier than finding my patients in good health."

She'd place a wager against that. Three pairs of eyes gazed at him with dog-like devotion.

He examined his pocket watch. "I regret to say I am expecting another patient presently."

"Doctor," Martha squeaked. "Forgive us for taking up so much of your time. You must come to tea soon. Our Bess here is an accomplished cook." She raised her eyebrows for emphasis. "We must get home. I'm sure my husband needs us at the shop. Maggie, we will pray on our knees nightly for Sarah's recovery, for she is very dear to us."

"Thank you." Their gazes met, and she knew her friend meant every word. Martha and her girls chattered excitedly as they made their way down the street.

Edward Carter looked at his pocket watch again and waited.

"Sir, I would like a word with you."

He tilted his head. "How can I assist you?"

"You can assist me by telling me why you so incompetently pulled poor George Forham's teeth."

"Miss, you are mistaken."

"I saw inside his mouth. Do you not even know the basics of tooth-pulling? George's father himself said you did pull an excess of teeth and caused pain that was not warranted."

His eyes narrowed. "I do not appreciate your accusations. You would believe the village idiot over a skilled physician?"

"I have yet to see the skill." Her face grew hot.

"The silly boy would not hold still. He made it nearly impossible for me to perform the surgery."

"George?" She scoffed. "He is ever the docile

lamb. If he struggled, he did so only because of your ineptitude."

"Now, see here, mistress." His eyes grew hard as agates, and he poked his finger toward her chest. "I insist that you cease your slander."

She would not be put off by his demands. "And another matter. Did you deliver my sister, Sarah Ackerson and mistake her for dead? How could such incompetence occur? You mistook her for having brain fever."

"I assure you, every symptom indicated she had brain fever and indeed she was dead. That she is alive now is something I cannot explain." A corner of his mouth lifted, and he drew a step closer. "Can you?"

"What are you insinuating?"

He smiled. "I have heard the rumors about town and smelled the fear. Perhaps there is a more satanic explanation for Madame Ackerson's return..."

His gaze crawled over her face. The menace was clear. She must keep her mouth shut about his treatment of Sarah, or he would fuel rumors that Satan returned Sarah from the dead.

She longed to leave with the last word, but was speechless with rage and barely noticed the sudden downpour on the way to the cottage.

****

Maggie made an effort to quench her anger upon entering the cottage. It was soon shoved aside by the sight of Sarah tossing and turning by the glow of the fire. Ruthie cringed in the corner. The exposed timbers of the ceiling, darkened with years of smoke, loomed toward her.

Samuel paced with the squalling babe in his arms.

"What am I to do with this lot, Maggie? The babe needs feeding, and I cannot budge Ruthie from her spot. I do not know how to make the babe's food."

Maggie hurried over to Sarah and laid her hand on her sister's forehead, then palpated her hot, hard breasts. It was as she had feared all along; she had milk fever. The midwife manual clearly said the life-threatening condition could be brought on by fear and shock alone.

The only treatment available involved emptying the breasts of milk and dosing her with herbs for fever and discomfort. She would have to act quickly or the fever would worsen, and it would not take long for the poison to spread to the rest of the body. Sarah could very well die unless she could nurse the child as soon as possible.

She hurriedly put warm compresses on her breasts to relieve her discomfort and set about restoring order to the chaos. "Samuel, I will fix some pap, and you will feed the baby just enough to make her cease her crying. Then Sarah must nurse her."

"How can a senseless woman nurse her child?" he asked.

"I shall give Sarah some feverfew in her pap to relieve her pain, and you will feed her so she has the strength to nurse the child. We will prop her up, awake or no, and hold the child to her breast."

Comprehension lit his face. He wasted no time in grabbing the pot and feeding the babe.

"Remember to give her just enough to stop crying."

Ruthie clung to Maggie, the cold sweat from her forehead wetting her apron.

"Ruthie," she grasped her bony shoulders. "What is

amiss?"

"I am afraid."

"Why, Ruthie?"

"I lay down beside Mother. She was asleep too, I think. When she's asleep, I can pretend she is the same mother I always had. Then, all of a sudden, her eyes opened. They were red, and she said—hissed, Aunt Maggie, a word I'd never heard." She began to cry. "In a voice not hers."

She found herself longing for Ian's presence, anchoring her with his bright, green gaze, his soaring voice settling on her like the dawn of summer.

"What did your mother say, Ruthie?"

She pulled away from her bosom. "That hissing voice chanted other words I've never heard, but I heard one word over and over. It sounded like...*ee-shell*."

At the utterance of its name, the presence lay waiting, heaving and powerful.

Chapter Eleven

Despite her unease, Maggie cradled Ruthie's cheeks in her hands. "Ruthie, all is well. We will save your mother, and you will help. You must feed her some pap that has feverfew in it. It will lower her fever, and then she must feed the baby. It is time to be brave. Can you help me now?"

Ruthie nodded. While Maggie and Samuel propped Sarah up, the little girl mixed the pap together according to her aunt's instructions and began to feed her mother. The feverfew and Lena's soporific ale would strengthen Sarah and perhaps relieve her pain, but would she be able to nurse the babe?

As if he had been summoned, Ian arrived, carrying a lute. She followed his eyes taking in the scene. They lit on her, enlivening and calming, glistening like newly garnered mint. Her body seemed to drift toward him, toward the respite the mere sight of him brought her, but she hid her own desire and apprised him of the situation. He removed his coat and vest, rolled up his sleeves, and asked if Sarah had taken the feverfew yet. Maggie nodded.

He reached into his coat pocket and showed her a packet of herbs, finely ground. "I concocted this for Sarah." He added the mixture to the pap boat.

"Thank you."

"I hope it works," he said.

It needed to. Sarah breathed rapidly, cheeks flushed. How could she best nurse the child? First, Maggie instructed Ian to shut the drapes and bolt the door. They could not be too careful. God only knew what someone might think they were doing.

Then, she instructed Ian to help Samuel move her lower in the bed. She had Samuel get into bed with her, behind her head with his legs straddled around her. Sarah leaned against his chest, head lolled, eyes open in slits.

"I can feel her heat through my clothes," Samuel murmured.

"It will take about a half hour for the concoction to take effect," Ian said.

Maggie changed the baby's clout. She took off her little nightgown, working on sheer instinct; perhaps it would help Sarah to feel the baby, skin to skin. Out of consideration for Samuel's feelings, she motioned for Ian to turn his head as she prepared Sarah for breast-feeding. When, God willing, their endeavor was successful, she could drape her to shield her breasts from view.

Sarah's petite size would allow Samuel to hold the baby in his arms in front of her; perhaps it would help to explain to her what they were doing. Sarah had once described the feeling of her milk coming down as a million tiny pin pricks all at once. In her state, how would she react when the baby took hold?

"Sarah, your baby must be fed and you must nurse. Do you remember nursing Ruthie? It will be painful at first, and then you will be much relieved."

She did not respond, but at least with Samuel's touch upon her, she had stilled. Perhaps Ian's medicine was taking effect now.

Maggie opened Sarah's night rail and exposed one hot, engorged breast. She circled her thumb and forefinger around the areole and as gently as possible squeezed the area slowly, rhythmically. Sarah stiffened as the early milk began to seep out.

She nodded to Samuel. "Ruthie, give your father the baby." He held the babe in his arms as Maggie positioned her at Sarah's breast. The babe fussed and rooted for the nipple.

"Samuel, you must be prepared to hold onto Sarah tightly. I do not know what she will do when the suckling begins. It is painful at first."

The babe made several attempts until suddenly, she latched on. Sarah stiffened and uttered an incoherent cry as the strong little jaw clamped down upon her tender breast. Maggie massaged the sides of her sister's breast to encourage the milk to flow, letting out her breath bit by bit as the baby drank greedily. For what seemed like endless hours, they waited.

Then, miraculously, a light of awareness rose upon Sarah's face like the sun. Eyes wide with shock, she looked down at the babe.

"Sarah." Samuel kissed his wife's cheek. "Your daughter. You have a daughter."

She searched his face and laid her hand on the baby's torso, stroking the smooth skin. "I don't remember," she whispered.

Ruthie blinked and placed her hand over her mother's. "I've been taking care of her, Mother."

At the sound of Ruthie's voice, Sarah smiled and reached for her daughter. She closed her eyes, tears rolling down her pallid cheeks. "My sweet Ruthie."

Maggie laid a blanket over the babe and slipped outside to give them time alone, telling Samuel he must have the baby nurse on Sarah's other side as well.

Ian followed her out. She had never felt so elated, so alive.

"It is cold out, sweeting." He draped her cloak about her shoulders, fastening it at the neck with care.

It must have been cold, but she did not feel it and felt as light as a gull on the wing. Sarah had returned to them.

Ian smoothed the hair back from her face. "You are clever beyond measure. You brought Sarah back from her nightmare."

"But you made the medicine that calmed her."

"I merely stirred things, but you, you are worthy of song, my Maggie." He took her face in his hands and kissed her, softly. His firm lips tasted of cloves, warm and spicy.

Sarah alive and conscious, and this man, odd musician-apothecary, like no other, at her side! Having his hands upon her felt as natural as breathing. As he touched her, a heavy weight slid off her shoulders and she saw her joy reflected in his eyes.

"We must get out of the rain," Ian murmured.

When had it begun raining? His fingertips, firm and warm, rested on her upper arms. She reached up into the darkness and laid her palm against the hair lying wet against his head, his shirt plastered to his wide shoulders. Joy magnified as she touched him, felt the elation coursing through him as if his body had joined hers.

The rain cooled the blush on her face as she led him to the barn. With a cold splash of clarity, she remembered what Ruthie had said when she'd first arrived at the cottage. "Something strange..."

"What is it, Maggie? What is troubling you?"

She struggled to focus on Ruthie's story, but in truth, after breathing in his spicy scent, she only wanted to be encircled in his arms. Still, she repeated the word that Sarah had called out in her sleep.

"Ee-shell?" The pressure of his fingers on her arms increased.

"Yes." She leaned into him in the darkness.

He nuzzled his lips in her uncovered hair. "So soft. I believe I've heard that name before. I cannot place it—in my travels, perhaps. I will think upon it when I return home." His voice rumbled in her ear, melodic, rusty.

She must touch him; he was soaked through, his skin warm against the cold shirt. The muscles of his chest played against her hand as he breathed. Without thought, she pulled his shirt out of his breeches and slipped her hands inside it to feel his bare skin. His muscled stomach tightened as her hands slid up his torso. So warm against her cold fingers.

Her palm circled the matting of crisp hairs upon his chest and closed over his heart. She wrapped her other arm around his back. His heart pounded against her palm and he moaned, his hands in her hair, lips upon hers. His manhood strained against her stomach, and she pushed against it.

Suddenly, he cleared his throat and backed away. "There is only one way this will end, my sweet Maggie, if we continue in this fashion. I want to touch you like the finest musical instrument, with delicacy and fervor and not as if you were a common doxy who exists merely to satisfy my itch. You do not deserve such treatment." He kissed her again, gently this time.

She made an effort to steady her breathing and cool the heat that rushed through her body. He left her at the cottage door and walked away, singing as he went. Without his body against hers, she felt as bereft as an orphan.

****

By the time she returned inside, the babe guzzled from the other breast with gusto, and Ruthie snuggled against her mother's side while Samuel rested his chin on Sarah's shoulder.

Samuel glanced up. His eyes narrowed upon seeing her soaked hair. But he merely pressed his lips together, no doubt choosing to ignore her in favor of his newfound contentment. She did not blame him. Why spoil this perfect moment?

As late as the hour was, there were tasks to perform. First on the list was getting Sarah to eat some soup. The babe rested with her wee head on Sarah's neck. Samuel had placed his big hands on top of Sarah's to help her hold the child there. The babe wore the drunken look little ones get when they are beyond sated. She removed her and put her in the cradle, then urged Ruthie upstairs to have a decent night's sleep.

Sarah looked pale, but so greatly improved that Maggie stopped in mid-step and offered a prayer of thanksgiving. Upon opening her eyes, she found Sarah staring at her, eyes slightly unfocused.

"Maggie," she whispered.

She embraced her sister, the first opportunity she'd had. Her shoulders felt parchment thin. "Yes, dear girl. How are you feeling?"

Sarah ignored her question. "What happened to me?"

"You have been quite ill, Sarah."

"I do not remember."

Thank God she did not. Would it be necessary to tell her what had happened before someone in town did? She must have a proper bath—she would soon notice the grave dirt in her hair, would she not? And what if Ruthie said something?

Maggie squeezed her hand. "You have been through a lot, Sarah. You must give yourself time. Give yourself a chance to rest, to regain your strength. Close your eyes and rest while I fetch some soup."

"I fear that if I do, I will disappear again," she croaked, her voice still hoarse from exposure and lack of use. She sank her head back onto the pillow and closed her eyes. "I am so very tired, Maggie. Surely more tired than a new mother should be."

"Do not worry. You'll get your strength back if you do as you're told," Maggie said, happy to play the older sister again. "Now let me see how you're healing."

First, she examined her breasts; they had already improved. After she fed Sarah and made her comfortable again, she wandered over to the table and noted with relish all the food the townspeople had brought, out of kindness and curiosity. For the first time in a long time, she tucked into a meal with fervor.

Ian had forgotten his lute. She ran her fingers over the neck of it, and imagined his fingers stroking, warming it with his caress, applying with delicacy just the right pressure upon the strings, upon her.

She took a deep shaky breath. What might have

happened in the barn if he had not stopped her? She had all but invited him to take her maidenhood, without hesitation, thinking nothing of the consequences. She barely knew herself anymore. But the feel of his torso against hers, smooth like polished beach rock...

What had she almost done, that she would let herself be at the mercy of a man's desires, just like her mother? That she had almost let a man take her on the floor of a barn? But the heat and pleasure rushed through her, and she understood what it meant to yearn. So there existed a man who could control his urges? Or perhaps he stopped because he did not desire her the same.

He had left the imprint of his lips upon hers and his own essence from his tongue in her mouth. The warm molten honey had flowed through her body and the only thought had been how she could get closer to him.

Reality washed over her like the splash of a rogue wave. It was clear: she was not one iota different from any other woman, from her mother. What stopped her from becoming her mother, powerless against the needs of a man?

Sarah sat up when the babe began to cry. Maggie placed the child in her arms again so it could feed. Sarah lay back and sighed contentedly. Their own mother came to mind unbidden. Never had contentment touched her face, only the pinched look of grim acceptance and suffering as one babe pulled at her teat and another reached his arms up for her, two more children playing in squalor at her feet.

Shortly after her mother's death, Father took his fists to the pub for a change of pace and died of knife wounds. By then, she was under the tutelage of the old midwife, and she and Sarah helped with problem deliveries for local farmers when they needed slim hands. Five years later, smallpox took their brothers and sisters. Samuel married Sarah, and they moved to King's Harbour.

How close she had come this evening to risking herself, becoming her mother, without hope, a victim of a man's selfishness. Had she forgotten the promise to herself? But what of the rightness of his heart beating against her hand, his touch awakening her body? What of her needs? She splashed her flushed face with cool water from the ewer.

She resumed her meal. There were other more pressing things to consider. How to make Edward Carter accountable for his malevolent treatment of Sarah? She had felt the threat of his ill intent when she questioned him about her sister. He had made it clear he would happily ruin them with his malice-barbed words, spoken with that unctuous charm. She had worked hard to establish herself as the town's midwife and would not let him destroy her reputation.

Jonas must be questioned again. Surely he knew something, for he certainly acted guilty. How to extract information without attracting attention? Would Edward Carter wreak vengeance on her as he had threatened?

The food soon succeeded in making her sleepy. As she stood up to go sit in the rocker, she noticed the heavy weight in her apron and pulled out the strange figurine that had been in Sarah's hand. With her handkerchief she dusted the dirt off, taking it by the fireplace to study in the dim light.

It was a statuette of red clay, hardened by age. An

old woman with a bent back carried a water vase, upside down. She had a hawk-like nose, with fierce, slanted eyes like a cat, her sharp chin jutting out, mouth agape as if speaking. On top of her head, a coiled serpent hovered, fangs sharp and ready to strike. A chill crawled on the back of Maggie's neck.

Suddenly, the statuette glowed like an ember snatched from the fire, but did not burn her. She hastily placed it on the mantel and prayed for calm. Where had this strange object come from? What did it mean? She climbed the stairs to sleep for a few hours. Surely she must rest or go mad.

****

In the deep of night, a woman's voice downstairs roused her.

"We can wait no longer," the voice commanded. "We have saved her. She must join her sister and avenge."

"Holy God, what is this?" Samuel cried.

She clattered down the stairs. Samuel stood with the fire poker in his hand. The fire roared in the fireplace behind him, sparks rising. He stared at the opposite wall, where reflected in the glow of the fire, the shadow of the old woman stood, her fierce eyes the only color glowing amber into Maggie's. The snake upon her head undulated, body coiled in a knot, forked tongue flitting in and out from between sharp fangs.

"I have waited long, midwife. We have saved her. I carry the power of the womb in every woman and will help you but you must avenge. *Tu hermana*—your sister—is saved so together you might destroy this womb killer."

Her legs grew weak. "What would you have me

107

do?"

The shadow of the fierce old woman swelled and threatened. Maggie's heart throbbed in her throat as the shadow of the snake took on skin and scales of yellow and green and uncoiled from its mistress's head, slithering down the wall into the dark recesses of the room.

Chapter Twelve

"*Intuicion, medicina,*" the spirit rasped. In a vapor the color of red clay, the old woman vanished.

Maggie heard a rustling beside her. Sarah was kneeling, hands raised in prayer, then collapsed on the floor. Samuel rushed to pick her up and carried her to bed. Upon examination, she was not hurt, merely weak.

"Sarah," she said, clasping her hand. "You are not strong enough yet to get out of bed. Why did you kneel to that apparition?"

"I don't know," Sarah whispered. "I only knew that I must."

"Light the candles, Maggie." Samuel stood guard over Sarah, one hand holding the poker and the other upon Sarah's shoulder, and darted a glance at the wall where the spirit had been. He wiped the sweat from his brow and motioned for a quivering Ruthie to crawl into bed with her mother. "Do not worry, Ruthie. I will watch over you."

"Samuel, I am not afraid," Sarah murmured and fell asleep at once, as did Ruthie. Maggie lit the candle on the mantelpiece with trembling hands. The figure of the old woman still rested there where she had placed it. She grasped it in her hand; perhaps holding it would give her understanding. The figures were the same, yes—the gnarled hands, serpent upon the head—and the water jar overturned—what did it mean?

Samuel shifted position and squinted, scanning the room. "Maggie," he whispered, in a strangled voice. "What was real? The snake, that woman—how can I protect my family against—what is it? Is it Satan? Sweet Jesus, fetch us some whisky."

She handed him a glass and took a sip of her own, the fire of it reassuring. This she understood: whisky burned when she swallowed. She was a midwife. Her life was dictated by the moon and the wombs of women. She dealt in what could be seen: A woman's belly swells with child and with a midwife's help and the force of her womb, together they bring forth her child. The force of her womb—power—power and pain—is that what the snake woman meant by "the power of the womb?"

Maggie examined the babe and found her sleeping as soundly as her mother. She and Samuel stood in silence, listening to their regular breathing, and before long her tight muscles loosened, just a bit.

Samuel swayed on his feet.

"Samuel, why do you not sit?"

He shook himself. "No, I must guard them. Maybe it's true what some of the town are saying, that Satan brought Sarah back. Perhaps if I get Vicar Andrews...no, I do not believe it." He rubbed his hand over his face. "I tell you, Maggie. Dawn cannot come soon enough."

"Samuel, what did the spirit mean when she said, 'we have saved her?' Who saved her?"

He did not answer.

A prickling of unease crawled from Maggie's forehead to her shoulders. The weight of her confusion pressed upon her chest. She felt herself sinking into cold depths and struggled to breathe.

And then soft hands rested upon her head and a voice of infinite gentleness whispered, "Do not be fearful, midwife. All is well."

"Who are you?" she asked, searching the room and noticing Samuel's alarm.

"What is it, Maggie?"

"I don't know. I only know she has reassured me. You did not hear her?"

"Her? Who?"

"I don't know. She said not to be afraid, that all was well." Peace settled over her as still she felt gentle hands upon her shoulders in blessing.

"Could she be an angel?" Hope brightened his face.

"Mayhap she is. I feel no malevolence from her, only peace. One thing for certain, Samuel; we must trust in Sarah's goodness."

"Yes, but what of the apparition and the snake?"

"I will speak with Ian." The thought of seeing him again helped steady her, as dawn seemed a lifetime away. The smile that cajoled the dimple under his eye to come out and play. The sound of his laughter, uninhibited and inviting.

Samuel snorted. "What makes you think he has the answers?"

"I don't know. He has seen the world, has seen many inexplicable things. And he speaks many languages."

A genuine chuckle rumbled out of Samuel's throat. "Why do you not just admit you are sweet on him?"

Despite the dimness of the room, she hoped he could not see her deep blush. It was a waste of time to lie, for Samuel knew her too well. "He is learned."

"Oh yes." He snorted.

She sputtered then gave up, deciding to save her strength.

"Make sure he does not teach you too much, Maggie."

Did the man think her an idiot? Midwives must adhere to a high standard of behavior, and no one knew that more than she.

She glanced at the window. A sliver of grey light appeared under the curtain. "Oh praise God."

Samuel opened the curtains wide. The long night had passed. A survey of the room revealed burning embers in the fireplace, the candles having sputtered out long ago. The steady breathing of Ruthie and Sarah and the more rapid breathing of the baby was a comfort. No one looking in on the scene now would ever believe what had transpired during the night.

There was much to do today. She slipped outside and around to the back to gather eggs and reveled in the fresh, crisp air. The morning melody of birdsong did much to invigorate her. She would make Sarah a posset today and send Ruthie off to Joannie's, so they could talk.

The familiar squeak of Henry's night soil wagon broke her reverie. She followed the smell to the front.

"Miss Maggie. Going to be a fine morning." Henry jumped off the wagon and grinned at her as he fed their mare a wizened apple from his pocket.

George came to stand at his side and smiled, wincing a bit.

"Hello, young George."

"Morning, Miss Maggie," he whispered, hiding behind his father's back.

"How are you feeling?"

He slid beside his father. "Better, ma'am."

Henry elbowed him.

George started. "Thank you."

Henry patted him on the back for his effort. "The apothecary, who if you don't mind my saying, is a bit of an odd fellow..."

Maggie nodded. It was true. She was enamored of an odd fellow. She was enamored. Oh God.

"...anyway, he gave him oil of clove as you said he would and was quite kind. I will spread the word, as diligently as I spread..." He swept his hand out to show the contents of his wagon "...this."

She laughed. "For that I thank you, for he is peculiar, but a good man."

He cocked his head, a veiled look in his eyes. "Did you hear the latest?"

"No."

"Old Jonas was in his cups at the Siren Inn last night talking about when he found your sister. What was he doing at the kirkyard at that hour, anyway?"

A good question, one she needed Jonas to answer today.

"He was blathering on about the ghosts. 'The ghosts, the ghosts.' Drunken old fool."

"Ghosts?" A chill trickled down her shoulder blades.

He glanced behind his shoulder at George, who idly petted the horse's mane. "George! Get the shovel out of the wagon. I'll be right there."

"Did he say anything else?"

"No, miss. I'd better get to work, then." He tipped his hat, his hazel eyes gazing into hers.

After they left, it occurred to Maggie he was several days early for his scheduled visit. How curious.

****

She set about making eggs with the reassuring sound of Sarah singing a lullaby. A well-rested Ruthie perched on the side of the bed, singing along with her mother. Samuel poured water into the ewer, rubbing his face and grunting. It set Ruthie to giggling and soon her mother as well. The sound did much to enliven the room.

After a hefty breakfast, Samuel went to the shop, and Ruthie walked to Joannie's house to see if she could be of help. By that time, Sarah had fed the babe and tucked her into the cradle.

"I am hungry." She stretched her arms upward and yawned.

"Well, and it's no wonder." Maggie handed her a plate. "Remember not to eat too fast. You haven't had solid food since..."

"Since when?" she asked.

Sarah appeared noticeably better, compared to last night. Her skin, always pale, bore a hint of rose. She moved with greater ease. She had not yet noticed that her hair, which had been wrapped in a cloth when Maggie had hastily cleaned her, was still full of grave dirt.

"What is it, Maggie?"

Oh, her sister was certainly more alert. Samuel must bring the bathtub in the house so she could wash her hair. For if she saw the grave dirt... "Nothing, my dear. Finish your breakfast and then you must rest."

Maggie hastened to Samuel's workshop to speak with him about the bathtub. He was repairing a scythe for Mr. Johnson, who squinted at her suspiciously and then lowered his eyes. The night she had sat with his daughter during the smallpox she had never seen a fever rise so high. She did not think she would make it, but toward dawn the fever broke, and she and Sarah returned daily to apply poultices to her sores. It was a miracle she had survived. Was her service to him so easily forgotten?

"Maggie, I'll be coming in after I finish here. Go and do your business."

Samuel would not want Mr. Johnson to know he was returning home to nap in the middle of the morning. He was not used to nightly vigils, all too common for a midwife. She couldn't resist winking at Samuel. He scowled.

After he returned to the house, Maggie set out into a windy cold morning. It buoyed her considerably to be out near the docks, where the dark clouds loomed over the slate grey sea. The hammering of repairmen working in the shipyard and bits of their singing and shouting mixed with the cries of gulls carried on the wind. A fishing skiff fought against the whitecaps and sidled in to dock at the bay. This familiar scene did much to chase the fear of last night away.

She'd often thought if she were one of the local gentry and had nothing to do but tend to her own leisure, she would spend all day watching the ships come in. King's Harbour had some of the most skilled craftsmen in the kingdom, and ships from other nations would even risk an encounter with the smugglers and Hawkhurst gang members to avail themselves of their skill.

She pulled her cloak around herself. She was not a

lady of leisure, and her women had need of her. Icy rain began to fall. She headed for the warmth of the Siren Inn to check on little Sabine.

She opened the heavy doors to the overpowering smell of rum.

"*Ach*, you drunken sot," her friend Lena yelled at the figure of her husband Josef crouching over a fallen barrel. "Five gallons of rum, on the floor. Go ahead, proceed, lick it up, waste not a drop, you *dummkopf.*" She towered over him with a broom in her hands.

At that, he straightened his lean, muscled back, menace in every muscle. He rubbed his hand over his pated forehead and stared at Lena with eyes in slits, body weaving ever so slightly. Lena took a few steps backward, silent now, her face red with suppressed rage.

For such a small man, his voice was surprisingly deep. "*Meine Frau,* do not push me too far. Mayhap I should have the magistrate wipe the rust off the scold's bridle."

Maggie gasped. Josef must be drunk indeed to mention the day that Lena, a new bride, was forced to walk around town, an iron mask upon her face. She was being punished for nagging and arguing with her new husband. She had just moved to town and had witnessed this short but effective form of discipline.

Lena's face now looked whitewashed, and she grimaced, as if she could still taste the metal tab in her mouth that had kept her from talking. "Oh, you would not do that," she said under her breath.

They stood nose to nose, both huffing and puffing. "No, I would not." And he laughed, swaying and whispered, "For I do love your sweet *willing* flesh under me, Lena."

Lena blushed and smirked. Maggie gathered that in the long run, the scold's bridle had resulted in more punishment for Josef than Lena.

She turned away as they locked their lips in a kiss. Before meeting Ian, she would have been puzzled at their behavior. Now the memory of his touch upon her skin made her yearn.

Lena pulled away from her husband. "Maggie, once again you look as if you slept not at all. Come, I have tea." She motioned her to a table by the window.

"I really do not have time, Lena, though I do appreciate it. I'm here to see Sabine."

"You can drink a quick cup."

"As long as none of your ale's in it. You heard about my shameful conduct."

"Oh *ja*," she said dismissively. "More interested I am in this man of yours."

"He's not my man," she scoffed.

"All right, all right. I can see you're in no mood to joke."

"How is Sabine?"

"*Ach*! The poor child. I have gone up to check on her as often as I could, but it was very busy last night. I brought her some breakfast, and she seems improved. Whoever did this to her, I could kill with my bare hands." Then her face softened. "The baby, she is an angel. I could hold her all day."

She patted Lena's hand. "You will be holding a baby of your own someday soon, Lena. The tea was delicious. Thank you for caring for the girl."

She made her way upstairs. Fortunately the willow bark had given poor Sabine some relief; the pinched look had eased, and she seemed more alert, flashing Maggie a smile of recognition, displaying a set of dimples on each side of her mouth. The babe lay in her arms dressed in a white embroidered gown that no doubt had come from Lena. An empty bowl lay on the bedside table, a napkin tucked under the girl's chin. Thank God her good friend had been administering to this girl. Maggie sat for a minute with her hand upon Sabine's and spoke with her, knowing she could not understand.

"Hello, Sabine. I am going to examine your privities, so I might make you feel better. Let's see how you are progressing." She hoped the girl could sense the comfort she tried to convey in her voice. She placed the baby in the cradle and pulled Sabine's bedcoverings down.

The girl gazed, toffee eyes glistening. She cried out as Maggie gently touched the area around her birth passage and took a deep breath through her nostrils to conceal a growing rage. When Edward Carter pulled the baby out, he had torn the outer area of her birth passage. She did not know what kind of damage he had done inside with his forceps.

Where had this poor girl come from? How did she happen to be in this Gerard Blanc's possession, and why would Edward Carter bring the child forth early? Merely to be brutal or so she could return to work? She applied a cool compress of lavender and seaweed on the young mother's privities. Sabine started and then sighed with relief.

"Leave this on for as long as you wish, the longer the better," Maggie said, knowing she could not understand. How to communicate with her? How was she to build a case against Carter if they could not communicate? She must find someone that spoke her language...perhaps Ian. How easily he came to mind, as if he were already there, waiting. If she ever slept, he would probably be in her dreams.

She gave Sabine a dose of willow bark and settled her in bed once again. Where was Gerard Blanc? Lena said he hadn't been seen since last night. How had a young, beautiful girl come to such a pass? Only time would tell if her injuries would fully heal.

She stopped downstairs to give Lena instructions on the medicines. From the sound of Josef's whistling and the glow of Lena's plump cheeks, it was clear what they'd been up to.

Around midday, Maggie ventured out into a hard, driving rain. She would visit Ian to ask him for his help in unearthing information about the strange figurine in her pocket and Sabine's strange language.

If she'd not known the way to the apothecary shop by heart, she would have been in danger of getting lost in the blinding gusts of rain from the channel. Salt water stung her eyes, and bits of dirt and pebbles flew into her face. She reached the shop with relief.

One would think he would have heard when the wind slammed the door behind, but he was oblivious, crouched over a teardrop-shaped string instrument. The fingers of one hand wrapped around the narrow upper neck of the instrument, while the other hand strummed lightly on the strings. He looked down, as if he sang to it in his rusty and rumbling voice, one eyebrow raised and the other hidden behind a lock of hair that had fallen into his face.

"No, you dolt," he muttered, stopping to glare at

the offending instrument. Completely ignorant of her presence, he tapped his foot on the stool and began again. His fingers lightly caressed the strings on the neck. How would they feel upon her skin, pressing, searching? She closed her eyes, the better to feel his voice.

But the spell was broken when he shook his head and growled. "No! Utter rot!" He sighed and began again.

She could not speak, could not move. The note rose into the air, floating, liquid, sweet, and settled upon her. His voice slipped inside to fill her emptiness.

"Maggie."

She opened her eyes to find his gaze intent upon her.

"I feel quite foolish," he murmured. "I had hoped to finish this song before you heard it, and now you have ruined the surprise."

Before she could take a breath, he appeared at her side. He put his hands on her upper arms.

She cleared her throat. "You are writing a song for me?" She leaned into him without thought.

He nodded. "That is sometimes what men—smart men, I say—do when they want to court a woman."

"Court me?"

He slid his hands down her arms to clasp her fingers in his. "Yes, Maggie. I am asking Samuel tonight for his permission to court you." He brought her hands to his mouth, kissing them.

"You don't have to ask him; I am of age."

"But I want to show him that I respect him and you, of course."

She wanted to say the work horse does not get

courted. She might get ridden, sold or bought, but courted? She bridled her tongue instead.

His eyes searched hers with intent. "Do I have *your* permission?" He grinned, showing the dimple right below his eye. "Of course, I will court you whether you say yea or nay."

"Oh, you will, will you?" She turned from him, to hide her smile. "You have a high opinion of yourself."

"I only know that you are rare, my Maggie, and I will not lose you." He turned her toward him, touched his lips to her forehead, and tucked wisps of hair under her cap. Then he moved away, handing her a cloth to dry herself. He settled her upon a stool to watch him work.

"Are you comfortable, sweeting?"

She nodded, blushing. He busied himself around the shop, pouring liquids, repositioning vials and bottles behind the counter at lightning speed. He sat, he rose, he talked, he sang, foreign songs and folk songs and bits of nonsense. What ailed the man? Was he always like this? His vitality both buoyed and annoyed her, and she smiled despite herself.

The wind blew sleet against the window, a reminder of her purpose here. The fool man was so distracting.

"I need more willow bark and feverfew."

He touched her sleeve. "Do you?" His eyebrows rose. "Are you certain? Could it be you merely wanted to see me again?" He waggled his sun-bleached eyebrows.

She sputtered and snatched her arm from him. "No! I have more pressing things to do than waste time here with you."

Her words had no effect on him. He grinned, edging close again, and stroked her cheek with the back of his hand. "I am happy to provide you with whatever you need."

"I must ask a favor of you, then. Would you visit Sabine and see if she speaks a language you know?"

"Of course." His breath swept across her face. She could not stop the pull of her lips toward him.

He stepped away, once again humming and darting about, polishing the already spotless counter. "Willow bark? Here we go." He wrapped up the herb with a flourish and gathered the other medicines she had mentioned.

Without warning, she felt the heat of the craven object burn in her apron. When she reached in to retrieve it, she found a hole in the pocket.

"My Lord!" She examined the burnt spot.

He rushed over. "What is wrong?"

She put it into his hand.

He shifted it from one hand to the other. "It's hot."

"Yes, this strange object is always warm, but never this hot before."

He turned it over in his hand, examining the curious bent shape of an old woman, with her hawk nose, slanted cat eyes and a snake coiled upon her head. "Where did you get this?"

"I found it underneath Sarah's bed a few nights ago. Do you know what it is?"

"No," he said, absorbed in his examination. "But..."

"What?"

"I have seen something similar to it, I don't remember where. It may be a talisman of some sort. Let us go into my parlor, and we will peruse one of my books." He took her hand, raised his brows in invitation, and pulled her along before she could think about the wisdom of such a venture. If anyone should see her alone with a man in his parlor, her reputation would be ruined for certain.

But it doesn't feel at all wrong, she mused. The warmth of his hand made her feel she had entered a sanctuary, where she could breathe in the peace and forget herself. But never had her body felt like this in church.

Is it a sin for me to desire a measure of peace and comfort in my life? No one with any sense would be out in this weather; why should I worry so? And I need someone's help. Why not this man?

She followed him through the narrow hallway to his private quarters. He stopped up short. Her bosom pressed against the long bands of muscles in his back.

"Oh, pardon me," he said, with such an obvious lack of sincerity she snorted with amusement.

He set the figurine on a table, lit some candles, and stoked the fire. The small room was unadorned by knickknacks or art. Lutes and other string instruments were lined up against the wall. Pipes, flutes, and what looked like an organ grinder's machine sat on the chairs. While the shop had been without a speck of dust, the tables and mantel of the sitting room were covered with a layer of dust. The bricks in the fireplace needed scrubbing, and the fire grate was black with soot. All in all, it lacked a woman's touch.

"Please excuse the sad state of this room," he said sheepishly. "I have not had sufficient time or indeed a reason to tidy it." He flopped down on the settee and patted the space beside him. Aware she might not be able to control the consequences of such proximity, she sat just the same.

He picked up the figure and placed it back into her hands; it had cooled. He cupped his hand over it, index finger lightly caressing the back of her hand. "It looks ancient."

"I heard Sarah say it," she said tentatively.

"Say what?"

"That word—Ee-shell."

"You heard it?" He peered at her.

"I know it sounds absurd, but I heard her say it."

He smiled. "Mistress Maggie."

It seemed everything he said, he sang, in the husky voice that made her want to soothe his muscular throat with her fingers.

He untied the string of her cap, lifting it off and smoothing her hair, slowly, deliberately. "Nothing," he said, "that has come out of your mouth in the time I have known you, my sensible Maggie, has been the least bit absurd. It is just that there is much in this world that cannot be explained." He skimmed her lips with his index finger. "Like the feel of your lips, petal soft."

Without thinking, she closed her mouth around his finger and leaned toward him to slide it in further; he closed his eyes. Her center warmed with moisture. After a time, he slowly pulled away, and replaced his finger with his lips, soft and warm, and then his tongue. He slid his hands into her hair, over her shoulders, undid her bodice, caressing her breasts through the thin shift while sliding his tongue slowly into her mouth so she could taste the essence of him, spice and male.

He lowered his head, kissing the swell of her

breasts. "Maggie." His lips closed over her nipple, sending licks of flame within her. She yearned to draw him in.

The clock chimed. She pulled away, the warmth of his life force ebbing from her. She stood, put clothing and composure together again.

He joined her, quite still for once. "I am sorry."

She nodded and struggled to slow her breathing. "I will not risk being held captive by your whims and desires, a fleeting amusement you pick up now and then like one of your musical instruments."

He took her hands, drew her closer. His labored breath grazed her forehead.

"Look at me, Maggie." He lifted her chin.

As she looked into his eyes, her center shifted.

"Do you not have desires of your own, my Maggie?"

"Better to deny my desires than to be at a man's mercy, ruled by his selfishness."

He held her face between his hands. "I admit I am not perfect. Although I have no claim on you, yet, your happiness has become my goal, my...home. I would not want to disappoint you." He kissed her with exquisite care.

She backed away. "There are more important things than tending to my own happiness. I need your help."

He picked up the figurine and walked over to a bookcase, placed it on top, and squatted down, humming to himself, a tune she'd heard in the Siren Inn, "I Love a Lusty Gal," or some such nonsense.

"I know it's here somewhere." With chaotic speed, he removed one book, flitted through the pages, and shoved it back on the shelf with a grunt. "No. Ah, here it is." He rocked back and forth on his heels as he thumbed through pages. She joined him as he pointed to the page.

"Ixchel, or pronounced 'Ee-shell,' is a Mayan Goddess of childbirth and medicine," he said.

"Mayan?"

"A civilization in the Central Americas. Very ancient."

"This Ixchel, who is she?" Maggie asked.

"She aids and protects women in childbirth and pregnancy. She is the giver of rain. See the water urn?" He kissed the top of her head. "Like you, my sweet Maggie, she is the giver of life."

She could not help it—his praise made her center glow with pleasure. Oh, this would not do, lingering alone with him. "What about the snake?"

"I don't know," he said. "But I will find out."

It was as if she'd summoned the snake: at the mere mention of it, the shadow upon the wall of the hawk-nosed goddess with the ears of a cat and the hiss of a snake reappeared to her.

"What is it, Maggie? You are afraid?" He cupped her cheek; she could not help leaning into his hand.

Why should she not tell him about the visitation? For there was no one else on whom to depend. Samuel was not a simpleton, but he was a simple man. It was not within his power to comprehend this. She certainly could not share this with any of the townspeople, including Lena.

"Tell me." He gathered her into his arms. "Share your fears with me, Maggie. You do not have to be alone."

The solid length of his body, his strong arms around her stilled her trembling, but she could not tell him anything else. If she said it aloud, it would be real.

"I need to return to the cottage."

He tucked his nose into her neck and breathed deeply. "Ah."

"I must get back."

"I will escort you." He stood, straightening his attire. She saw the bulge of his desire.

"No, I can manage on my own."

"I *will* escort you," he said with a dark look she'd not seen before.

He guided her to her door through the blowing sleet and said he would return that night to ask for Samuel's permission to begin their courtship, although as he said, kissing her forehead, their courtship had already begun.

Maggie opened the door to find Sarah slowly moving about. Ruthie shadowed her anxiously. While she was gone, at Sarah's request, Ruthie first helped her stand, and they discovered she could walk short distances without dizziness or trouble. She moved a bit gingerly like any mother newly delivered. Ruthie had pulled her mother's hair up in a simple bun, emphasizing her high cheekbones and translucent skin.

Maggie stood for a moment in the center of the room, searching high and low for the serpent, walking around and peering into recesses where it might hide. She could feel its eyes upon her, waiting.

"Aunt Maggie," Ruthie said. "What are you looking for? May I help?"

She started. "Oh nothing important, Ruthie. Never mind."

Sarah perched at the table. "I feel inordinately weak, Maggie. I find I must sit and rest every few minutes." She talked slower than usual, as if she listened with one ear to another conversation. "I don't remember being so fatigued when Ruthie was born." She shifted on the bench. "I had to lie down after I combed my hair." She grimaced with revulsion. "Maggie, I had dirt in my hair! What happened to me? I feel...different."

Oh no. The bath. While she was at Ian's, thinking of her own pleasure and puzzling on things she didn't understand, she'd forgotten about giving Sarah a bath. She'd feared this would happen. How do you tell someone that they had been buried alive?

Samuel trudged in, covered in soot from the forge. Instead of going straight to the ewer as he usually did, he walked directly to Sarah, and teeth white in his black-smeared face, placed a smacking kiss upon her lips.

She sat dumbfounded, a blush creeping up her neck. "Samuel!"

He made for the ewer then, and there Maggie apprised him of Sarah's questions, hating to spoil his ebullient mood. But if they did not tell her, one of the townspeople would.

"Ruthie," Samuel said. "How long has it been since you practiced your letters? Go over by the fire and do your schoolwork, if you please."

She obeyed, casting an anxious glance at her mother. Maggie helped Sarah back to bed. "Sarah. There is something we must tell you. When your birth pains began, I was in Winchelsea. Do you recall?"

She closed her eyes for a moment. "I felt very ill

that day—my ankles so swollen I could not lace my boots, and my head pounded." She swallowed with effort. "The pains came on sudden and strong when I was at the Smyth's. I arrived home in the wagon. Everything seems blank for a while, and then...I saw a man standing by the bedside. He said he was the new doctor."

She looked up, eyes brimming with tears. "I wanted you, Maggie. I did not want him to touch me, but the pains were powerful. He gave me something to drink, said it would help. And then... I recall nothing, not even when the babe was born. Why can I not remember?" She put her hands over her face. "I don't remember delivering my own child!"

Maggie glanced at Samuel. They could keep the truth from Sarah no longer.

He grasped her hand. "Sarah. We do not know how this happened, but after you delivered the babe, you appeared to be dead. Of course now we know you were not."

She stared, face ashen. "How can this be? I don't understand."

"Samuel speaks the truth, Sarah," she said. "And you were buried with great haste. The doctor said you had brain fever. We don't think that was true, for no one survives it. We know nothing of the man who delivered you other than his reputation has been less than stellar in this town in the short time he has been here. I am trying to find out what happened."

"I was buried—alive?" She pulled at her hair, the bits of grave dirt falling on the quilt. She moaned and rocked back and forth. Ruthie dropped her book and ran to her.

"Sarah," Maggie urged. "For Ruthie and the baby's sake, you must try to remain calm. It is a lot to take in. Rest while I make you a calming tisane."

Sarah's voice faltered. "Who rescued me?"

"A man named Ian Pierce arrived at the graveyard and saw you on the ground in your winding sheet," Samuel said.

"He brought you home, Sarah," Maggie said. "He saved you, and that is why you are here now."

Sarah rose and grabbed Samuel's shoulders. "How could you mistake me for dead?"

He flinched as if she'd slapped him.

"Sister, all I know for certain is that the doctor, this Edward Carter, made an error to which he won't admit. But you are safe now, Sarah. You are safe and back with us again, praise God."

She did not respond to that, but said, "When did this happen?"

"Three days hence."

"Why do I not remember?"

Maggie looked helplessly at Samuel and struggled to find the right words. "You were insensible."

"And finally, the nursing of the babe seemed to bring you to your senses," she added.

Sarah began to shake and frantically brushed her hands over her body. "I was buried. I do not remember that." Her voice rose. "I was buried? I wore a shroud? I was in the ground. I was buried." She plucked at her skin and clothes, moaning.

Holy Lord, do not let her lose her senses again.

"Sarah, please!" Maggie cried. "For the babe's sake, you must calm yourself. You must think of the babe and Ruthie. I promise you I will find out what

130

happened. There will be justice. I promise."

She ceased her frantic movements and in a monotone whispered, "A bath. I must cleanse myself. I must...sweet Jesus!" She began to cry in great, gasping sobs.

Samuel held her, crooning, "You will have your bath, my sweet. I will fetch the tub. You will have your bath and Maggie will scent the water with lavender, your favorite."

Maggie laid more wood in the hearth and set about heating the water. "Ruthie, fetch *Robinson Crusoe* to read to your mother." This would occupy both Ruthie and perhaps soothe Sarah, along with the tisane she gave Sarah.

Before long, Samuel helped Sarah into the tub and with Ruthie reading in the background, he washed her hair and bathed her with great care. After Sarah's bath, they fed her and tucked her into bed. She fell asleep after the baby suckled. Ruthie took the babe from her mother and placed her in the cradle. Maggie sighed and eyed Samuel. He sat in the rocker with a generous glass of whisky. She poured one as well, and they sat in silence, listening to the rain beat against the windowpane. It had grown dark.

When there had been plenty to do, the events of last night could be swept aside. Now in the quiet, she grew cold despite the fire. Somewhere in this room, a serpent waited, coiled and ready to strike. A spirit loomed over them. Mayhap she was benign as Ian had said. But how could they know for sure? Where was the snake?

Chapter Thirteen

Maggie's song echoed in Ian's head as he beat its rhythm upon her door and crept in when no one answered. Immediately, he inhaled the raw exhaustion on her skin and helplessness radiated from her. Would music soothe her as it soothed him?

She did not hear him enter and did not know about his visit to Samuel after he'd walked her home earlier that afternoon.

Samuel glanced up when he entered the barn, then resumed pounding a horseshoe. The forge fire warmed the spacious barn and cast shadows on the farm implements hung in an orderly fashion on the wall.

Ian waited, heart pounding. While the blacksmith worked, he amused himself by having a staring match with a large tabby curled on a saddle. It served to calm him a bit. Eventually Samuel paused in his work, black brows raised in expectation.

Ian bowed. "Good afternoon." Much to his dismay, he had to clear his throat.

Come on, man. You have sung for King George II himself. Surely asking this simple man for permission is not as daunting as all of those dour German faces gaping at you.

Yes, but King George does not have bandy forearms that could crack me like a walnut.

Samuel wiped the sweat off his face, glanced at the

plow on his right, and waited. "What do you want?"

He fortified himself with a deep breath. "I would like to ask permission to court Mistress Maggie."

He nodded. "Yes, it is time for her to marry. You are a decent man; you saved my Sarah." He squinted. "But you're a restless sort, aren't you? You have been wandering for years. What will keep you here?"

Ian met his eyes, tried to still his trembling eyelids. "Maggie will. I will do my utmost to be worthy of her, as a man and a husband."

Samuel folded his arms. "So you will marry her?"

He lifted his chin, ignoring the buzzing in his ears. No. He would not give in to this affliction now. "If she will allow it. But I would like to court her first."

"Oh, she will allow it." Samuel studied him, eyes following the tapping foot. Ian tried to still it, but no use.

"You are impulsive," he stated.

"Yes."

He leaned forward. "I wonder. Are you a man of substance and constancy? Or will you flit off again to parts unknown, leaving Maggie alone with a brood of children?"

"I am not going anywhere. I am bound to continue the legacy my father began, to serve the needs of the people of King's Harbour as best I can." He clenched his hands into fists to still them.

"During your courtship," Samuel growled, "you will refrain from doing anything that will sully her reputation. We are under scrutiny from the town, all of us."

"I will guard her virtue, and I will stay. I must."

Samuel nodded and stood, glancing at his

mandolin. "I suppose you will be playing your infernal music constantly?"

Ian shrugged. "Most likely."

Samuel sighed and shook his hand. "As I am indebted to you for Sarah's life, I will allow your courtship of Maggie. I promise you I will break your neck if you are as frivolous as you seem." He lifted a massive plow upon the work table as if it was a feather.

He dismissed Ian with a wave. "Go forth, Mr. Pierce. Go court my sister-in-law."

****

That evening, Ian returned in his Sunday best: buckskin breeches, a brown silk jacket with jade buttons, made to order in China. Never had he thought it would be worn for such an occasion. He could not resist fiddling with the neck cloth as he paid his respects to Samuel. Sarah lay in the bed, eyes closed. She was noticeably paler than when last seen. What had happened?

He'd brought along his mandolin; putting his fingers to work helped to calm the music playing uninvited in his head. The last time he'd played for them, it seemed to soothe them. He strummed a whisper.

Maggie took in his attire, grey eyes almost black. The intensity of her gaze burned into his skin.

She set the table for tea, the corners of her mouth flitting up. "How like you to show up in time for tea. I assume you have forgotten to eat again."

He nodded, watching her mouth move, remembered how it closed over his finger, moist, warm. A blush crawled up the smooth column of her throat. She remembered too, he could tell. His eyes followed the path his lips had taken earlier that day.

They were interrupted by rustling in the bed. "Maggie?" Sarah cleared her throat. "Is that the man who saved me?"

Ah. So Sarah knows. That explained Maggie's distress.

Maggie motioned for him to follow her to the bed. "Yes, Sarah."

Her large, blue eyes seemed to see through him. "Good evening, Mr. Pierce."

"Good evening, Madame Ackerson. How are you feeling?"

She closed her eyes for a moment and swallowed. "I am confused, but grateful. Thank you for rescuing me."

"It was an honor to bring you home."

She nodded. "I am sorry about your brother. Maggie and I did everything we could to nurse him back from the smallpox, but to our sorrow we could not save him. He was a fine man."

"He was. Thank you for your efforts on his behalf. Now I have kept you talking long enough. Can I bring you a plate of food?"

"I am not hungry, just now, but I thank you." She closed her eyes again; a fine trembling coursed through her.

He went to the hearth to fetch some warming bricks, but guessed it would take more than that to remedy the chill the knowledge of her death and return had given her.

Tea commenced after Maggie insisted upon setting Sarah up with a small meal. Conversation at the table waxed and waned. Ruthie sat beside him and nudged him with bits of news and reports of her reading progress. Maggie was mostly silent, keeping her eyes upon Sarah. She busied herself tidying up, moving about with her usual efficiency. Samuel had returned to the rocking chair, pipe in hand.

"Miss Maggie." Ian grabbed hold of her hand as she went by.

She avoided his eyes.

"Sit a moment. I have something I must ask you."

She shook her head. "I expect to hear from young Polly Jamison's family this evening. She looked fair to popping yesterday when I checked on her. I don't have time to dawdle about."

"Please," he croaked.

She plopped down, mutiny on her face.

"You recall my saying I would court you," he began.

"Court me?"

"Yes," he whispered. "In the shop this afternoon, remember?"

"What? Yes, yes, but I did not take you seriously. You were singing at the time."

"So what has that to do with it? The song was about you."

"You meant it?"

"Of course I meant it, woman! I may jest from time to time, but about music, never."

"Well, I..." She held his gaze, pink suffusing her neck and bosom.

At that moment, devil take it, there was a pounding at the door.

She shot up. "I told you it would not be long."

Vicar Andrews entered with a wide smile for

Maggie and a wary look reserved for Ian.

"Vicar Andrews, won't you have some tea? Are you hungry?"

He swept off his hat, splattering water on the scones and shepherd's pie. "Oh, so very sorry, pardon me," he mumbled, taking a dingy handkerchief out of his pocket and swiping at the table.

He spotted Sarah. "Madame Ackerson! God be praised. He has indeed answered my prayers. Good e'en to you, Miss Ruthie, Samuel."

"Yes." Sarah clasped his hand. "I am grateful for your prayers, Vicar."

The vicar kept glancing over at Maggie, with a look of...oh ho! Surely not. She idly stirred her tea. Odd, that.

"Vicar Andrews," she called. "Come warm your belly with some tea and a bit of lamb and fresh scones."

"Please excuse me." He patted Sarah's hand and ventured over to the table. "It is indeed with Mistress Maggie that I must speak."

"What brings you out in this dreadful weather?" She set a plate heaped high before him.

He ignored the food. "Well, actually, it has cleared, and the stars are now out. It is tolerable." He held the teacup in his hand and stared into its depths. He flushed, and ventured forth. "I am afraid, Miss Maggie, that I have received considerable complaints about your, er, conduct at the marketplace yesterday."

He fixed Ian with a gimlet eye. "Your conduct in the marketplace was most scandalous. I could scarce prepare my sermon for tomorrow because of parishioners visiting me. They say when Sarah...came out, she brought Satan with her, and they say the devil has wormed his way into your heart, Miss Maggie."

Maggie gasped. "That is nonsense, Vicar!"

Samuel rushed to stand by Sarah. She appeared to be asleep, thankfully. "You cannot believe such tales, can you, Vicar?"

"No." Vicar shook his head emphatically. "I am nothing if not assured of your wife and Miss Maggie's virtue." His gaze lingered a bit too long at Maggie. "Even though it appears *others* have forgotten that of late."

Maggie glared at this bit of ecclesiastical censure.

Vicar rubbed his hands in distress. "What can I tell my flock to assure them all is well? I am at a loss."

Maggie sighed. "I will see you in church tomorrow, barring any unexpected birthing. It is not my fault sometimes God chooses to bring forth life during your services."

Ian coughed down a laugh.

She fisted her hands at her sides. "Vicar, do you not realize we have only ever striven to do God's work?"

He nodded. "Indeed, I do realize that, Mistress. What could be more righteous than to bring one of God's little lambs into the world?"

"Vicar," Maggie entreated, palms up, "I thank you for your understanding and your confidence in us." Her hair had slipped out of its cap again, and she brushed it out of her face. "I ask you to please do whatever you can to still the rumors. For I assure you, I am truly sorry for my conduct and will do my utmost to discover the nature of Sarah's travail."

With assurances he would do what he could and with one more dirty look in Ian's direction, the vicar set off. Maggie stared after him, feet planted on the floor, her fists opening and closing, mouth open and eyes black as a cauldron.

Samuel sidled away from her. "Maggie," he warned. "Calm yourself." He made haste for the rocking chair. Mayhap he had seen her in this state before?

While Ian may have never courted anyone before, he knew this was not a fine time to woo a fair maiden.

But I have myself been beside myself a time or two, ah—how intriguing a line—have myself, been beside myself——stop, man.

So perhaps he could be of help. He lightly touched Maggie's shoulder.

"What?" She snapped.

"My lady, would not a walk be a fine idea?"

"Good idea," Samuel grunted.

"Oftentimes a man will attempt to take the woman he is courting for a walk," Ian said.

"Now, in the dark?"

"Vicar says there are stars out."

"Vicar can go to..."

"Maggie!" Samuel barked. "Go."

Ian laughed. She shot him daggers.

"Do not argue with me, Maggie." Samuel's voice was strangled. "Bundle up."

She put on her cloak, and when he tried to hold her arm, she jerked away. His love song would have to wait.

The sleet had left the ground slippery. Fingers of frost crept up the folds of his cloak, but Maggie did not seem to notice the cold as yet. He had never seen her in a temper before. It was most entertaining and not a little frightening. She strode ahead, leaning into her bad leg. He should not call it that at all, for surely it is a very fine leg, straddled over his, in bed. He did not mind being behind her, not one bit, for she treated him to the sight of her sweet backside.

She muttered to herself, every so often barking out epitaphs like a mad dog. "I give my life over...for the sake of the women of this town...miscreants...I do nothing for myself, nothing! Up at all hours, no one, no one...son of a shit...ingratitude...how dare..."

Oh, so my Maggie is not always in control.

The ground was treacherous. If he did not come to her aid, she would surely fall.

"Maggie, let me help you."

He ventured up to her and grasped her arm. She glared but did not pull away. She stood, gasping for breath. Her hair had fallen into her eyes again, and she swiped it away impatiently.

"What do you want from me?"

"Your love," he said.

She took her cloak off and threw it at him. "Make yourself useful, then, and carry my cloak. I am overheated."

"You will catch your death. It is freezing out."

"I don't get ill."

****

She couldn't have tolerated being in the cottage for another minute. To be chastised like a common doxy! For all she did to serve the people in this town! For the endless years of toiling, bringing babies safely into this world, since before she had even had her first monthly courses.

Her head seethed like a boiling pot. She must walk

until it cooled, for she was beyond the desire to control herself. Her feet slipped on the icy cobbles, and she slowed her pace with effort.

The infernal troubadour trailed behind her like a hound dog. Then he was beside her, taking her arm. Why resist him? Why deny that his touch made her tremble? Made her body feel alive for the first time? What had being virtuous done for her, when the regard of the townspeople was so easily lost? When these good women could so easily distrust and forget what she had done for them. She felt like an instrument of the devil, full of poison and a heartbeat away from screaming like a harpy and clawing her way through town.

He held her upper arm firmly, and she felt his fingers through her cloak, cool, calm. A deep rumbling arose from his chest, and he began humming, then louder, to match the ferocity of the wind. That was the preamble, apparently, for suddenly he released her arm, leaped in front of her and began to sing.

"My woman, when she's angry, puts Medusa's hair to shame.

She rouses all my senses and sets my soul to flame
When she unleashes fury, a virago gone insane
I'm only very thankful I am not the one to blame."

Arms and legs akimbo, he sketched a courtly minuet, bowing, gesturing, pantomiming like a court jester.

Rage leaked out of her like holes in a faulty bucket. The moon had come out, and his hair had come loose. He looked mad, capering about, repeating the song and every so often eyeing her hopefully, like a jester seeking the queen's approval.

"You are a fool," Maggie gulped.

He bowed. "I am not just any fool, my queen. I am your fool." He grinned, cross-eyed.

She laughed grudgingly, all other thoughts gone but the sight of the madman in front of her. "You are a fool," she repeated.

"Well," he admitted. "There have been a few occasions when I have been forced to act the fool for a fee."

The clouds gulped the moon. Ian bent toward her; she grasped the solid strength of his shoulders and breathed in his warm scent, licorice root and lemon, and found his mouth. If she had already been labeled a wanton, what harm would it do to give in to her desire? His lips warm, so alive, his tongue tangled in hers. She slipped her hands inside his cloak to his back and pushed his lower body into hers, feeling the bulge of his desire against her belly, and she strained against him.

He kissed her face, her neck, slipping his hands under her bodice, stroking the tender skin of her stomach through her worn shift. His other hand cupped her bottom, pushed her against the thick length of his member. She ground against him, her center pulsing, searching to feel his hard heat against, inside her.

Without warning, he pushed her away.

"Miss Maggie." A shocked voice at her elbow belonging to young Ben Miller, slapped her like a wave. She turned away to regain composure; she had not heard the boy's approach.

Ian grabbed his arm. "What is it?"

"Miss Maggie," the boy said again, tugging at her sleeve. "You are wanted at the Siren Inn. Madame Lena told me to fetch you. She said the foreign girl is bad." He stamped his feet and rubbed his hands together. "It's frightful cold out here, Miss Maggie. I went to the house to look for ye, and, and...er."

"Ben, go to my home and fetch my bag. Hurry!"

He nodded and ran off.

They didn't speak as they fought the wind to the Siren Inn. Dismay iced her gut upon grimly considering her predicament. She had been seen clinging to Ian like a wanton by the son of Mae Miller, the worst gossip in town. She was ruined.

What was Samuel thinking, encouraging them to walk out together tonight, when it was clear she cannot stop touching him? But there were more important matters at hand now, were there not? Sabine—what had happened to her?

They burst into the warmth of the Siren Inn. Lena had a good crowd tonight. Sailors and merchantmen alike lolled about the tables, singing and muttering epitaphs at a deafening volume. Out of the corner of her eye, Maggie noticed three known members of the Hawkhurst Gang sat in a corner, heads together, guns on the table.

Ian narrowed his eyes. "Do you often frequent this place at night?"

"What do you think, jackass?" She snapped, as they fought their way through the swaying bodies. "It is not as if women deliver babies here often."

They worked their way up the narrow staircase and down the hallway to the Sabine's room. Ian's presence buoyed her as she thought of the girl's keeper.

She knocked on the door. "Sabine, it is Miss Maggie, come to check on you. May I enter?"

Lena opened the door. "Thank God you're here, Maggie."

The room was in great disarray, with clothes and articles flung upon the floor, the stench of dirty clouts, beef broth and dried blood assaulting her nostrils. Sabine lay sunken into the bed, her dark eyes stark against the covers, her face covered with bruises.

"This morning," Lena said, "when I brought her porridge, Gerard Blanc took it at the door. When I asked him how she was, the idiot nearly bit my head off. It is Saturday, *ja*? I have been too busy to check on her, and I have not seen the bounder since. Oh I should have checked on her!" She backed out of the room. "I must return to the kitchen."

Maggie felt the girl's forehead. "Her skin is clammy."

Ian stood at the other side of the bed. He lifted up her arm and held two fingers on the inside of her wrist. "Her pulse is erratic."

"I must examine her. Will you stay, in case she speaks and you can translate?"

He nodded, eyes steady on her. "I would not leave you here alone, Maggie. She speaks Cantonese, of which I'm familiar."

"How did you know that?"

"I came to see her earlier, at your request, remember? I will tell you later what I discovered. Now I will make a poultice for her face and make sure nothing is broken."

"Oh. Thank you." She smoothed the girl's dark hair back from her forehead. "Sabine."

Her eyes flickered open, a hint of recognition showed, then they flickered shut again.

"I am going to examine you now."

Maggie lifted the covers. The linens beneath

Sabine were soaked with blood. She needed her bag. For now she could only hold a cloth on the poor girl's privities in an attempt to stanch the bleeding that had resulted from the beating.

The door swung open. "Miss Maggie, I have your..." Ben entered. "Oh—what have you done?" He threw the bag upon the floor and ran out.

No time to think about the ramifications of the boy witnessing this bloody mess. She and Ian worked together to do what could be done to stop the bleeding. In the course of a few hours, the bleeding slowed.

A cold sweat prickled her forehead. Why would anyone do this to Sabine?

Ian stood over the girl, his lips pressed together. "My God," he said. "Someone must have seen me questioning her and meant to punish her for talking. I should have been more careful."

"No." She felt her bile rise. "How could you have known?"

Lena entered with the baby.

"Lena, can you continue to care for the child?"

She nodded.

They sat vigil with her for a while longer. She did not show great improvement, but on the other hand, she had not worsened.

She gave Sabine an extra dose of feverfew. As she and Ian left, the bell tolled four in the morning. She staggered under a weight of foreboding. There was great depravity afoot; a man who would bury a woman alive would not balk at beating a defenseless girl. She had accused Edward Carter of wrongdoing yesterday, and now Ian had been seen questioning Sabine. A young boy would go home and tell his scandal-loving mother that a girl lay in a pool of blood, and Maggie Wilson was at the bedside. Not to mention she had been seen in an indecent embrace with a man.

As if reading her thoughts, Ian said, "Maggie, my dear." His hoarse tenor bit into the cold air. "Do not worry."

"My reputation as a midwife and a respectable woman is in tatters," she said. "And this poor girl may die because of a scoundrel I have no grounds yet to accuse. The townspeople will think I am responsible for Sabine's death if she dies."

His eyes gleamed in the dark. "But you are not responsible, and the truth usually has a way of coming out."

"Would that I could be as optimistic as you are."

He put his arm around her waist. She had not the strength to resist him. The warmth and comfort of his touch softened the ragged edge of her tortured thoughts. Her eyes closed of their own accord, and she let him guide her home.

"I will tell you what I discovered from speaking to Sabine. She was sold by her father and taken to Hong Kong by a man who...trained...her, and when she was sufficiently trained, was then sold to Edward Carter. During the journey, it was discovered she was with child, and he brought her here until she delivered, before her time. She thinks he will take the baby and sell it into slavery."

She stopped, chills coursing through her. "We must stop him. We must gather evidence against him. All we have is the word of a foreign girl against Carter."

"I will not sleep tonight, but you can." He soothed her forehead with his fingertips. "I will see what can be discovered about Edward Carter's activities."

He kissed her at the door, lips warm in the frigid air. "Sleep, Maggie. Nothing can be done about our troubles tonight." He disappeared into the darkness.

Once inside the darkened cottage, she washed at the basin, the rapid breathing of the baby and Sarah's steady breaths accompanied by Samuel's snoring comforted her with their normalcy.

She built up the fire and covered the baby. When she turned toward Sarah to do the same, something moved on the bed. Her breath caught in her throat, and she forced it out. It was merely her sister's hand, under the covers.

Then, in the light of the fire, the iridescent scales of the snake glowed. It wound up Sarah's body to her shoulder, coiled. Yellow eyes glowed into Maggie's. Her mouth would not open to scream, and her body hardened to a pillar of salt, arms leaden at her sides.

She could not draw her eyes away from the snake's eyes, the center a thin sliver, like a shadowed moon. The forked tongue of the serpent flicked toward her, commanding compliance, and she fought the weight of it upon her body, dry, cold, tried to scream, but salt filled her mouth and she could not.

"It is time. You must fight," it hissed. "You must fight for them."

The serpent rubbed against Sarah's cheek, forked tongue close to her mouth, as if it whispered secrets. Then it crept down her shoulders and slithered off the bed, disappearing into the darkness.

For a moment Maggie could not move, then ran her hands over Sarah's body. What had the snake done to her?

She stirred. "Maggie? Is everything okay?"

It took all she had to answer in a normal voice. "Go back to sleep, Sister. Everything is fine."

She had read the Bible; the snake was an instrument of the devil. Was this not proof that Satan had brought Sarah back from the dead? What did it mean when it said to fight for them? Fight for whom? It was the same thing the strange goddess had told her, though. Was she meant to fight for the women Edward Carter killed? Were there more victims like Sarah? How was she to find out?

She sank into the rocking chair and gave in to her fear and exhaustion. Where had the snake gone? She must contact the vicar for help. Satan, in the form of a snake, was here.

Chapter Fourteen

Maggie dozed off in the rocking chair for a while. Upon awakening, she could barely button the bodice of her Sunday best, fatigue making her fingers stiff as a crone's. Samuel and the vicar had made it clear she must attend services this morning. She sipped a cup of tea while the household still slept.

"I feel wonderful." Sarah sat in bed and stretched her arms into the air, yawning loudly. The pale skin of yesterday had been replaced with the warm glow of health upon her cheeks. "I'm getting up." She bounded out of bed.

"Sarah, be careful."

Her sister stood at the cradle, put the babe to her breast, and sat in the rocking chair. She turned her head, grinned, showing the space where her tooth had been pulled. "She is a hungry little mite, isn't she?" She sighed lustily. "It is good to be alive, Maggie."

Samuel awoke and soon Ruthie clattered downstairs, eyes wide as Sarah now moved about the cottage, greeting Ruthie with vitality so pronounced from the night before that chills skittered up Maggie's spine. How could she be so improved in one night's time?

The serpent's visitation from the night before crowded her thoughts as she and Ruthie walked to church, sliding into a pew at the last moment. Mae

Miller, Ben's mother, shot them a look of such venom she surely thought she must have imagined it. Others stared in similar fashion. She busied herself with the prayer book, heat prickling her face.

Mae leaned toward her. "Well, indeed we have experienced a miracle you are in our midst, especially after your *eventful* evening." She sidled away as far as she could and whispered in her husband's ear.

Worry lay like a hot stone in Maggie's belly. To what was Mae referring, her shameless embrace with Ian or the horrid scene at the Siren Inn?

Fortunately, the choir began singing, and before long, Vicar Andrews walked to the pulpit. For the moment, she found comfort in the familiar words as the Litany began.

A rush of cold air swept down the aisle as the door burst open. The vicar's eyebrows lifted as Ian slipped into the empty spot beside her. The cool wool of his cloak brushed her sleeve, bringing a refreshing change to the stuffy room.

Her face pulsed with heat. What could the fool be thinking? After the evening's events, the last thing that needed to happen was for them to be seen together, adding fuel to the fire. Stupid man.

When the congregation knelt as one, he bowed his head, sneaking a sideways glance at her. She glared at him when they sat and attempted to concentrate on the vicar's soothing voice. Ian's foot tapped a silent staccato rhythm; the muscles of his thigh bulged and lengthened against her leg. His scent drifted out of the folds of his clothes, clove, salt of sea, and sweat. She imagined him on a ship's deck, sun aglow on his face, the swell of the waves reflected in his eyes.

Later, as the congregation sang, he burst out in his tenor, all smiles and exuberance, earning shocked gasps from the people nearby. But a look of such innocence shone on his face, she could not help smiling and lost her place in the music. He nodded in rhythm to the music. Did he move even in his sleep? The hymn faded as the thought of watching him in his sleep, tousled and warm, filled her head. Her mouth grew dry.

She made a last feeble attempt to listen to the Lord's word. She had a thankful heart, she did—he had given Sarah back to them, but what was happening to her now? She must speak to the vicar. She glanced at Ian and for one brief moment, peace and warmth enveloped her, whether it made sense or no.

Eventually, the service ended, and the townspeople brushed past hurriedly without meeting her eyes, and no one spoke a word to her but Ian, whom she did her best to ignore. She was good and truly ruined.

Vicar stood with Mae Miller and in a booming voice intoned, "Remember that Christ said, 'Let ye who are without sin cast the first stone.' Let us not judge others, my good lady."

As she and Ruthie made their way home, Maggie tried to avoid Ian by walking ahead, but his legs were very long. He paid her rudeness no heed, instead attending to Ruthie's enthusiastic chirping. When they arrived home, she was surprised to find Sarah had already laid out the table for noon meal.

She clasped Ian's hand. He winced, grinning at the strength behind it.

"My good man," she exclaimed, "nothing I say could express how grateful I am to you. Thank you for bringing me home."

Ian bowed and kissed her hand.

Samuel's countenance as they ate together indicated he had heard about Maggie's behavior the night before. Between bites he scowled in her direction, but kept quiet. Perhaps he did not want to upset Ruthie and Sarah with his anger.

Ian amused Ruthie with talk of his time with King George II. His face shone with animation, eyes alive. He simply could not hold still. He drummed his fingers on the table, making Ruthie giggle, and Sarah's lilting laugh filled the room. More than once the fool jiggled the table, meriting a venomous look from Samuel. He seemed oblivious to the strained atmosphere—or was he? His eyes followed Sarah with interest. Every so often he eyed Maggie with a warm, assessing gaze, making every inch of her skin feel bathed in cream.

Later, Sarah returned to bed to nurse the baby, and Ruthie trotted off to Joannie's house. After they left, Samuel picked up the water bucket and motioned for Maggie to follow him out the door. She waited as he filled the bucket from the well.

Finally he spoke. "What has come over you? Have you no mind for your reputation or that of the family? Have you no morals, no...decency?"

She swallowed hard on her anger and strove for honesty. Why did Ian affect her so? When he touched her or merely looked at her, his eyes took her away to a place of respite, her body awakened and answered to his. Why was that wrong? Did she not deserve a measure of comfort when all around them chaos reigned?

"Samuel, I don't care to discuss it. I assure you I had not intended this to happen. But I..."

He put his hand on her arm and shook his head. "If he is an honorable man, Maggie, he will marry you."

"Marry me?" It was as if he'd thrown the bucket of water over her head. "I have only just met him. I do not know him. It is too soon. Marry me?" she repeated.

"You desire, er, feel an affinity for him, do you not?" He reddened, wiping the sweat off his forehead with his work-scarred hand. "These are women's matters, and if Sarah was herself, I would not be discussing this with you."

"I feel for him, yes, but I do not know him. What kind of a man is he? I do not know."

"If he is any good at it, he can make a good living as an apothecary."

"I make my own living and have done so for nigh on ten years."

"Do you not want children of your own, Maggie?"

"I...yes, I don't know!" The image of Mother rose unbidden in her mind, the day she learned Maggie had started her monthly courses and put her head on the table and wept. Is that what she wanted, to be like her? To be at the mercy of a man and the moon? Because were not all men much the same as her father, selfish at heart?

Samuel eyed the door furtively, shifting the bucket from hand to hand. "He seems a decent man. And Ruthie likes him," he added.

"Oh, for that alone I should marry him," Maggie drawled. "She is fond of him because he is continually in motion, like a child. Have you noticed? He's like an organ grinder's monkey, always scrambling about."

The monkey himself poked his head out the door. "Can I assist you?"

She ignored Samuel's chuckle. At least his mood had improved. "I must ask you a question."

Samuel took the water inside. Ian followed her on the path to the barn, where they might talk more privately.

"What is it, Maggie?"

She told him about the visitation of Ixchel and the snake.

"I knew there was something you were not telling me." He laid his hand on her cheek. "Sweeting, you do not have to struggle alone."

"When you left me at the door last night," she continued, encouraged he did not think her insane, "the snake was curled upon Sarah's body, and I could not break my gaze from its eyes. It spoke to me! I did not imagine it."

He smoothed a strand of hair back from her face. "No, I am sure you did not."

Dread rose in her as she said the words aloud. "There is a serpent, the devil's instrument, in the cottage. How do I cast it out? Do I summon the vicar? I do not know what to do."

He grasped her by the shoulders. "Look at me, Maggie. The snake upon Ixchel's head—in the Mayan civilization, it is a symbol of medicine, of healing."

She stepped back. "It was a snake who tempted Eve with the apple. It is because of the snake's temptation that my women must suffer so!"

"I have learned in my travels that there are many different ways of believing, Maggie, in civilizations more ancient than ours. For the Greeks as well, the snake is a symbol of medicine and healing."

"But," she sputtered.

He took her hands. "I have learned not to question the ways of other countries, but to accept."

"That's wonderful for you," she retorted. "But how does that help now? Some of the people in this town think Sarah has risen from the dead like Christ. Others think it was Satan. I know neither one is true, and a childbirth goddess tells me I must avenge the death of the women whom this Edward Carter has killed? What am I to do?"

He wrapped his long arms around her. "Consider this, Maggie mine: Sarah is markedly improved. We can all see it. Perhaps the snake is not destructive but has come to heal her."

"But why?" His touch gave her no small measure of strength, and she began to sense his logic. "Oh. This Ixchel means for Sarah to help in this endeavor. But how? She cannot be seen about in public yet, she must be churched first, and it has not even been a week since her travails. What must I do?"

"You are a most capable woman, Maggie. You will do what needs to be done, like you always do. And you are not alone. I am here." He kissed her.

She drew in his breath like a baby draws its first.

He walked her to the cottage door, touched his lips to hers in farewell. "I will return this evening."

Back in the cottage, she told Samuel about the snake.

His eyes grew wide with disbelief. "How can this be?"

"Look at her, Samuel," she whispered.

She lay on her side asleep, hands under her chin. Her normally pale complexion glowed with vitality, as if lit from within.

"We cannot deny that she has improved. A day ago, she could not move about, and now she can scarcely be contained. There is something at work here, Samuel."

He shook his head. "I do not understand such things." Despite it being only early afternoon, no one could blame him for pouring a measure of whisky for himself and sinking into the rocking chair.

Chapter Fifteen

When Maggie opened the door for Ian later that night, her dark brows rose. Perhaps she approved of his attire: buckskin pants, top coat of dark green with a silk sheen to it, and a silk cravat he'd bought in Cathay. It is not every day a man like him proposes to the healer of his soul.

The room crackled with vigor as Maggie set the table for tea with quiet efficiency of movement and that single-minded way of hers. As he approached Sarah and grasped her hand, he felt the river of strength coursing from her into him. "It is wonderful to see you looking so well, madame."

She laughed. "I would not be in this fine condition were it not for you."

They sat down for tea. Samuel sat beside Sarah, sliding glances at her from time to time, brows puckered in concern.

Maggie leaned over the table slicing bread, cheeks flushed, making her eyes glow like the moon. She handed her sister a cup of tea. "Mind you it's hot, Sarah." She stared at her plate.

Sarah ate with the gusto of a sailor, devouring a slice of eel pie and looking inquiringly around the table before she cut another. "I could help you on your rounds tomorrow, Maggie."

Maggie jerked her head up. "What? Sarah, you

157

know you cannot leave the house until you're churched." She shook her head and exchanged a glance with Samuel.

He noted Maggie's utter stillness as Sarah said, eyes glowing with cheerful defiance. "I see no reason to be idle when in fact I feel teeming with good health."

Even he, a hapless bachelor (but hopefully not for long) knew that after childbirth, a woman must stay in her home for a month. After the baptism of the baby, she is allowed to return to society.

Maggie's look of utter astonishment would have been comical if he did not feel her distress resound in his bones. "You cannot, Sarah. You know this!"

Sarah shook her head. "I could be helping you, Maggie. You have worked yourself to the bone of late, and why should I not work if I'm able?"

"This is not like you at all, Sister. We women must do things according to the tradition and for your health as well. Most women are not even out of bed at this point. Besides, we are under enough scrutiny from the townspeople already." She scowled at him.

Sarah folded her arms and glared at all of them in turn. "You cannot keep me imprisoned here. I am needed."

Samuel pushed up from the table. "Sarah, go back to bed. You are overwrought." He took her arm. As he led her to the bed, she jerked it away from him. "I am not tired," she snapped and stomped off to sit in the rocking chair. Samuel returned to the table, looking as if he'd been slapped.

Maggie's eyes met Ian's. Worry swam in the grey depths. "Never in all of my life have I seen her behave so badly. My sweet Sarah would never have spoken to her husband like that."

"Ever?" It seemed hard to believe.

"I have always been envious of how my sister can control her temper. Indeed, nothing seemed to vex her." Her high color began to fade. "I always tried to be more like her, but I never could."

He resisted the urge to kiss her palm and hold it to his heart. "You should be no one but yourself, my Maggie."

Sarah picked up the crying baby and returned to the rocking chair, humming in a monotone voice that matched the rhythm of her rocking.

Samuel shook his head. "What are we to do with her? What is happening to my wife?"

"She will have to be watched closely," Maggie said.

Samuel nodded. "She must not leave the house."

What an inopportune time to ask for Maggie's hand in marriage. On the other hand, it might distract her from her troubles. The song he'd written for her beat against his heart and insisted he share it soon, whether he willed it or not. He had wanted to be at his best tonight, to present himself to her as a person worthy of her, but could not slow the blood bursting through his veins, could not stop fiddling with his neck cloth.

Ruthie came through the door, going immediately to her mother. She wrapped her arms around her neck and kissed her.

"Aunt Maggie," she chirped, as she bounded over to the table. "You should have seen that boy of Joannie's. My, his head is swollen."

"Oh!" Ian saw the resolute focusing of her eyes on

Ruthie. "Jimmy is the tall one, is that not correct? Will he be okay?"

"Certainly," he said. "I had to stitch him up, but he'll be recovered in no time."

"We have need of Joannie." Maggie lowered her voice. "She can keep an eye on things."

Soon thereafter, Samuel helped Sarah back to bed and lit his pipe by the fire. Ruthie played with her dolly by the hearth. Maggie busied herself with tidying up, and he tried to avoid staring at her but could not help himself, for the more he saw her, the more he must breathe her in. A man of three and thirty, suddenly shy! He had travelled the world, met women beautiful and bounteous. But no one like Maggie. He missed his lute, for music helped his hands to still.

She bustled around the room, lifting things up, putting them down again. He grabbed her hand as she wiped down the table.

"Sit a moment, will you please, Miss Maggie? I must ask you something."

She jerked her hand away. "I have bigger concerns than a conversation with you."

"Please, I beseech thee."

She plopped down, irritation wrinkling her forehead.

"You recall my request to court you."

"Court me?" She blushed then scowled.

"I..." He faltered and she held his gaze.

"It seems that I have discovered that I...that I..." He, who spoke with a golden tongue to kings, sheiks, and fierce warriors throughout the wide world over, could not speak to this woman with the dark, winged brows, who stared intently at him as if she could unpeel him layer by layer. He could not put his thoughts together as she glared.

"It seems," Ian croaked, "that with my full heart I know that I must ask..."

At that moment someone knocked upon the door. The vicar, again. Blast the man! His visits were as regular as a horse's bowels.

He stood at the threshold. "I must speak with you, Mistress Maggie. I have spent this Lord's day listening to the most horrendous rumors about your conduct last night, and again, I defended your virtue." He eyed her expectantly.

She stood with her arms folded, lips pressed together.

"I would not give credence to them until I asked you if they were true. It concerns a parishioner who saw you and Mr. Pierce in a passionate, most indecent embrace. Late at night. Behaving in a manner *most* unseemly." He paused. "In full view of the public."

Maggie took a deep breath. "I will not lie to you, Vicar."

He sighed and shook his head. "I am deeply disappointed in your conduct, although I do not think you are to blame." He eyed Ian pointedly. "Miss Maggie, your reputation is most certainly ruined, but it's much worse than that."

"Just what is going on, Vicar?" Samuel demanded.

"Rumors have increased that your wife has brought Satan out from the grave with her." His hands fisted at his sides as he turned to Maggie. "They say your indecent conduct is evidence of the devil's handiwork, you who have always been a godly woman. And there are rumors you harmed that poor foreign girl."

"No," Ian stepped forward. "That rumor is most untrue. Maggie only came to her aid."

"He's right," Maggie said. "I have done nothing wrong."

"It doesn't matter," Samuel whispered, glancing at Sarah. "It is what they think. What can we do, Vicar?"

"I will marry you." Ian met her eyes, begged her to acquiesce. "Mayhap it will appease them. It would not be the first time someone let their passions get the best of them."

Her eyes grew wide.

"I cannot guarantee that it will work," he said. "But I think it will help."

"I see no other recourse." Samuel nodded.

Vicar cleared his throat. "Some say, Mistress Maggie, that you summoned the devil to bring your sister back from the dead."

Maggie gasped. "Who would say such things?"

His Maggie had told him about Edward Carter's threat to spread rumors. He would pay him a visit. Tonight.

"It is not fair." She slammed her fist upon the table, making the babe cry.

"You have no choice," Samuel yelled. "You will marry."

They stood toe to toe, Maggie's chest heaving, Samuel's dark eyes in slits.

The vicar glared at Ian expectantly. Now? This is not how he planned it, but he would do whatever necessary to ease her way. So he kneeled in front of her. She stood, arms folded, staring down at him like an avenging angel.

"Maggie, my heart. You are a woman most unique

and rare." He took her hands. "Would you live with me, be my wife and companion? I will honor and love you. I will serve you, with all that I have within me. I will sing you my soul."

Her eyes glinted like black onyx. "Yes, damn you."

The vicar gasped, "Mistress Maggie!"

Ian kissed her fisted hands. As his lips brushed against her knuckles, her flesh yielded toward him, just slightly. She smiled.

Vicar cleared his throat. "I will ask for a special license from Doctor's Commons. The wedding is day after tomorrow."

****

Ian had proposed and now set about readying the house for his new bride. He straightened from dusting and saw the parlor with a stranger's eyes: threadbare rug, a worn divan, dingy lace doilies, and a fireplace in need of polishing. A miniature of his mother sat upon the mantel along with a Chinese figurine from the Ming Dynasty he'd sent home to Daniel.

He smiled at the thought of Daniel receiving the object in the post. He could hear his practical brother say, "It is just like Ian to send something completely useless."

He had found the vase in Hong Kong while in search for a cure. The hunger and chaos of the crowded markets beat at the base of his throat, the smells of dumplings, sweat, and fear that pierced his skin like needles. He had walked endlessly, days on end, every movement and sound flowing through his veins, into his mind, heart and filled it to bursting—joy, pain—making him throb from the inside out. In his jagged thoughts Ian wondered if his condition was an affliction or a blessing. Until the descent into the dark pit.

Remembrance faded like wisps of smoke, and he slowly became aware he'd broken in two the flute held in his hands. He could not control it then: how would he hold himself now, close his senses off to everything around him?

He shook himself. He would not dwell on doubts. There must be a combination of the many herbs and tinctures in his travel chests that could alleviate the torment, if only he would work harder. He would trust his instincts, how the glow of her eyes and her purposeful movements quieted him. He would put himself in her hands, and pray God she would never know what plagued him. Pray God he could worship her body so well she would forget all else.

He climbed the stairs to the sleeping chamber, struggling to catch his breath in anticipation of their wedding night. In two days he would sink his face into the valley of her waist, cradle her lush hips in his hands, taste her sweet nipples, and make her back arch with desire. Precipitous and obligatory their wedding might be, but he would make sure she would not regret it.

He scanned the room, looking for what might be needed to make it more welcoming for her. It had not altered from when Daniel had lived here alone. It was Spartan but large with a simple bedside table and a brass bed. The walls were bare, and the only spot of color was a satin bedcover of imperial blue that had belonged to their parents, who had died his fifteenth year.

That very winter, Daniel seamlessly took charge of the shop, though only two years older. Restless as always, Ian had spent most days wandering the outlying areas and travelling to London for needed herbs, assisting him when necessary.

Daily, he heard the creaking of the ships as they crept into the harbor, heard the sailors' cries beyond the fog, their songs and tales of adventure, and his restlessness pursued him. His travels grew lengthier, and he and Daniel made plans for the future that would satisfy both his wanderlust and his ambition.

Ian would go to medical school in London, train under the great doctors there. Daniel would remain in King's Harbour. When he returned with his degree, Ian would treat the patients, and they would purchase their medicines from Daniel. With great excitement and enthusiasm, he set off to London, determined to excel at his studies. And indeed he did for a time. Enough of the past. He would not let it diminish the joy they would share in this room. Instead he envisioned what Maggie might need at their bedside. A fine bottle of wine and goblets? Some oil to ease her maidenhood? His cock throbbed in anticipation. He would bathe tonight; she seemed a fastidious soul, and he would not offend her. In the corner by his steamer trunk stood a lacquered screen bought for its beauty in Japan. Perhaps it could be taken downstairs to go round the tub for her privacy. He would find some oil of roses to scent the water, for he'd smelled a hint of it on her skin.

The basin and ewer in the corner was acceptable, nothing fancy. In the mornings, she would rise and splash her face with water, wash the sleep out of her dawn-hued eyes. The knowledge they would greet the morning together coursed through him in a rhythm that beat through his bloodstream, and a song rushed out with great wings that demanded to be released in an assurance of joy.

He took air in through his nose, slowly, listening to his breathing as the old man in Varanasi had taught him to control the rush of sensations. There was something he'd to do yet tonight. He must protect Maggie from Edward Carter, no matter the cost.

Ian's footsteps resounded on the cobblestones, cool air upon his face refreshing with clarity. Drinking songs burst out of the Shipwreck Hotel, the thump of mugs upon the table, snatches of hearty laughter. There's nothing as satisfying as a drinking song. Everyone knew the words, and the chorus of voices, out of tune or no, never failed to stimulate him. But he did not need that right now. Perhaps later.

He would be polite, in control. There was no response to his knock on Edward Carter's door, so he turned the doorknob slowly and crept in. A single candle illuminated the desk, and a light shone from a door in the back recesses of a hallway.

"No, please!" A scream scorched the tiny hairs upon his skin. Ian made his way toward the sound and then heard Edward Carter's voice.

"Have I not told you to keep your mouth closed to what goes on behind these doors? That girl of yours should keep her mouth shut."

He heard a strangled gurgle, and a young man's voice as he struggled for air. "Please, I promise. I promise." There was labored breathing and the scrabble of feet on the floor.

"Perhaps I shall shut her mouth for her. With my cock."

"No."

"She won't want you after I loosen the rest of your

166

teeth. One more?"

That voice. Ian had heard it before. Fire coursed through him as he rushed toward the door, swinging it open. A boy of about twenty was strapped in a chair, his mouth held open by a chunk of wood. Blood trickled from the corners of his mouth.

A man stood at his side, a pair of bloody pliers in his hand, but he did not know him as Edward Carter. "Ah. I wondered when you'd show up. Just taking care of my assistant here." He kept his eyes on Ian as he wiped the boy's mouth. "Off with you. That should do it." He untied him, patting him on the back.

"Now then." Carter wiped his hands on a rag. Smiling, he said, "How is my favorite lunatic?"

"I see you haven't changed. Still on your quest to alleviate suffering."

"Yes, quite," he said.

Ian followed him out into the front room. "Why did you come to King's Harbour?"

"Doesn't a man have a right to make a new start?" The *doctor* eyed him from head to toe, smoothing back a lock of hair that hung over his forehead. He'd missed a spot of blood under his fingernail. "You're looking well, for a Bedlamite."

"That was a long time ago. I would never have been there, if not for you."

Breathe deeply.

"Oh yes," he drawled. "You were ever the faultless hero, the professors' golden boy."

"I held no malice toward you."

"You could not leave well enough alone, could you? Had to report me to the authorities, when I was hurting no one."

"You were desecrating the dead. And I did not report you."

A tiny light of comprehension brightened Carter's eyes, then shuttered over.

The reason for the miscreant's arrival became clear. He had thought Ian responsible for his expulsion from medical school, and he was going to exact his revenge.

Had Carter not done enough already?

And while he bided his time, he would amuse himself. Sarah's missing tooth, bodies for sale to the highest bidder in London...but how would they prove it? Perhaps it was as the spirit said, there were others besides Sarah.

"You were always lording your superiority over us," Carter drawled. "Until we saw the real, raving mad, you."

Wisps of memory floated back: the anatomy room, the corpse laid out, the sinews and muscles calling out their melodies. Ian had not been able to keep it to himself, their songs pounding in his head. He had to share it with his fellow students, if they would only listen. The man known as Carter appearing at his elbow, persuading the professors he would take him where he needed to go.

Ian straightened. "I am not here to discuss my past or yours, only to insist you stop your malicious rumors about the midwife and her family. Stay away from her."

"Yes, I've heard how you fancy her. Odd taste, that."

They stood nose to nose. He would not respond to Carter's goading. "You are to stop," he said, "or everyone in this town will learn that you are a fraud."

"You would not do that." Carter grabbed him by the shoulders.

Ian grasped his wrists, turned them, and shoved him backward.

He lost his balance, quickly righting himself, straightening his vest. "Does your woman know where you've been?"

"Yes, she doesn't care," Ian lied.

Carter tried another tack. "Would the fine people of King's Harbour trust an apothecary who could go insane at any moment?"

"We are at a standstill, then." Ian fought to slow his heart and the urge to slam a fist into his smirk. "I warn you, leave her alone, or I will kill you."

As he turned to leave, the bastard laughed. "I will never forget how you pissed yourself when they beat you because you would not stop singing."

Once outside, Ian gulped the salt air...Maggie had a right to know what she married, regardless of whether she had a choice or not.

Chains upon his wrists burning, screaming the song, melody and harmony at war.

That man was not Edward Carter. His name was Phillip White, the man who sent him to Bedlam. Memories long buried began to surface like a drowned corpse.

Chapter Sixteen

The next morning Maggie replenished her midwife's bag and set out to check on Sabine, with plans to question Jonas about the night of Sarah's trial. He was usually at the Siren or the Shipwreck this time of the day. She also needed to pay a visit to Emma Neal, who was due to deliver any day. It seemed odd she had not heard from her.

The bitter cold of a few days ago had given way to a mild sun that flirted in and out of the clouds and cast shadows on the ocean. Shouts of jubilation erupted from a fishing boat docking as the shiny scales of a net full of fish flashed in the sun. The cheerful banter of the men with their haul did much to cheer her into the day.

On impulse, she stopped into the bake shop to pick up a treat or two for Lena and Sabine. Martha whistled as she frosted a cake, but upon seeing her enter, dropped her knife on top of the cake.

"Good morning, Martha."

"Maggie." She wiped the knife off with her apron and resumed her work, avoiding her eye.

"It smells heavenly in here. Is that gingerbread baking?"

Her husband appeared from the back room and just as quickly retreated. Certainly Martha did not subscribe to the rumors that circulated about her and Sarah?

"Martha, have you not been my friend these many

years? Please tell me you do not believe what is being said about us?"

"They say you brought your sister back from the dead, Maggie."

"Who says?"

"Everyone." She wrung her hands in her apron.

"When did you hear this rumor?"

"Yestermorn."

Was Edward Carter fueling these rumors? It was hard to tell in this small town, where rumors were as prevalent as seaweed. Perhaps Martha could be reasoned with. She was a practical woman. "You have known us well for five years, Martha. Sarah and I nursed Isadora when she nearly died from smallpox. Remember her fever, how we could not get it down? But we were there, praying with you, day and night. I am the same woman."

"I know, Maggie. But I'm afraid."

"Trust me, Martha."

She set her shoulders back and nodded. "You are right. I let it get the better of me. What would you be wanting, Maggie? I have gingerbread, of course, and sticky toffee pudding." She bustled behind the counter. At this sign of normalcy, Isadora and Bess entered and greeted her like an old friend.

Maggie exited a few minutes later, greatly relieved, the bundle of goodies warming her hands. It looked as if she could count on Martha's family. But they might be the only one, for as she walked the short distance to the inn, a number of people out enjoying the sunshine did not bother to greet her. Only a fool would miss the undisguised looks of revulsion levelled in her direction.

She entered the Siren with a sense of relief. As

predicted, Jonas lay in a corner by the massive fireplace. Lena never had the heart to throw him out, for he was a miserable soul indeed: skin and bones, white hair wild and sparse on his pate, drool pooled on the floor, his skinny ankles sticking out of baggy breeches.

There was no sign of anyone about. She set her things down and crouched by Jonas.

"Jonas. Wake up." She shook his shoulder, and eventually he opened his eyes and scrabbled backward like a crab.

"Jonas. I need your help." She opened up her bundle and handed him the gingerbread. "Here, I brought you something."

He settled himself against the stone wall and devoured the food.

"Now you must answer some questions. What were you doing at the graveyard the night my sister was buried?"

"No, I mustn't speak of it." He moaned.

"You must. It will be my secret, I promise."

"He will kill me."

"Edward Carter?"

He put his hands in front of his face as if she would strike him. "He will kill me if I tell. That he sent me there. And if he does not kill me, the spirits will."

"The spirits?" Maggie tried not to gag as she patted his shoulder. The smell of gin seemed to seep from his skin.

"There was a nun. And an old crone. And a snake. And the old crone...no, no more!" He scrambled to his feet and exited before she could even rise.

So now they knew for certain Jonas worked for Carter. Doing what? She went upstairs to check on

Sabine, who showed some improvement, thanks to Lena's nursing and Ian's herbs.

When she told Lena about her marriage to Ian the next day, she wrapped her in a tight hug.

"*Liebchen*, does God not surprise us all? *Ach*, I have a dress that will suit you. I will bring it over in the morning."

"No, you needn't fuss over me. My church dress is adequate."

"You say you do not want to marry this man, Maggie. But I have seen the way you look at him, as if you'd like to eat him. Stop thinking, my friend. I will make sure you look beautiful tomorrow, as a woman should on her wedding day." She hugged her again. "He is a good man, a kind man."

"He is an odd man," Maggie muttered and amidst Lena's laughter, set off for Emma's cottage.

The fog had moved in. The short distance to her client's home seemed interminable, the fog oppressive. Though it was the middle of the day, she felt inclined to look over her shoulder, as if someone followed her. Foolish.

She received a chilly reception from Emma's mother. Emma had already given birth to a little girl, delivered by Edward Carter the night before. The bastard had stolen her patient right out from under her! Maggie tried to hide her hurt and displeasure upon hearing the lavish words of praise for *the great doctor*. How quickly they'd forgotten she'd delivered Emma's other children safely.

As she returned home, greatly disheartened, footsteps echoed behind her. When she stopped, they stopped, but by the time she reached the cottage, it was like it never happened. Nearing the barn, she heard Samuel's voice raised in anger.

"Sarah, you must return home."

Her sister paced about the barn. What was she doing out of the house?

"I must go and speak to Edward Carter. They tell me he has buried other women, mothers like me."

"They?" she and Samuel said in unison.

"The goddess and the holy sister," Sarah said impatiently.

"Sarah." Maggie clasped her shoulders. "You must stay at home. I promise you we will make Edward Carter pay for what he's done to you."

"There are others," she cried. "Others who did not live."

Samuel grasped Sarah's hands. "We will take care of it, woman."

She fought for the words to make her sister understand. "Sarah, think of Ruthie. You are frightening her. And you must care for the baby. Think of your own baby right now. Do you hear me? And you must understand that your—return—has frightened people."

"They are saying that you have brought Satan from the grave with you, Sarah," Samuel said.

She paled. "How could they say such a thing, for all that we have done for them?"

"They are saying it, and we must be careful, or they will run us out of town or worse."

The fire had gone out of her, and Samuel led her into the house. Perhaps she understood now, just how precarious their situation was.

Later that evening, Maggie took the pins out of her

hair and had Ruthie run upstairs for the hairbrush. It was silver, the only thing of Mother's she possessed. She sat on a stool by the ewer, and let Ruthie brush her hair, enjoying her long, gentle strokes.

If she closed her eyes, she could imagine her mother's hands ministering to her as they had when she was a child, softly counting the strokes, stopping to let her fill in the numbers. And her singing, sweet and high, songs from her childhood, before the unending toil of countless children made it hoarse with fatigue and hopelessness.

Maggie trembled with apprehension so violently that Ruthie dropped the hairbrush.

Would my life be as my mother's was, at the mercy of a man who cared only for his own needs and did not consider mine? And what of Ian's strange behavior?

"Aunt Maggie, what is the matter?"

She endeavored to put her mind at rights for Ruthie's sake and searched for the strength to calm herself. The poor girl had endured enough in her young life. "Oh naught but a chill. Now, off to bed with you. Tomorrow is a big day."

She gave her a hug of reassurance, and the little girl climbed the stairs to bed. Maggie washed with warm water, hands shaking. What ailed her? Was the prospect of marriage turning her into a hysterical ninny? She had never before been prone to hysterics.

The hour grew late. She was probably overtired, and just a bit of sleep would do her good. She surveyed the room and built up the fire, crawled into bed upstairs with Ruthie, and closed her trembling eyelids, praying for respite. Her breathing came quick and shallow, heart beat against her ribs, and the night wore endlessly on, measured by restless turnings.

In the dead of night, a soft voice resounded in her bones. "All will be well, my sister. All shall be well and all manner of things will be well."

A feeling of peace and warmth came over her, and at last she slept.

Chapter Seventeen

The calming effect of last night's echoing words dissipated like sea mist as soon as Maggie opened her eyes to the day. Samuel greeted her, eyes gleaming like polished chestnuts.

Ruthie could not stop chattering. "We are riding a carriage to the church! I wish that I could pick some flowers for you, Aunt Maggie!"

She tried not to think of what this day could have been like, had Sarah been herself. Her only blood relative would not even be able to attend the wedding. She poured a cup of tea and sat. Nothing could be done about that. Maggie swallowed the loss of what might have been, the sisterly words of advice Sarah might have given her. But she merely sat with the baby in her arms, a blank, inward look in her eyes.

Before long, Lena bustled in, a cream-colored dress in her arms. "*Ach*, the sun shines for your wedding day, my friend!" She hugged Maggie hard.

Maggie opened the curtains and looked on the new day. Although cold, the sky was cloudless, rare for this time of year. But the trembling in her belly would not cease. She stood at a precipice, and there would be no going back once jumped. And circumstances grew stranger by the day: upon examining Sarah's privities last evening, Maggie discovered her womb had inexplicably healed as if she'd never borne a child.

How could she leave Sarah now? She was needed here.

Lena handed her the gown and swept off her cloak to reveal Sabine's babe wrapped tightly against her torso, its tiny head snuggled between her ample bosom.

Ruthie knit her brows. "Whose baby is that?"

"I'll explain later." Maggie met Lena's eyes. "How is Sabine?"

"Better even than yesterday. Your husband-to-be visited early this morning. He brought a draught that helped her sleep and left some ointment for her battered face. He is a fine apothecary, Maggie." She laughed, the babe moving up and down with the rising of her bosom. "He said he wanted to spare you a trip and would return to check on her later." She eyed her friend wickedly. "No doubt he wants his *Fraulein* to rest and prepare herself. No doubt he has plans for you."

She blushed. "Never mind that, Lena. How...kind of him." Much as she wanted to fight it, warmth suffused her body and she felt—cared for. "She is resting comfortably?"

"In a deep sleep, the best thing for the poor girl."

Lena glanced at her. "Sarah, it is so good to see you well. How are you?"

"I should be doing something." She glowered at Samuel.

"It is good to have you back with us," Lena said. "Now look at the dress." She spread it out upon the table.

Her stomach grew slightly queasy. Once she left the house with this dress on, there was no turning back.

"You." Lena tapped her on top of her head. "Stop thinking. You knit your brows, and I know what you're doing. Stop thinking."

She steered Maggie over to the stool and barked at Samuel. "She must get ready. Go see my husband at the pub. He is tapping a new barrel of ale. You will bring some back for the celebration. Now go."

Samuel made haste out the door. Ruthie hopped up and down excitedly. Lena unstrapped the baby and handed her to Ruthie. She reached into her pockets and put some jeweled combs in Maggie's hand. "These I wore on my wedding day. Now I dress that lustrous hair of yours and make you beautiful for that tall strudel of a man."

The dress was exceedingly beautiful, finer than anything Maggie had ever worn: cream satin soft as a dove, the bodice dipping low. The panel in front had tiny embroidered pink roses with climbing leaves. The roses continued down the underskirt. Round panels of the most delicate pink color shaped like blossoms encircled the waist. The sleeves were tight on the upper arms and belled at the elbows. A small bustle in the back and a lightest pink satin overskirt completed the confection.

Ruthie sighed. "Aunt Maggie, it is...oh my!"

Her heart raced. "It is too fine for me to wear. Lena, where did you get such a thing?"

"Try it on, *Liebchen*."

"I cannot. It is too fine."

"Maggie. Try it on," Lena commanded.

"Yes, Maggie. You will look beautiful." Sarah crept up behind her and placed a hand on her shoulder.

Lena dressed her hair, and she felt suddenly shy, not accustomed to being the center of attention. The dress fit remarkably well, although a bit tight in the bodice, showing a shocking expanse of bosom. It grew quiet. She thought she must look wrong indeed.

"Oh Maggie," Lena whispered. "*Wunderschon.*"

"Aunt Maggie, you look beautiful!" Ruthie breathed.

"They will approve, the two of them," Sarah intoned.

Lena made Maggie put on the heeled slippers and held the mirror for her, moving it slowly up and down. She could not believe her eyes.

Could they be right? Could I, the workhorse, look beautiful?

Who was this woman, dark brows, grey eyes shining and looking not at all like a workhorse, but someone she did not know? The creamy satin made the skin above the bodice glow with a light pink flush. The bodice emphasized her waist then flared out to display womanly hips. The skirt fell in stately folds and when she moved, the gown rustled in approval. She would not wear anything this fine again. And her hair, swept up and back, the rubies in the combs in stark contrast to the black hair, curls cascading down her back—so lovely.

"Aunt Maggie," Ruthie cried. "You look like a queen. Mother!" She turned to Sarah.

Sarah looked up, eyes growing wide. "Oh yes, oh they will most certainly approve, Sister. It is as it should be."

Maggie grasped her friend's hands. "Thank you, Lena."

"He will be overcome when he sees you, Maggie."

"It is so sudden. I do not know him. He is a stranger to me, and so odd."

She shook her head. "No, Maggie. You are

thinking again." A low chuckle rose in her throat. "I have seen the way he looks at you, like you are a piece of warm strudel fresh out of the oven, and he must devour you. Do not think. Feel."

Her cheeks warmed as thoughts of their nocturnal encounter rose to the surface.

Lena placed her hands on Maggie's cheeks. "Ah, *meine* friend, I can see it in your eyes. You are drawn to him, and sometimes that is all we need to start a new life. Trust your instincts, for behind desire love often hides."

While they waited for Samuel to bring the carriage, Lena forced her to practice walking on heeled slippers, and Maggie could not help getting caught up in the excitement.

Samuel peeked around the door and stared, clearing his throat. "Maggie, you are...like a bride. I have the carriage waiting, and after the ceremony we will return here. Lena's kitchen has prepared a wedding breakfast."

He picked Ruthie up and swung her around. "You look lovely, little one. You have your Sunday best on, I see."

Maggie smiled, a most nerve-wracking mixture of excitement and trepidation roiling inside her. They made haste in the carriage to St. Agnes' Church.

Today I do not feel like a workhorse, but like a gift waiting for someone to open me.

****

The church stood stone-faced at the top of the hill. The high arched windows and flying buttresses around the church made it look otherworldly and ancient. Indeed she felt as if someone or something eyed her from the high Norman tower, judging if she was worthy of walking into its ancient doors. She offered a prayer for courage and that she, a sinner, might be deserving of God's mercy. The chapel was nearly empty; it seemed most of the congregation had chosen not to come.

Vicar entered from the back of the church, dignified in his robes. "Welcome, welcome." He reddened when he saw her, opened his mouth again to speak, and shut it. Finally he croaked, "Are you ready for this most momentous day, Mistress Maggie?"

She nodded. "Has Mr. Pierce arrived yet?"

He grimaced and shook his head. "I'm sure he'll be along shortly."

She sat in the front pew with Ruthie and Lena, watching sunlight play upon the stained glass windows. Samuel paced the aisle, scowling at the door.

Ian arrived. Maggie's throat pounded as he walked down the aisle with that wide-shouldered grace, eyes on her. He wore a dark green suit, hair tied back neatly. His shaven face accentuated his high cheek bones and smooth tanned forehead. Most of all, he wore an air of expectancy that fair crackled as he stood before her, without speaking.

His eyes held her and lifted her up in a swell. He whispered, "My heart stopped beating when I saw you, and the promise of living my life with you has started it again." He took her hand and led her to the altar.

The service began. As they knelt for the prayers and listened to Vicar's exhortations on the sanctity of marriage, the trembling rose within her again. Ian squeezed her hand, but she could not meet his eye. What was she doing? With the repeating of the vows, she became his. This man she did not know, who confused and perplexed her, whose moods changed like the sea. This man who now owned her body and could do with it what he wanted.

Maggie watched the movement of the vicar's mouth but heard nothing. Her heart raced and she struggled to breath, cursing herself for her weakness. The panting created dizziness. Out of the corner of her eye, she saw Ian's concern but could only tell her lungs to take in air and breathe it out.

Near the vestry, a misty image of a woman in a white wimple and brown robes, surrounded by light, beckoned to Maggie. She appeared before her, eyes alight with serenity, face aglow, and put her hands upon her head in blessing. Peace flowed through Maggie's body at the woman's touch. As the nun faded from view she said, "All shall be well, and all *shall* be well, and all manner of things shall be well."

Maggie returned to her fate, looking into Ian's eyes and in them saw the fullness of life.

****

After the ceremony, the small smattering of friends attending congratulated Maggie and Ian heartily: Martha and her family, Lena and her husband, Joannie and her brood, and a few others. The assurance of Ian's hand in hers, warm and solid, did much to chase any remaining doubts away.

Samuel kissed Maggie's cheek. "I'm sorry your sister is not here."

She nodded. "It cannot be helped. But I thank you, Samuel, for taking me into your home all these years. I guess you will have it to yourself, now."

"You will be missed, my sister." The catch in Samuel's throat gave away his emotion, and she embraced him.

He turned to Ian and shook his hand. "Congratulations. You are fortunate."

"I agree." Ian kissed his new bride.

Once outside the church, jubilation died on their lips upon seeing a group of townsfolk gathered on each side of the walkway.

They stood silent and watchful, with an undercurrent of threat in their eyes that made Ian put his arm around her and Samuel do the same with Ruthie.

Vicar said, "Can you not congratulate the happy couple? They are part of our flock, are they not?"

No one spoke aloud, but whispered behind their hands with hissing malevolence. The happiness of the occasion gave way to apprehension.

Chapter Eighteen

By the time they returned to the cottage, Lena's husband had laid the table with a lace tablecloth, and the aroma of beef, oysters, and freshly baked bread filled the room and dispelled much of Maggie's anxiety.

Joannie, her husband, and their brood stood near the fireplace and greeted them heartily.

After shaking hands with Joannie's husband, Ian bent down to the boy with the bandage around his head.

"Oh ho, Jimmy! How is that noggin of yours?"

He felt around the bandage and gently tugged Jimmy's earlobe, then made as if to pull a coin out of it. Presenting it in front of him, he exclaimed, "Sink me, look what I've found!"

Jimmy giggled and Joannie's husband exclaimed, "Well, look at that!"

Ian placed the coin in the boy's hand and proceeded to greet the rest of the brood, finally lifting Joannie's hands to his lips and making her blush. He slid a hand around Maggie's waist and squeezed. She felt Ian's vitality ripple from him like wavelets. He spread his fingers possessively over her hips. For some reason she could not explain, she avoided his eyes and instead watched Sarah, already seated at the table, oblivious to the celebration.

Lena, bustling around like a hen, seated the bride

and groom at their place of honor. As the table was not overly large, Samuel, of course Sarah, Ruthie, Ian and Maggie sat at the table and the rest of the company filled their plates to stand together in groups.

She mentally shrugged her shoulders. She was married, whether she had chosen it or not, and so might as well enjoy this day. The food tasted delicious and she ate heartily, particularly enjoying the oysters and Lena's excellent chowder. All the while, she felt Ian's eyes upon her, even as he talked animatedly to others, they never left her face, body. From time to time, he would eat another oyster, grinning wolfishly at her when one of the men urged him to eat more, for he would need them, they laughed. Lena had also provided heaping bowls of peas and beans, known to give men stamina for bed sport.

Good-natured ribaldry was tossed like a summer salad, particularly by Samuel and Ed the Butcher, compounded by Joannie's husband having to be pounded on the back for choking, so heartily did he laugh. The ale flowed freely, and food disappeared from the table. Indeed, Maggie could not remember a better time with such congenial company and sincere well-wishing.

Samuel's heartfelt toast would stay with her always. "To our Maggie and her husband, Ian. May God bless your union and may you find joy and comfort in each other always."

To cheers and catcalls, Ian kissed her full on the lips, lingering just a bit more than was decent. She reddened. He whispered in her ear, "I do so love to see your skin glow, Maggie mine."

Soon there was no more delaying the departure.

She kissed Ruthie and Sarah goodbye, received assurance from Joannie she would stop in tomorrow to help Ruthie with dinner and check on Sarah.

Samuel embraced her. "Take care of our Maggie," he said to Ian, the undertone of threat apparent to all.

Ian nodded. "I assure you, sir. I will honor and adore her."

A storm had blown in from the Channel. The wind blew salt water mist into their faces, a refreshing change from the crowded room. He took her arm to guide her around the puddles and for moral support against the riffraff outside the Siren Inn shouting their greetings and bawdy suggestions. This, however embarrassing, raised Maggie's hopes that perhaps her behavior would be forgiven by some.

They reached the apothecary shop, and as Ian placed his hand on the latch, she took in his scent, different tonight, sandalwood. He turned. His eyes shone like polished emeralds. "I hope you find your new home inviting."

He ascertained that the closed sign faced outward, and they passed by the well-ordered apothecary counter. "I try to keep a clean shop," he said, "though neatness is at times a challenge for me."

"Well, that bodes ill for me," she drawled to hide her nervousness. Who was this man? He was now her partner for life, and the only thing she really knew of him was he was an apothecary, he was a musician, and he made her ache and yearn so when he touched her. Maybe Lena was right. Maybe she should stop thinking for a while.

"Do you not have a girl to help you clean?"

"No, I prefer to employ my considerable energy to

the task. It helps me...settle."

He took her cloak and placed it carefully on a hook in the hallway to the parlor. Then he returned, resting his hands on her shoulders briefly, letting his fingers play up and down her neck. Chills trickled like warm water down her back. He guided her into the parlor.

"I hope you find it pleasing," he murmured, his breath teasing the tiny hairs on her neck.

Find what pleasing?

He pulled her against him; the hard length of his cock against her stomach both alarmed and pleased, her breasts yielding to his chest.

After he released her, she glanced around the parlor. He had tidied up since her last visit. He lit an already laid fire, and soon the room glowed with a homey light. The furniture shone with beeswax, and the room smelled of sandalwood. He lit a candle and came to her.

"Please, my bride. Sit down. Let me wait on you." He cocked his head, eyes glinting with amusement. "Have you ever, in your life, had someone attend you?"

That is not the life of a work horse.

"I was born to wait on others, not the other way around. Like women everywhere," she added. "As soon as I could walk, I worked."

"Not tonight, my bride." He gently pushed her onto the settee and lifted her feet onto a cushioned stool. He undid the laces of the more practical boots she had put on before they left the cottage. He pulled them both off and waited.

"Kindly take off your stockings, madame."

"Why?" she croaked.

"Obey your husband," he growled playfully. "Take

off your stockings, or should I assist you?" He grinned. "Not just yet? I will pour us some wine. We'll enjoy the fire for a while."

He pretended not to watch as she rolled the stockings down, taking care not to damage the dress. She found herself taking her time merely to torment him. Where had this coquettishness come from? And what was he about? Surely he would not take her here, in the parlor?

"Do you like champagne?" He handed her a goblet of fine etched crystal with a delicate, twisted stem.

Her hands felt big and awkward holding it. Where had he gotten something so fine? "I don't know. I have never had it."

He set his wine glass down and put her feet upon the stool, then sat on the settee beside her, very close. They were silent for a while, listening to the fire crackling.

"Are you comfortable?" he asked.

Was she comfortable? No one had ever asked her that before. "I...yes."

They resumed their reverie. Indeed, she was not used to silence; living with a large family had meant there was always someone crying, hollering, pots clanging, children playing, her father bellowing. And a house with a new baby was seldom silent.

Ian cleared his throat and turned to her. "There is something I must say to you before anything else— something for which I must apologize. Believe me when I say that I do not regret our joining, being ever aware that I do not deserve you. My inability to control my impulses has resulted in taking you away from where you are needed, away from your sister and her family. I promise you that I will do everything I can to help you care for them—I have seen the worry in your eyes, and I will not keep you from them."

He lifted his glass. "To my wife, beautiful and strong. To our marriage, sudden but most precious."

The reflection of the fire danced in the champagne's bubbles. He watched her mouth as she touched her lips to the rim and took a sip.

"Oh, it's wonderful! Wherever did you get it?"

He grinned. "Maggie, when you smile, my heart capsizes, and I fear it will never right itself again. In answer to your question, I resided in France for a time."

He compressed his lips and gazed into the fire. There were deep shadows under his eyes; it seemed he did indeed fatigue, although one could never tell from his level of activity.

He peeked out from under his lashes and murmured, "I played for the court of King Louis for a fortnight. He gave me that bottle as a gift."

She nearly spit out the precious mouthful. "You played for King Louis XV?"

He shrugged. "I had been travelling, and one of his counselors heard me perform in the market and brought me to court." He spoke as if he'd merely gone to buy a loaf of bread. "Mind you, I would not spread that information about."

She nodded. England's relationship with France was always on edge, and the threat of another war loomed ever near.

He filled her goblet. "I saved this bottle for a special occasion."

He set it down and knelt in front of the stool. He reached into his pocket and opened a vial. The scent of eucalyptus tickled her nostrils. He cradled her foot in his hand, massaging the oil into it, his fingers strong yet sensitive. She could not help moaning with pleasure. His eyes gleamed like sun on sea as he glanced up from his ministrations from time to time, mouth slightly open, lifting at the corners.

She set the goblet down and eyed him warily. Should she not be waiting upon him? Of course she knew what the marital act entailed, but had no knowledge how the night would transpire. If she'd had the time to imagine her wedding eve, she would never have imagined his strong fingers massaging the arch of her foot, one firm hand upon her calf.

His fingers gently kneaded the bottom of her foot, below the toes. Bit by bit, the muscles gave way. Her breasts tingled with warmth. He had not touched them! How could this happen merely by touching the foot?

"What..." she jolted upright.

"Maggie," he rumbled. "Let me care for you."

He pressed his thumb on a spot on the inside of her ankle, below the bone and moved in a circle, slowly, gently. "Lay your head back and close your eyes," he growled playfully.

She cooperated, letting her mind rest and soon felt only the movement of his long fingers upon her feet. Her womanly parts softened and reached for him.

He stopped, and she felt at once cold and lost-but not for long. Hands cradling her face, he kissed her, soft at first, then with a growing intensity she matched, joining her tongue with his.

"Do you like kissing me, my Maggie?" he murmured.

He smiled against her lips. His tongue tasted of

wine and a flavor unique to him. She felt the fire of life course under his skin, hot and eager.

He took the pins out of her hair and massaged her scalp. "Your hair is like polished obsidian, Maggie. So soft it slips through my fingers."

"Where did you learn to manipulate the feet like that?" Her voice sounded different to her ears, softer, more womanly.

He sighed. "Can we discuss this later?"

"I would like to know now...husband." She had watched other women do this since childhood but had never attempted it herself. She lowered her lashes and peeked out from under them, ran her hands slowly down his shoulders over his muscled upper arms. "Please."

He groaned. "You are no match for me. I suppose you have a right to know where I have been. I had hoped to have this conversation later—much later." He glanced up the stairs where their bed awaited.

Then he continued. "I spent a year in China and sought the help of one skilled in the art. I had need of it at the time as a remedy for something that had been plaguing me."

"And what was that?"

"I had succumbed to—I am not proud of it. You see," he traced her collarbone. "I had been seeking a solution I thought would help, but it did not." He laughed without humor and looked away.

His melancholy made Maggie's stomach twinge with distress. She laid her hand upon his cheek. "It doesn't matter now."

He kissed her open lips tentatively, and she answered back, pressing against the hard length of him into the cushions and matching the increased pressure of his lips with her own.

She reached up to caress his neck and feel his heartbeat, and as she had longed to do, pressed her lips against his neck, so she might feel his pulse enter and enliven her. She must get closer to him.

He sat her on his lap and slowly unbuttoned her bodice. "Maggie, may I love you? I promise to the best of my ability, to take the time you need."

He removed her bodice, his breath upon her neck. The fire warmed her breasts through the thin shift in contrast to the cool air on her back. Her nipples stiffened.

Ian's eyes swept over her, dark with intensity. "Oh, Maggie. You are magnificent."

To cover a twinge of embarrassment, she said, "And you are overdressed."

"You're right." He removed his coat and unbuttoned his linen shirt and stood bare-chested before her, crisp light brown hair at the base of his throat, curling over his broad, muscled chest, and around his nipples. Below the muscled planes of his stomach, a trail of hair led to the waistband of his breeches. Maggie's belly grew warm. This man knew how to make a good fire, in the hearth and in her belly.

He held his hands out to her and smiled, long lips curling up at the edges. "Maggie, do you want me?" His eyes held such hope and fear, she caught her breath.

"Yes," she whispered. "Must I say it?"

He chuckled, pulling her to her feet. "No, I can see it in your eyes. I will do my utmost to please you. Let us go upstairs. Let me love you."

She followed him to the bedchamber, watching the

hard muscles of his buttocks flexing through his breeches with each step. At the landing, he took her hand and led her into the room, lit two brass candle sconces in the corner walls. The four poster bed was made of sturdy oak, and the bed covering made of blue satin with birds embroidered with leaves in a pattern throughout.

"Is it to your liking?"

She nodded, awed by the size of the room. What a family would normally share was theirs alone. In the far corner was a dressing table with a pitcher and basin, and a looking glass. At the other end of the room was a window, where she would see the morning light from the bed. He shut the curtains. She stood in her bare feet, arms covering her breasts. She must look ridiculous with the skirt of her wedding gown still on, but on top only the shift.

"You must be cold, standing there," he murmured and led her to the edge of the bed. "May I remove your overskirt?"

She nodded. "Take special care with it. It is Lena's."

The heat radiated from his chest. His breath upon her barely clothed stomach as he knelt to undo the skirt sent waves of shivers through her. He took his time, sliding his hands down her thighs. Her center clenched.

He carried the dress over to the dresser and laid it carefully on top, then returned to caress her face and kiss her. She returned the kiss with increasing intensity. Her heart pounded in her throat.

"Maggie," he said, eyes resting on each breast in turn.

Her nipples hardened in response to his gaze.

"Please."

"Yes," she breathed and reached back to untie her shift, letting it fall to the ground.

"Ah," he smiled. "You are...I have no words, so my body must speak for me."

He kissed her again, holding the back of her neck, and her body melted into him. Eventually, he stepped back and slowly removed his breeches, throwing them aside. His legs were long, with narrow hips, muscled thighs and calves covered in light brown hair. His manhood stood straight and erect against his belly. The air left her lungs as he took her in his arms again.

His manhood pulsed hot against her bare skin. Their mouths met, deep, rough, tongues melding. His lips found her neck, biting, kissing, and chills ran through her, liquid heat pooling in her middle. She pressed her breasts to him, and he guided them to the bed, lowering her. The shock of their bare bodies together and the pleasured heat of it! He circled the nipple with his tongue, took it into his mouth. His rod leapt against her stomach, imploring and she knew she must get closer.

She grasped his shoulders. "Please," unsure of what she wanted but yearned for.

He ran his hands through her hair. "Yes?"

She nipped his lower lip. His cock surged against her entrance, and she urged him on.

He eased into her and she started at the shock, gasping as he eased his way further, and she felt the burn of her maidenhood breaking.

"I am sorry," he whispered and kissed her.

She lifted her hips as he pushed the length of his silken hot cock into her. He held very still and their eyes locked. She rose to meet him, her womanhood squeezed around him and every nerve came alive as she urged him to fill her, fill her more, and he sent light and fire coursing through her, as she bucked under him, dissolved into him.

As pleasure rocked her, he nipped her neck, and she was lost again, suspended in the air not knowing where her limbs and his began as he pumped his essence into her. They moaned together and rolled onto their sides, slick with sweat and still one. He throbbed inside her and trails of sensation lingered as they lay in silence for a while.

Kissing her forehead, he groaned in pleasure and murmured, "Are you well, Miss Maggie?" The rusty edge of his voice made warm honey trickle between her legs, and his member swelled within her in response.

She sighed. "I have no words."

He smoothed hair back from her face. "I had meant to take more time, to be more thorough, to ease your maidenhood."

She snorted. "Did you not hear me cry out? And not with pain." She ran her hand down the muscled length of his back and sighed again, snuggling closer.

"I quite like to hear you sigh," he whispered. "I vow to make it happen often."

****

Later, they sat against the headboard and feasted upon wine and plates of savories.

"I am ravenous," she mumbled, mouth full of meat pie.

He peeled an orange and dripped juice upon her bare shoulder. "My apologies." He slowly licked it off, nipping the shoulder lightly.

"Ouch," she shrieked, spilling champagne onto her privities.

"Oh, that will not do." He lowered his face to her lap, unbound hair tickling her thighs. She squeezed her legs together in protest, but he edged them open with his face, kissing the insides of her thighs. Parting her womanly folds with his finger, he covered his mouth on the nub of her pleasure bud, which had stiffened and grown. One hand caressed her breast. He increased his pressure on her pleasure bud and lowered his mouth to fill his tongue into her in and out, slowly. And before she knew what happened, he replaced his tongue with his cock.

I cannot get enough of you," he growled and held very still, then slowly entered and paused. "Do you like the feel of me, Maggie?"

"Yes," she gasped. "More."

His smile played against her lips. He sank his cock a little deeper, stopped again.

"Please, more." She must feel him inside of her. All of him. "Will you make me beg?"

He rolled them over. "Have dominion over me, Maggie, for you do rule my heart."

A force stronger than herself bid she ride him until they cried out together.

They rested, replete, and she understood now. Understood why women risked their lives in childbirth for the pleasure of a union, with a man who could make the blood sing in their veins, bring them such pleasure that the rest of the world disappeared for a while. That lying in bed with the feel of a man's rough, muscled flesh against hers could give her this loose-limbed peace and well-being.

He held her face in his hands. "Oh Maggie, I do not deserve such joy. I do not deserve the bounty of your body and your soul. God knows I am not worthy of you."

"Why would you say such a thing? It is not as if I'm the village princess. More like the village workhorse." The words were out before she could stop herself.

He let out a short burst of laughter. "Come again?"

"I am a workhorse, valued by how hard and long I can work."

He tightened his hold on her so she could barely breathe. "Maggie, what rot. You are exquisite in every way possible. For as long as I live, I will write your song and never do you justice: your hair, silken, your eyes, dark as dusk, grey as dawn, the bounty of your body and the welcome of your hips. And your giving spirit, generous and strong. Your sense of purpose buoys me, strengthens me, and now without it I could not survive. I only hope to be worthy of you, my wife."

"Ian, you have made me come alive. I did not know how much I needed you until now."

"May it always be so, my love."

She could not speak but could only hold him, knowing her life had changed this day, in every possible way.

Night fell, and she lay boneless and glowing with pleasure. Ian made forays downstairs to get supplies and even at one point, heated water, filled a basin, and helped her cleanse her privities.

His energy seemed boundless, his appreciation of her body boundless as well. He clearly knew his way around a woman's body, and being above all a practical woman, she did not mind. Indeed, thankful she was for it, more than once.

A miracle had happened: for several hours her only concern had been her own pleasure. And her husband's. Eventually, they made their way downstairs to the parlor. She watched idly as he bounded about the room, candlelight playing on unruly hair spread out over his shoulders. He stocked the fire, down on his haunches, naked and primitive, making her heart pound in her ears, blocking out all rational thought.

They sat together, he stark naked, she in a thin silk robe from China. The silk whispered against her body, making her feel like a decadent queen.

She traced the scar that ran up the side of his jaw to his ear lobe. "How did you get this?"

He grew still. She did not recognize the voice that rasped out in a hard monotone. "There is so much in my life I am not proud of, Maggie. I would not have you think less of me."

"You are my husband now. It does not matter."

"Does it not?" He grasped her hand. "I pray that you will always feel this way."

"We are joined," she whispered. "So I must accept you, all of you, as you must accept me and my shortcomings."

He rested his forehead upon hers. "It is only fair that you should know, and I must risk it. I feel like a fraud, for I have been hiding something from you."

She pulled away to see his face. "Just tell me."

He stared into the fire. "Even as a child, I had the vigor of two boys. I was the terror of my parents. As I grew into a gangly young lad, this energy began to overtake me; the songs coursed through my blood in an endless melody, the sea breeze burned on my skin, every sound—the chirping of birds, conversations, resounded in my ears, and I could shut nothing out. I could not still myself, no matter how many times Father beat me. He was not a cruel man. He just did not know what to do with such a boy."

"Was there no potion he could give you that would calm you?"

"Believe me, he tried." His voice grew hard. "I had periods of calmness that enabled me to concentrate on my schooling, and Mother and Father would think it merely a phase. Then, without warning, I would feel the affliction return, the tingling on my skin, the brightness of the gull's wings, the heightened emotion that poured from me."

She had difficulty imagining the inability to control her impulses. Was it not just a matter of will?

"After our parents died, Daniel tried to keep me busy procuring herbs, but there were times I could not apply myself."

"Your brother was a good man," she said.

"He accepted me, as I was, unconditionally." He paused for a moment and wiped his eyes.

She put an arm around him.

He pulled back his shoulders and continued. "A year or two after our parents passed, for a while it seemed that my affliction had abated. I went to medical school. It would be the perfect partnership."

"It sounds like a fine plan."

"Yes, it was." He sighed. "Until, without warning my affliction rose up in me, and my stellar reputation at the medical school was shattered in one display. I could not help the melodies that the muscles sang to me, on the dissection table, as they glistened red and I only wanted to share the beauty of their names. So there, in front of fellow students, I unraveled. And the man I knew as Phillip White, who now goes by the name Edward Carter, persuaded the doctors I should go to Bedlam. And he would deliver me there."

"Bedlam?" *Oh God.* "Why did you not tell me sooner? And Edward Carter has an alias?"

He clasped his hands in his lap. "I am sorry. I should have done. But what kind of a proposal do you think that would have been? Marry me. I have been in the bowels of Bedlam? Would you have married me?"

"It's not as if I had a choice in the matter anyway," she snapped and instantly regretted it. "But I am not sorry, Ian." She grasped his trembling hand. "It must have been horrible."

He took in a ragged breath and slowly released it. "Daniel got me out and took me abroad, and no one in King's Harbour ever knew I had been there. No one but Phillip White. When I was well, I began to travel in search of a treatment for what the Swiss doctor Bonet calls 'manico-melancolicus, for when the mania ends, despair begins, until the episode is over.'"

She sat for a moment without speaking, trying to absorb his confession. She'd never heard of such a condition, but it made sense: his constant movement, the look of fatigue, the endless music that poured out of him. "How long did you stay abroad?"

"I wandered for five years, searching for a cure and procuring herbs for my brother."

"And you paid your way by singing?"

"Yes, trying cures along the way—fasting cures, Indian snakeroot..." He grew still, drawn inside himself.

"What is it?"

"Indian snakeroot, used for the heart but also in cases of mania. In my case, I experienced a deep melancholy I hope to never experience again. But Maggie—your sister—the bitter smell upon her breath."

Her head spun at his mercurial change of subject. "You mean when she came out?"

He bounded off the bed and paced the floor. "Yes, I could not identify it at the time, but Indian Snakeroot is also used to deaden nerves, to mimic death. He could have given it to her for that reason."

"But why?"

"The man is capable of anything." He poured them some wine and sat again. "So now you know my story. It is unfair that you are chained to me and my affliction. But I will tell you true, sweeting, that was the past and you are the future. For since I met you, I have found peace in your eyes and your steady grace. Your love has healed me."

He put his hands on top of hers. "Do you accept me now, Maggie? With all that you know?"

She took his face in her hands. "I do love you." And it was only when she said the words she realized their strength. She kissed him with all the fervor in her heart.

"So now," Ian said lightly. "You know your bridegroom is not perfect, which I'm sure has come as a shock to you. It is getting late, and I know you must work tomorrow, and so must I."

"It is no small thing that I have not been summoned to a birth," Maggie said. "Nothing short of miraculous." She yawned loudly. "I can't say I'm sorry. I feel glorious."

She smiled at the smug expression on his face.

****

She lay with him again in the early morning hours, this time slow and tender, saying with her body all that could not be expressed aloud.

She awoke long before dawn and found his side of the bed empty. As she descended the stairs, she heard a lute playing a most minor tune, and Ian singing, low, mournful, as if he had gathered all the loneliness in the world and poured it into the song. She did not want to intrude, so keen was his grief, but as she entered the shop he looked up. Her gut wrenched when she saw the haggard hollows of suffering on his face. On the counter sat a beaker filled with brown fluid and herbs and bottles scattered around it.

"What is it? Can you not sleep?"

"Go back to bed, my love. I am accustomed to this sleeplessness, although I dosed off for a short while after our last...endeavor." He held her palm against his cold cheek and grinned, but it did not reach his red-rimmed eyes. "I will take you up to bed."

Hours later, she woke again to an empty bed and found him still playing downstairs, head lowered and fingers still tireless. Disquiet washed over her. How could he survive the day without sleep?

He put down the instrument immediately and embraced her. "I have the pot on for tea. I was going to bring you a tray."

"Oh no, what time is it?" She then became self-conscious of her appearance; her hair must look like a flock of ravens nested there. He, meanwhile, although weary-looking, had already shaven and dressed and smelled of the sea and his unique spice.

The clock chimed eight. "What? Why did you let me sleep so long? I should be making my rounds by now!"

"You deserved a good lie-in this morning." He grasped her bottom with both hands, pressing his erection against her. "See, Maggie? All I have to do is look at you and I want you again."

She should push him away, but instead softened with desire. Would it always be thus?

A good while later, they sat at the table eating a breakfast of fresh rolls, thick slices of ham, washed down by fine black tea. She could not stop looking at those fingers, long and elegant, that made music on fine instruments, on her body.

She held up the tea cup. "Is this tea from your travels? It's delicious."

He wiped his mouth on his napkin. "From India."

"You will have to tell me stories of your stay there."

He averted his eyes. "Would that all my tales were pleasant." He rose from the table and began to clear the dishes.

She gaped at him open-mouthed.

"I have fended for myself a long time, Maggie. There is no reason to stop now." He returned and kissed her hard on the mouth. "Besides, I have my selfish reasons. You work hard and long. I want you to have energy left over at the end of the day, to love me." He grinned. "For there is much more for us to experience."

She found it hard to believe there was more to love-making than they had already experienced.

Chapter Nineteen

She made her ablutions upstairs for the day to the tune of Ian whistling in his shop. She felt rested, albeit more than a little sore in places never felt before. But her privities glowed where he had touched her, and the mere sight of the rumpled bed made her blush.

She walked into the apothecary shop just in time to see Widow Jenkins at the counter, her gnarled fingers on Ian's wrist.

"Young man, I cannot tell you how much that willow bark helped with my rheumatism." She leaned into him with all the subtlety of a mare in season. "Why, there's no telling what I am able to do," she tittered. "And whatever you put in for flavor made it so very tasty." She eyed him as if *he* was tasty indeed.

He winked at Maggie, hair already slipping out of his tie. He fastened her package, bowing as he handed it to her.

"Hello, Mrs. Jenkins," she said.

"Well, well," she cackled. "So our Maggie has a husband."

She eyed her up and down, rheumy eyes widening at the red marks on her neck. She had keen eyesight for her advanced years. Despite her best efforts, Maggie blushed, from bosom to forehead.

Widow Jenkins nodded, a gummy smile on her wizened face. "Ah, dearie, I see you have been well loved." She leered at Ian.

Maggie looked to Ian for help. He grinned and handed the old woman the package.

"Mrs. Jenkins, thank you for coming in. Do you need help home? My lovely bride will be going your way. Mind you, remember to only use the amount I have prescribed for you."

He walked her to the door and waited as she grabbed her supplies. He wrapped her in an embrace.

Mrs. Jenkins cooed.

"My wife," he purred. "Beauteous, bounteous, and beloved."

Her face grew hot. Did he not realize in the course of a day she had turned from the village spinster to a newly bedded married woman? And he knew it was highly improper to kiss her so, drawing her in with the sea in his eyes, tasting of black tea and sugar, lips warm and soft.

Mrs. Jenkins cackled, and Maggie pulled away, but a ridiculous feeling of joy lifted her as she took the old woman's arm and headed out into a weak sun.

The people of King's Harbour were out enjoying the fine day. They lingered on stoops with brooms, gossiping and waving. Some smiled and waved at her, but many sent such looks of malevolence she had to fight not to recoil. Word of her marriage had spread swiftly and did not seem to make a difference to those who thought her tainted with evil. The old woman patted her arm.

"Pay them no mind, girl. Those that malign you are not worth your trouble. Those with memories so short should remember the nights you spent at their family's bedsides. You nursed my grandson back, you did."

Johnny had been three and not expected to live, but Maggie had stood vigil for two nights, watching him helplessly. How did God decide who lived or died? On what did it depend? Certainly there did not seem to be rhyme or reason to it. Did he decide at all? The good book says, "The rain falls on the just and the unjust," but does God not make the rain?

She spotted Joannie walking bare-headed in the dim sunlight, face to the sky, bandaged Jimmy tugging at her hand.

Happy to be distracted from sacrilegious thoughts, she called, "Good morning, Joannie. Where are you headed?"

Joannie started with surprise and ran to embrace her. "Oh, and it's right lovely you look this morning, Miss Maggie! We are headed to have your husband check Jimmy's head. Did you enjoy your evening, then?" She waggled her eyebrows.

Ed the Butcher yelled from his shop, "And where's yon randy groom this morn? Can he not walk?"

John the chandler hollered, "I see young Maggie's moving slower than normal, is she not?"

Guffaws and cat calls resounded in the street, and even the women joined in the traditional post-wedding ribbing. It was quite unfair her husband let her run the gauntlet of ribaldry alone. She could only hope he would suffer the same indignities at the shop today. But judging from his reaction to Mrs. Jenkins's ribbing, he would probably enjoy it, stupid male.

With a chorus of titters trailing behind her, Maggie took Widow Jenkins home and arrived at her sister's. Sarah tidied up the breakfast dishes, with more energy and more color in her cheeks than ever before.

She put down the dish rag and rushed over, hugging her with enough force to take the breath from her. How could someone so thin be so strong?

"Sister! It is so strange not to have you here after five years. Do you like your new home?" She peered at Maggie like she could read her mind. "How about your husband?" She glanced at Ruthie, who sat at the table, sounding out words from a primer and casting longing glances out the window. "Is he...satisfactory?" Sarah giggled.

Maggie sighed. "Must we speak of it? He is quite adequate."

Sarah giggled.

"Sarah, you seem more yourself, today."

Ruthie looked up from her reading. "No, Aunt Maggie, she's not herself." The last word ended on a shrill note.

Sarah ignored the remark. "I feel so much better this morning. We all slept—even the babe. When I awoke, my breasts were bursting with milk."

"Keep in mind that you must get extra rest and eat frequently. You always were forgetting to eat, but you cannot afford to do so now. There is nothing to you. Perhaps Ian has a tonic that will help you put on a stone or two."

She smiled and patted her arm. "Oh Maggie, how much you have gone through for me! I would truly be dead were it not for you and your new husband. I feel quite restored now, though. And you look, um, well-rested."

Maggie huffed and tried to dissuade her sister from her excessive sentimentality, much like old times. "Has anyone come by for me this morning? I expected to hear from Mrs. White. Surely she is ready to deliver by now, and I am concerned about her. I will drop by today." She avoided Sarah's eyes. "I overslept, I must admit."

She had not been prepared for the pleasure his body would bring—those hands, that voice, his member, delighting in ways she could never have imagined...

Sarah giggled. "Maggie! I can see from your dreamy countenance that he was, er, adequate, as you say. You are fair glowing."

This was the old Sarah. She fished for details about their first evening as man and wife. She would not get them.

"The marriage was adequately consummated." She blushed. "Rather more than once. Can we not cease this discussion?"

"Splendid—well done!" Sarah hugged her again. "Waste no time in getting with child." The playfulness was gone. "Waste no time. The goddess will bless you, as she has so many others."

"Ruthie." Hiding her concern, Maggie rummaged in the tea can for coins. "You may go outside now. Run to the bakery. Buy a meat pie for your father and Uncle Ian. Deliver them and then you may go to Joannie's house to help with the children."

Ruthie threw on her cloak, all the while chanting, "Uncle Ian, Uncle Ian," slamming the door and waking the baby.

Sarah held the figurine of Ixchel in her hands. "She saved me."

"What?"

"I remember how I came to have this. I lay

underground in darkness, cold and gasping for breath. I tasted blood and something bitter in my mouth. I could not think, could only gasp for air. I grew faint again. So I thought of the babe and tried to feel my stomach for her, but my arms were bound. I tried to open my eyes against the shroud wrapped so tightly, and I could not even open them. White heat flashed through my head as I passed out again, and knew I would die there, wherever I was. And then blackness overtook me."

"You do not have to speak of this." In truth, she did not want to hear anymore.

Sarah took in great gulps of air, mouth open, as if she had just now emerged from the grave. "And then, hands ripped the shroud off my face, gentle hands on the side of my head and lips upon mine, breathing into me! There shone a light, warm, yellow. Through the narrow opening of the shroud, I saw the long fingers of tree roots, as if I was in a cave, but I knew then I had been buried, but that there was a space empty above me that had been cleared. And I saw, strangely, as if in my mind, but I knew she was still there, because I could see her, an old woman, gnarled with clawed hands upon my shoulders as she placed her dry lips upon mine. And I felt a great hollowness in my center and blood draining from me."

"And as her lips left mine, I began to breathe on my own again. She chanted words I could not understand, but they comforted me, and she tucked the figurine into the shroud, its weight reassuring as consciousness faded again."

"It is Ixchel," Maggie said, and explained to her what she and Ian had learned. "We think that the statuette is a talisman, but I do not know..."

As Sarah tightened her grip on it, there began a low-pitched hum, not heard but resounding within Maggie's bones.

Sarah nodded. "Could it be its powers that have so quickly healed me? How can I not worship this goddess? She saved me."

"Sarah, tell no one about this and show the figurine to no one." Maggie grasped her hand. "It could be interpreted as the work of the devil, but I think it is not."

Sarah rested and Maggie stood at the hearth stirring soup when Lena knocked softly. She walked in, her face drawn. Immediately Sabine came to mind, and Maggie readied herself for bad news.

"Lena, what is wrong? Please, sit and have some tea. You look as if you need it."

Lena still stood by the door, casting a glance at Sarah. "This morning, Jonas and Edward Carter sat down at a table. After I served them some ale and returned to my work, I heard them whispering. My hearing is good, *ja*?"

Maggie nodded, smiling despite herself. If someone whispered all the way in Winchelsea, Lena would be sure to hear them.

"Jonas looked terrified, and Carter hissed at him, 'mind you see that you keep your mouth shut about that night except to do the task I have asked you to, cretin. Take care of him. Do you understand?' Jonas nodded and Carter slapped him so hard he fell off his stool. Carter left, and Jonas kept drinking."

"I need to speak with Jonas, and soon."

"It would not do you much good now. He is asleep on the floor. And Maggie, the girl's keeper or lover or whatever he is, has not been seen for two days. My husband, he is afraid we will get no money for the room."

She embraced Lena. "Thank you, friend."

Where had the keeper gone? Had a smuggling trip gone awry?

"How is Sabine, Lena? And the baby?"

"The baby is beautiful and growing by the day. Sabine looks better, whatever your husband is giving her—oh—husband, yes," she cried, eying her intently. "I have not forgotten that you had your husband last night!"

Maggie eyed the toes of her boots.

"*Ach*, so married life has put some roses in your cheeks!" she crowed. "Is that green-eyed man as lively in bed as he is out?"

Yes," she said. "He was quite...tireless."

"So you did as I suggested? You did not think? You were satisfied?"

Maggie nodded, abashed.

Lena whooped, startling the baby and waking Sarah, who sat up, all ears.

"Ha—I knew it! You looked at him as if he was a juicy knockwurst and you were starving."

"What? That is most incorrect."

"Yes, *Liebchen*." Lena poked her roughly. "I shall be calling him 'Knockwurst.' A tall, tasty hunk of knockwurst. I could sample his long, manly..."

With her back to the door, Lena did not hear Ian slip in. Maggie tried to gesture to her that he was there, to no avail. She bit her lip, caught between embarrassment and hilarity.

Lena continued, "I would like to sample that

knockwurst, not a chore at all, that man of yours."

Maggie burst out laughing. Ian pointed to himself, eyebrows raised in question, looking both pleased and alarmed. She nodded.

Lena stopped and finally turned around, her face the color of a stewed prune, put her hand over her mouth, and disappeared out the door.

There was an awkward silence until Ian cleared his throat and lifted Maggie's hands, kissing each palm in turn.

"How are your healing hands today, my wife? You healed me last night, I know."

So foolish to be blushing after last night's activities.

"Your capable, strong hands," he murmured. "My salvation and my pleasure."

"You talk such nonsense," she scoffed. "It's not as if you need to seduce me. We are married."

"I hope to seduce you every night, my lady." He kissed her, slowly and thoroughly.

She pulled away as she saw Sarah watching with a secret smile.

"Let us walk before tea." Ian fetched her cloak, helping her into it. "It's lovely out now." He eyed her in that intense way he had. "And I would like to show my new wife off to the town."

She could not remember when she had last walked out for the sheer pleasure of it. They strolled along the Strand, water lapping against the dock, dock workers shouting as they loaded cargo on a visiting clipper ship. She pulled down the hood of her cloak and let her uncapped hair blow in the breeze with a sense of childlike freedom. She glanced at Ian and grinned.

"Oh Maggie, when you smile it soothes me so." She felt the tremor run through him as he laid his head against hers.

They gazed at the Channel in the distance, calm and forgiving this day. Small fishing boats bobbed, seabirds swarmed above them for the leavings. His body warmed her as the wind picked up, and after a while they continued on their way.

The whole town seemed to be out for a walk. Ed the butcher and his wife walked arm in arm, with friendly smiles and encouraging news of the new grandchild delivered the day of Sarah's burial. Buried and found alive. She relayed to Ian in a whisper Sarah's remembrance of the underground.

The chandler's wife skirted away from them, her young daughter Polly tittering behind her hands. Maggie sighed; she would be paying for her candles from then on.

Joannie and her husband strolled arm in arm, their brood trailing behind them like ducklings. "Ah, so good to see you out, Miss Maggie, Mr. Ian," Joannie cried. A child peeked out from her skirts, head wrapped in a bandage.

"Jimmy!" Ian cried. "How are you, my boy?" He picked him up and examined his head.

Jimmy stared, index finger in his mouth.

"You poor lamb, does it hurt?" Maggie patted his back. She glanced at Joannie.

"Not overly much, I don't think, as he's bedeviling his sisters again." Joannie gave him a buss on the cheek.

The other children gathered around Ian, having heard he often carried sweetmeats in his pockets. He was wonderful with children, she admitted, watching as he took three oranges out of his bottomless pockets and juggled them.

The six year old twins, Abigail and Mary, stared at her, unblinking.

Abigail whispered in her sister's ear, "Is she the devil, then?"

They stared at the top of her head. For horns? Edward Carter was no doubt at the bottom of these accusations. How many more patients would he steal from her?

Abigail's sister whispered, "I don't see horns."

"You silly chits! Where did you hear such a thing?" Joannie shook her head.

"From Polly."

"Shame on you! This is Miss Maggie who brought you into this world. Now, say you're sorry."

"If she is anything," Ian announced, "she is an angel. Look upon the face of my sweet bride, and what do you see?" He held his arms out to Maggie, as if presenting her to his audience. She frowned. He put his hand to his heart with great drama. "Ah, she scowled at me! What am I to do?"

The children giggled and sang their apology, then skipped away to shriek at the bloated carcass of a seagull.

Henry, the night soil man and his son, George emerged out of a side street. It had been a long time since she'd seen them away from their work in the light of day.

Henry's eyes lit up as he saw her. He gave a low bow. "A pleasure, Miss Maggie." He had a lovely deep voice, cultured and well-spoken. His black curls were tied back from his freshly shaven face. His toffee-colored eyes shone with enthusiasm and good humor.

He nodded at Ian, jaw clenched. "I hear congratulations are in order."

"Yes," she said.

"Then I must congratulate you, Mr. Pierce, for you are a fortunate man indeed." He shook Ian's hand, which turned white from the pressure of Henry's grasp.

George did not even pretend to disguise his displeasure. He glared at Ian, who smiled and waited to shake his hand. George vociferously shook his head.

"George," Henry said, "Mind your manners."

The boy shook Ian's hand but would not look at him.

"George," Maggie said. "How are you feeling since Mr. Pierce saw to your teeth?"

"Better, thank you, mum." He cradled his jaw protectively.

"Fortunately," Henry growled, "I have not laid eyes on Edward Carter again, the filthy miscreant." He flexed his hands. "For I see some missing teeth in his future...at the very least, a bloodied nose."

"Good man," Ian nodded. "I would not blame you."

Henry gave him a long, measured look. "Have you met him?"

"I am afraid so," Ian said. "Anything you might hear about his activities would be useful. We are certain he is behind the near death of Maggie's sister."

"And anyone else he may have harmed," she added. "Because we're sure Sarah is not the only one."

Henry nodded. "We will stay alert to any news." He ruffled the boy's hair. "We must be on our way. We are going to the Shipwreck Hotel for tea. A rare treat and a welcome relief from my cooking, as you might imagine."

George made a face, displaying his missing teeth, the gums still discolored.

"We have not replaced old Mrs. Downing as our cook yet, may her soul rest in peace. Well"—he nodded to Ian and bowed to Maggie—"again, congratulations. You are a most fortunate man." He narrowed his eyes at Ian, and the two went on their way.

After a time, she became aware of Ian's increasing agitation. He looked one way, then another, started singing a sea shanty under his breath, hand beating a rhythm on his chest. He stopped suddenly and faced her. "Oh ho! I had competition for your affection and did not even know it."

She laughed. "What? Henry? No."

"Maggie, have you eyes? Come now!"

"Well, Sarah had mentioned it from time to time, but I paid no heed."

He grasped her hand and kissed it. "It is a good thing I did not take my time. I have sealed the deal," he boasted.

"He is quite attractive," she said baldly, not knowing where this playful side came from. "He is *quite* attractive when cleaned of the town's shite. If I had only known."

His hand clenched hers. His eyes had turned dark. "It is good that I have already made you mine." He drew her near and nuzzled her neck, his lips tickling her ear. "Mine, Maggie, and I will remind you of it when we get home."

She shivered.

He broke from her and strode in the opposite direction. "I have an idea. Let's visit Sarah's grave before we go home. We have not been back. Perhaps the spirits left something there." He shot ahead.

"Slow down. Your legs are twice as long as mine."

Immediately he returned, tucking her hand on his arm. "I'm sorry."

They walked around the church toward the kirkyard and stood over Sarah's empty grave. Seeing it again underscored the horror of all she had been through. She held firmly to Ian's arm to chase her revulsion away and stamped her feet against the increasing cold. An object poked through the upturned soil in the dim light. She bent down and pulled it out of the ground, to reveal a pair of pliers, brushed the dirt off them, and recoiled at the dried blood.

Ian took them from her and wrapped them in a handkerchief.

"What could pliers be doing here? Could this be the tool used to pull Sarah's tooth? And if it is, who used it?"

"I saw Jonas at the grave that night," Ian said.

"Then we must speak to Jonas. I have tried, but to no avail." She told Ian about the conversation between Jonas and Edward Carter Lena had overheard.

"Whatever devilry they have committed, they did it together," Ian mused.

"We know Edward Carter has done this, but why, beyond just the desire to kill? There must be something else."

Ian drew her to him so she leaned back against him. His Adam's apple thrummed against the back of her head as he hummed the minor tune she had heard this morning.

"As long as there is pain in the world," he said, "there will be someone eager to inflict it."

Chapter Twenty

When they returned to their cottage, Ian poured some ale, and they sat by the fire to discuss the discovery of the pliers.

"Why would Jonas want to pull Sarah's teeth?"

He thrummed his fingers on his folded arms. "There is one possibility." He reached over to remove the pins from her hair, fingers stroking her neck.

She swatted his hand away. "Cease your fiddling and tell me."

He stopped moving long enough to grimace. "Good healthy teeth can bring a considerable amount of coin."

"Whatever for?"

He cocked his head. "Maggie, have you not heard of the latest thing? Surgeons are experimenting with transplanting teeth into the mouths of their patients. They have not been successful, but they persevere."

"So Jonas and Edward Carter are in the business of selling teeth for profit?"

"Yes, that could very well be true." Ian picked up the hurdy gurdy machine. "And it seems likely, considering we found the pliers and Sarah's tooth was missing."

"That would explain another motive for their activity, beyond depravity."

"There's more." He sat, the instrument on his lap,

and breathed deeply, eyes closed. He folded his hands and set them on the table. "There are doctors in London who will pay a dear price for fresh corpses. When in medical school, I..."

What ailed the man? Why was it so hard for him to still himself? He grasped his hair, loosening it from his tie, and shook his head. "I must tell you more about the history between Edward Carter and myself."

She nodded.

"One night, on the way to my lodgings after an evening at a pub, I passed by the graveyard near the hospital and saw dirt flying in the air by the light of a lantern. Immediately alert, drunk as I was, I stopped there. I recognized Edward Carter, or Phillip White, and another man. He carried a burlap sack, and once the grave had been unearthed, he bent down. I hid behind a tree and watched his arm reach down and pull back as if he yanked at something. He was wrenching teeth out of the dead body's mouth. I saw a glint of silver and the furtive loading of items into a sack."

"Being inebriated, as I said, and subsequently clumsy, I stumbled, and they both looked up. In the light of the lantern, we recognized each other. Over the graveyard, Phillip White hissed, 'If you speak a word of this, Pierce, I will carve you up.'"

"I was not overly worried about the threat. I had no intention of letting this gross injustice continue, but in my inebriated state I had no idea how to handle it. As it turned out, I did nothing about it." He sighed, head in hands. "But he got his revenge. We had never gotten along, White and I."

Maggie rose to pour more ale, trying to absorb this new information.

His hair had come out of his tie and fallen into his face. He shoved it out of his way. She smoothed his hair, tucked it behind his ear, and traced the scar that ran along the side of his jaw. As if it were her own, she felt the agitation running through him like a flood-swollen stream.

"Ian, what happened to you that day you went to Bedlam? Why could you control your—infirmity—and then not be able to?"

He laid his forehead against hers and searched for her lips, slowly, with great care, wrapping his hands in her hair. He lifted it and kissed her neck, his lips so warm, so firm. Her bones softened with desire.

He moaned hoarsely against her neck. "Let me love you. Have we not talked enough? Nothing we say or do will change what transpired today, nor will it alter the course of tomorrow." He nipped her gently and sighed, making every nerve rise to the surface of her skin. "That neck, so soft. Come."

He raised her up, his hands on her waist and guided her up the stairs. He stopped at the top and held her close so she could feel his cock against the cleft of her bottom. She ground against him to feel the heat pool in her privities. He spread his palms over her breasts, and unfastened the bodice with agonizing slowness.

It was dark in the room; he released her to light a candle against the dusk. "I want to see you, every inch."

Heat radiated from his skin as he removed his shirt. Then he stood there, one wide shoulder cocked up, and smiled in invitation, eyes on her opened bodice. His chest glowed in the candlelight, the hairs curling at the base of his throat, trailing down to his navel and beyond. She yearned to follow that trail, to touch him, like a wanton. And so she did, cupping his face in her hands and gliding both palms down his neck, across his shoulders, to whorl her fingers around his nipples and feel his body tense in response. She skimmed her hands down his stomach and tucked her fingers under the waistband, sliding his breeches down, bit by bit, stopping to feel the play of muscles in his thighs, his calves. She grasped his cock, the heat of it warming her hands in the chilly room. She cradled the weight of his sac in her other hand, enjoying the contrast of soft and hard, both of them hot. She breathed in the musky spice of him.

He moaned and lifted her up, stripped off her bodice and shift, and tossed them on the floor. He laid her upon the bed, lifting her arms over her head, holding them with one hand. His other hand trailed up and down her ribs. He circled a tongue around her nipple and took it in his mouth, sucking, drawing warm currents from her center. His heart pounded against her breast.

"Please," she cried. "Enter me, now."

His eyes glowed with pleasure at her entreaty, the green intensity sending a shock wave through her body.

He lifted his head from her breast. "No need to hurry," he rumbled.

He rolled her over so she lay atop him. "I promise you I will. We will take our time. First, touch me again, Maggie. I ache for you, no matter how many times I take you. Touch me, please."

She trembled and rose above him and circled her fingers around his manhood. Her hair swept across his chest, and she watched his face, his member pulsing in her hands. Pride and power swelled within her, that she could move him so. She tasted the salt on his chest, his stomach as he quivered and wrapped her mouth upon the rigid strength of his cock, sampled him with mouth and tongue both gentle and firm. He groaned and lifted her away from him, so they might kiss, their tongues entwining.

She slid up his body, rubbing herself against him. "Come into me. Please," she gasped. "I must feel your heart beat within me. Now."

He held her waist and thrust into her yearning warmth, his thick rod filling her, and she bucked against him, needing to be one. A tingling spread throughout her limbs as his strength flowed into her. He cried out her name and they lay together until the last tendrils of pleasure subsided. His heartbeat pulsed within her still, and he gave one last thrust for one last jolt of pleasure.

She tried to tell him, that she wanted to keep him there, in her body forever, so she could feel his heart beat within her, but she drifted off into a dreamless sleep, limbs tangled with his.

****

She woke before dawn, feeling a most pleasing lethargy and contentment. The space next to her was empty and already her legs were cold without the warmth of his muscled legs wrapped around her. The muffled chords of a dulcimer echoed up the stairs, and Ian's rusty tenor sang a minor, cacophonous tune that unearthed every heartbreaking moment of her life. The clock struck three.

He played, head lowered, with an alarming frenzy. He did not hear her approach, but continued to sing, voice rising, increasing in speed, until he finished with a crash.

"My darling." His fingers rested on the edge of the instrument, and a bone deep tremor coursed through them. His hair had fallen into his eyes. She combed her fingers through it. Purple stains of fatigue pooled under his eyes. His pain welled within her as if it were her own.

She sat with him in the predawn darkness. He resumed his playing and sang in a foreign tongue, a lullaby, she thought, for it did not take long to fall asleep.

She awoke at sunrise, finding herself in bed. Had he carried her there? Downstairs, he stood by the fireplace, hair standing on end. He teemed with energy, as if he'd been sleeping alongside her for hours.

"My beauty," he crowed, voice both hoarse and hardy. "Let me take that to the cesspit for you. I have made some porridge this morning, with raisins. Do you like raisins?"

He sailed out the back door and returned promptly to hand her a cup of tea and a buttered roll. Should she not be waiting on him? Uneasiness crept over her as she watched him bustle around the hearth, stirring the oatmeal and checking the water he heated for her ablutions. His moods ever-changed; just a few hours ago, he had been sunk in sorrow. This was her husband's infirmity then. Was it not just a matter of will? Could he not control it if he tried?

They sat at the table and discussed their plans for the day. She would go check on Sarah. Later this morning they would meet at the Siren Inn to question Sabine about Edward Carter.

It was hard to think logically with him standing

there, behind his chair. He could not remain seated. His eyes kept falling upon her open dressing gown, and he ran his tongue around his lips, eyes rising to meet hers, so green, so bright, like kelp drying on the shore.

"It is early still," he murmured. His silk robe gaped open to display his powerful chest, the brown hairs curling. His shoulders, wide and straight, tapered to his waist, like an arrow aimed true to his power and source of her joy.

She recalled the moment he had cried out, as his life force flowed into her and she took it in, her whole being centered upon his shaft, and the moment when everything spun into the air, pleasure on the edge of pain flowing through her, as his essence flowed through her soul.

Her breasts tingled with anticipation as his desire rose beneath the gown.

He took her hand. "Let us greet the morning together, wife." He led her upstairs.

****

Later, when Maggie arrived at Sarah's cottage, the door stood wide open. Samuel stood in the yard, calling for Sarah.

"Samuel, what's wrong?"

"She's gone. I went into the shop this morning, just for a moment," Samuel said, panting.

"Where are Ruthie and the babe?"

The trestle bench was overturned, dishes broken on the floor.

"Samuel, where is the baby?"

"Ruthie took her to Joannie's, to see if Sarah was there. Sarah was belligerent this morning. What is wrong with her?"

"Samuel, I'll find her. I'll go down to the pier and look for her at the Shipwreck Hotel." She grabbed Sarah's cloak. "Was she even dressed?"

He shook his head grimly. "I'll go toward Siren Street. Maybe she is just visiting Lena."

Maggie headed along the Strand toward the pier, not daring to ask anyone if they had seen her for fear of calling attention to the fact her sister was out before her churching. She rounded the corner to Pier Street. A crowd of people gathered in front of Edward Carter's shop.

"What is she doing here?"

"Satan has taken control of her, can't you see that?"

"It is true. See how she glows with his fire?"

"Here she is in all her glory. Do you need further proof?" Edward Carter's smooth voice carried over the crowd.

Sarah's voice boomed even louder. "The Goddess tells me you are the one, the defiler of women. For what you did to me and to other women, she says she will help me destroy you."

"I have defiled no one," Carter said. "Surely you people can see who the evil one here is. Have I not healed your wounds? Am I not your physician? This woman must be put away."

Voices rose in fear, shock, and an edge of anger increased in volume as people poured out of the Shipwreck Hotel.

"See her eyes, they glow."

"No, they don't."

"'Tis true!"

The crowd parted. Edward Carter held his hands up

in the air as Sarah, clothed only in her night rail, approached him and struck him with a clawed hand. The crowd roared. Sarah, face contorted, hissed at Carter.

Maggie hurried toward her and felt Ian's hand on her shoulder.

"I'll get her." He shoved through the crowd. "Good sister. You must come with me." He put an arm around her middle and dragged her out of the crowd. He dodged her blows as she reached for Carter.

"Murderer," Sarah cried. "Violator."

"There goes the woman brought back from the dead by the midwife." Carter pointed, holding his scratched face with one hand.

As Ian and Maggie made their way back to the cottage, a crowd followed them, taunting Sarah, who still hissed, but had given up struggling in Ian's arms as he carried her.

"Go away," Ian yelled. "Can you not see that she's ill?"

But the crowd would not leave them. Even after they entered the cottage and bolted the door, human voices buzzed like wasps outside. Thankfully, Samuel and Ruthie were back already. Samuel sent Ruthie upstairs with the baby.

He took Sarah from Ian. "Sarah. You must calm yourself." He embraced her, and she pinched his arms, kicking her legs back.

"Let go of me," she screamed.

"She has the strength of two men," Samuel gasped. The sleeve of his shirt was torn, and blood ran down his arm.

She tore from his grasp and ran to the door. She

struggled to unbar the door. "He must be stopped."

"Sarah. Can you not hear the crowd? Listen." Maggie grasped her arm.

The crowd cried, "Witch, necromancer."

"Come away from the door, Sister."

She clawed at the wood. "She tells me I must stop him."

"You cannot, Sarah."

She turned, ice blue eyes flaming. "Nothing has been done," she roared. "I implored you to seek justice. But you have done nothing."

"No, Sarah." Maggie said. "That is not true. We have. But it takes time."

"Time enough for another woman to die? The goddess tells me I must sacrifice myself to bring him to justice."

"No." Out of the corner of her eye, Maggie saw Ian approach. Samuel carried a rope and as one, on each side of her, they wrapped the rope around her to restrain her. She bucked, howling. They carried her to a chair in the corner and tied her to it.

"It is for your own good," Ian said. "Samuel, hold her head. This will calm her." He had a vial in his hand and poured the medicine in her mouth, holding her nose so she would swallow it. He backed away.

For the next hour they watched as she screamed, rage burning her face a dusky red. She struggled against the restraint but could not loosen the binds. Slowly her features grew slack, her muscles relaxed, and her head sank to her chest. She fell into a deep sleep.

They sat at the table, watching, waiting.

"Lucky that you still had some of the calming herbs that I had mixed." Ian's cheeks trailed with scratches from Sarah." I gave her a hefty dose."

"You are hurt," Maggie said. "Let me dress those scratches."

"Don't bother with it." He snapped, closed his eyes, breathing deeply. "I knew we must restrain her, but no one should be tied up like an animal."

"Listen to them." Samuel cocked his head toward the door. "They want blood."

The whole town must be outside. Edward Carter's voice rose above the din.

"Clearly, good people, you have seen her doing Satan's bidding today. Out in public half-naked, displaying her body. Look at my face—I have been struck by the devil's own maidservant."

Another wave of shouting crashed against the cottage walls.

Maggie recognized the voices of those she had served: the chandler's wife had labored a day and a night. She had watched over the woman and saved her baby's life by unwrapping the cord from his neck.

Ian rose and paced the room, arms folded, fingers flexing and unflexing. "People get much pleasure out of seeing others lose control, watching them, taunting them. Making entertainment out of despair."

"This spirit, this Ixchel will not leave us until Edward Carter is convicted," Maggie said. "We must convince the crowd that Carter is to blame for the deaths of these women and for Sarah."

"I will go to Hastings tomorrow," Samuel said. "I will talk to the constable and inquire about Edward Carter or Phillip White. Maybe he hurt women there and was run out of town."

"There must be a way to convince Jonas to talk,"

Ian said. "I will do that."

"After Joannie gets here," Maggie said, "I must go see Ed the butcher's daughter, and then I will tend to Sabine. Ian, will you meet me there later to speak to her?"

He nodded.

"How do we get out of here, alive?" Samuel asked.

Ian put his hands on Maggie's shoulders. "And when superstition overpowers reason, how does truth prevail?"

Cold washed over Maggie; somewhere in the room a snake hid, curled at rest, ready to strike.

There was a lull in the din outside for a time. Then she heard the voice of Vicar Andrews, stern and authoritative, and Ben Sutton, the town magistrate's deep voice. The townspeople roared their objection.

A moment later there was a knocking on the door. "Open up," Vicar Andrews called.

"We must speak," the magistrate said. "There has been an agreement made."

Samuel held the door open enough to let them in, then shut and barred it quickly.

Vicar wiped the sweat off his face and strode over to where Sarah sat. "I did not see your sister during her, er, display, but our good magistrate tells me it was frightening."

The magistrate cleared his throat. "They want you both tried as witches." He looked at Maggie. Ian braced an arm around her.

"But," the vicar said, "we have not tried a witch in this town in many years, nor do I want to. We do not know where the constable is—he has disappeared, and in any case would probably be no help. The crowd will not be pacified with mere words."

"We have compromised." Vicar looked down at the floor and then tried but failed to meet Samuel's eyes. "They will agree to leave the family alone, and Maggie may stay." He paused, clutching the sides of his jacket. "But your wife must go to Bedlam Hospital."

Ian jerked as if a knife had been plunged into his back.

Samuel stood over Sarah. "You will have to kill me first."

"Look here," the magistrate said. "We cannot stop them from killing her. We were able to allow Mistress—Pierce to stay because otherwise there would be no midwife in town. But Sarah must go away. To Bedlam."

Vicar sighed. "I am sorry. It was the best we could do. Just because we no longer allow them to burn witches, doesn't mean they won't, on their own."

"We can prove Edward Carter's guilt," Maggie said. "We just need some time. Can you not give us a day or two? And if we cannot lay the guilt on him, then I will go to Bedlam and let Sarah stay."

"No." Sarah's voice carried over to where they were whispering by the door. "I will go. The spirits will take care of me."

"She cannot be talking like that," Vicar cried.

Ian rubbed his wrists, and in a monotone said, "You do not know what you are saying, to make a woman go to that place. You are not human there. You are an animal, and they are your keepers."

"See here, man." The magistrate strode over to Ian and put his finger in his face. "We have no choice in the matter. Something must be done. Your sister-in-law's behavior is destroying this town. Listen to those people out there. We must appease them somehow."

"Out of respect for the service that you and your sister have done for this town, this was the only alternative. She would not be safe here, at any rate," Vicar pleaded.

"Please." Maggie touched the magistrate's sleeve. "Give us the rest of today and tomorrow to prove Edward Carter is guilty of burying her, and other women, alive, and of assaulting the foreign girl. Is it not evidence of guilt that he goes by another name, Phillip White? If we cannot prove his guilt by tomorrow night, then take me if you must."

"You must understand," Ian said. "It is the trauma of being buried alive that has unhinged her. It is not her fault."

Clever of Ian. The townspeople didn't know Ixchel possessed Sarah. They had seen nothing but her strange behavior. The magistrate drew Vicar Andrews over to the window for a consultation. They argued back and forth for a moment.

Vicar turned. "You have until tomorrow, five o'clock, to do what you've requested. We will pacify the townspeople with that promise, but you must make sure that she is not seen."

Samuel's face was ashen as he let them out.

They listened through the door as the magistrate explained the situation and gave the crowd an ultimatum. "Anyone caught loitering here will be thrown into gaol. I will act as constable in Pete Stowe's absence. Now go about your business and let us take care of the matter."

The voices rose in anger but eventually faded from

the cottage.

Maggie closed her eyes for a moment. Her heartbeat slowed with relief that they had gained more time. But not much.

"Do you think we can untie her now?" Samuel faced Sarah and kissed her forehead.

She shivered. "I'm very tired. Where is the baby?"

It seemed she was herself again, but for how long?

"She will sleep again, I think. It is a powerful mixture," Ian said.

"She must feed the babe first. Untie her."

Pray God they were doing the right thing. Ruthie brought the babe down, and Maggie attended Sarah to make certain she was strong enough to hold the babe while she nursed.

"I must go now to see if Joannie can come to keep an eye on Sarah." Ian embraced Maggie and held her at arm's length. His hands shook, and his eyes had gone dark. "She must not be left alone. Then I will hunt Jonas down and see who else I can question about his activities that night. I will make him talk." He bent to kiss her hard on the mouth. "I will stop at nothing to keep you from that place."

Before she could open her mouth to reply, he was gone.

After a short while, Joannie arrived with her husband in tow. "He did not want me to travel alone, once Mr. Ian explained the circumstances. And he will escort you to the Siren." She took off her cloak and walked around to view Sarah. "Poor girl. It is that monster's fault she is in this state."

"Thank you, Joannie. You are a true and loyal friend. I will never forget what you've done for us."

"Aw, don't fret about it. Mother came to watch the children, and I could use the break." Joannie hugged her. "It will be okay, Miss Maggie."

But as Maggie grabbed her cloak by the fireplace, she saw the exchange of worried glances between Joannie and her husband.

Chapter Twenty-One

The owner's old wife at the Shipwreck Hotel greeted Ian and dispensed his ale. Did she know how beautiful she was? How beautiful all women are, their softness, their glow, the round curves that sing of home? He took a swallow of summer wheat, honey, the drone of bees, warm breast, cool air.

Was that Jonas slumped in the corner? Just as he expected. No glow around him, no, none at all.

"Jonas, my good man! You are troubled?"

His eyes were red—he'd had a few. Mouth quivery, gulping. "She will not leave me be, the old woman, the snake woman, she is punishing me, oh I have sinned, have sinned."

"Tell me, old man."

"She says that I will suffer—the snake, wrapped around her head, tells me I will suffer for what I have done."

"What did you do, Jonas?"

Ian struggled to focus on him, to not drink in the man's despair.

"I cannot tell you. He will kill me!" He covered his face with his hands.

"Tell me, Jonas."

"That night, when you came upon me in the kirkyard, I dug her up, I shouldn't have done! But have been doing since I'd known Carter. I dug her up to pull her teeth for us to sell, and to ready her for the wagon going to London. Carter sells the bodies for money, good money. Sometimes he delivers the babies and sells them."

Ian called for more ale and nudged it toward him. "Go on."

"That night, I lifted her out, like always, uncovered her face, like always, and opened her mouth. Pulled the first tooth. She moved! I could not think, could only scream. Miss Sarah, who had never done a bad thing to no one, always kind to me she was, I had buried her and she was alive."

He gulped his ale down. "And now the dreams, the old woman screams, how I will suffer, how I will suffer for my deeds. What must I do to be rid of her?" He began to cry in great gasps.

"Jonas, you must help stop this, you must confess, so this does not happen to anyone else."

"He will kill me!"

"We will keep you safe, Jonas."

He looked around and rose, knocking his ale over and shoving his way out the door.

He hoped he had persuaded him. For if Edward Carter did not kill Jonas, his guilt would.

More ale, perhaps some whisky as well, to help calm his nerves, warm the cold chill of guilt falling on him like snow, stop the guilt that Jonas had wrapped around him. Carter would hurt Maggie if he stayed.

Despite the desperate circumstances, his skin sang with the brightness in the day, the piercing sadness of the curlew's call, taste of rain upon his lips, sweet drink of mermaids. The people sitting at the table, the sacred lilt in their voices. Every word had heightened meaning, great purpose. Oh, he longed to drink, to wash the stink of Bedlam off, to wash the memories clean. And pretend he could stay with her.

Before dawn today, he had watched her sleep, a small smile playing at her lips, black hair spread over the pillow. He woke her again, embraced her warmth, the comfort of her arms, her yielding softness. For a short time after they found their pleasure, he fell asleep, enough to taunt him. Life could be like this, if only he was not plagued so. And knew then, watching her breathe, it could never be as he wanted.

At first, he had thought perhaps it had gone from him, that finding someone he could not live without would quiet the pounding, the relentless buzzing and beating and cacophony that drummed inside, the pumping of the blood, the throbbing in his veins, the crawling, the crawling like a centipede on every inch of skin, if he could only reach inside himself to silence it. It seemed she has not healed him after all.

So he would drink the summer down, drink it down to warm him.

Chapter Twenty-Two

Accompanied by Joannie's husband, Maggie checked on young Betty, who seemed to be healing nicely, then entered the Siren Inn, anxious to hear what Ian had learned from Jonas. She appraised Lena of the situation.

"I am sorry for this, *Liebchen*." Lena put her work-roughened hand over hers. "But I am sure that all will be well."

Maggie smiled at the familiar words. Her friend set a bowl of chowder and a thick hunk of brown bread in front of her. "You have much to do, but you must keep your strength up."

Her cheery demeanor and hearty food did much to quiet the restless anxiety that roiled around in her belly.

"Our Sabine ate a bowl of chowder I had brought to her a while ago. She felt strong enough to get out of bed for a bit."

That was good news indeed. "Thank you for the chowder, my friend." Maggie stood and brushed the crumbs from her apron. "I will check on Sabine. Have you seen Ian?"

There was hardly anyone about at this hour, except a pair of sailors, intent on playing a game of chance.

"No, I have not seen him."

"He should have been here by now. We were going to talk to Sabine again."

What could be taking him so long? Of all times for him to be missing...she headed upstairs. Lena was right. Sabine was a resilient girl and showed every sign she would heal properly. Before long, she headed back, accompanied by Joannie's husband, to Sarah's cottage, anxious to relieve Joannie and hoping Ian had returned there, merely forgetful they had made plans to talk to Sabine.

She sent Joannie and her husband home, and the afternoon dragged by as she tended to Sarah and tried to keep poor Ruthie busy cooking and playing with a top Ian had given her. Where was her husband?

Samuel returned, dusty and tired from the road. He rushed over to Sarah, who sat in the rocking chair, feet up on a stool. "How is she?"

"As you can see, much the same. I dosed her up again, just to be safe."

"I have some news. The constable there said that two women, who seemed healthy enough to him, had died during childbirth during the time Phillip White practiced there."

Maggie handed him some ale and a bowl of soup. He sat down, attacking it with relish.

"I'm going to look for Ian." She made sure her head was covered, to help hide her identity.

"Be careful, Maggie."

"Do not worry, Samuel."

He frowned. "Where has the man disappeared to?"

She avoided his eyes. "Well, I..."

"What is it, Maggie? Has he treated you ill?"

"No, I just do not know where he is," she admitted. "He never met me at the Siren Inn, and I have not seen him since."

He glowered, fists clenched. "I knew it. I knew he was lacking."

"Samuel! You mustn't jump to conclusions."

Quite uncharacteristically, he embraced her.

****

She bent her head and strode through a lowering fog, the echoes of ships' bells accompanying her. She searched the path to the Shipwreck Hotel and made sure her hood was up. Upon arriving, she found Ian standing amidst a group of laughing people, singing an extremely bawdy song, with great arm and leg movements. She was in no mood for this raucous environment. Sarah's life was at stake. What could he be thinking? Meanwhile, her husband's performance had his admirers clapping and hollering, stamping their feet.

The owner's wife passed by with a tray of drinks in her hand and shook her head. "He is our entertainer tonight."

She elbowed her way through the crowd and grasped his arm. "Ian."

He stopped mid-song and took her in his arms, swinging her around amidst hoots and catcalls. "My beloved! You've come to join me!"

"I've come to take you home," she yelled above the uproar.

"Oh now!" Someone in the crowd called out. "The bride wants her groom home, does she? Miss Maggie is making up for lost time! Take her home, Pierce! Pull out that giant pestle of yours. Give her what she needs!" The men called out drunkenly.

To his credit, Ian did not delay but put his arm around her and swept out of the inn. The fog crawled at their feet, and their footsteps echoed as they made their way home. He could not keep still but continued his crooning, occasionally stopping to laugh and nod his head.

She shook his arm. "What is the matter with you? You disappear for hours with no word of where you'd gone. You promised you would help my family." As she spoke the words, saying them aloud gave them credence, and thoughts of her father came unwillingly and made her voice harsher than intended.

He looked at her with such self-reproach she swallowed anger with effort.

"Oh Maggie. I am sorry. I thought it would help."

"Help what?"

He ignored her question, murmuring, "Forgive me. My intention was to help, and—oh Maggie. All I want to do is love you." He stopped and kissed her with slow and lingering tenderness.

"Enough about that right now." She urged him on and down the street, and as they walked along the Strand, she switched to his other arm to guard him from the edge of the water, so crooked was his gait. How much drink had he consumed? The moon's reflection on the water revealed a half-moon, milky white and innocent.

As if in answer to her unspoken question he said, "I got Jonas drunk and questioned him about the night I found Sarah. He did admit he was there to pull her teeth and more, that he was readying her corpse for Edward Carter to take her to London to sell."

She nodded.

"And best of all, he has agreed to confess to the magistrate, tomorrow morning. If he does not remember, I will remind him."

A sense of relief washed over her, that he had a purpose to his trip and been successful. He hadn't gone there just to fill his belly with drink. Still, his demeanor was alarming. He vaguely reminded her of a puppet, as if he had no control over his movements. Is this what excessive drink did to him?

"Jonas said he'd been plagued with dreams of the snake woman, Ixchel, and her promise to make him pay for his crimes, in most horrible and bloody detail. I told him that confessing was the only way to rid himself of her."

She nodded.

"And if I had a tad too much to drink, it was worth the cost, wasn't it?"

He had indeed done good work today, but she would not tell him so. They were that much closer to being able to present a case against Edward Carter. Especially when Jonas confessed.

"I can speak of this no longer, Maggie. Can we not put our minds on other things and forget our troubles for a little while?"

"But Sarah..." How could he act as if nothing were wrong?

"Maggie, we can do nothing until morning."

It was true. Sarah was safely home with Samuel. Nothing bad was happening at this moment. Why not take what comfort they could from each other?

As soon as she latched the cottage door and lit the candles and the fire, Ian began removing his clothes. He stood in his breeches, swaying slightly, powerful chest bare and bathed in candlelight. His upper arms bulged with sinew, raised in a stretch above his head, loose breeches sliding down over his hips, the trail of hair from his navel to the hair at the base of his member. His eyes stripped her of her clothing, and she felt his need like her own heartbeat. She removed her clothing slowly, forcing him to wait as she had waited all those long hours, not knowing where he'd gone.

Once upstairs she pushed him against the wall. Their tongues met thrust for thrust, deep waves of warmth coursing through her. She removed his breeches and skimmed her hand up his muscled legs, his hands grasped her hair. She wrapped her lips around his member and grasped with the other hand the weight of his stones. Need swelled within her. She trailed her lips up his body, followed by her hands, sliding up the length of his body.

He lifted her to the bed. "Ah, Maggie, such joy you give me, and I do not deserve it." He kissed her, hands possessing her so every inch of her throbbed with need, his lips upon her nipples, hands demanding response, seeking her flesh to sing. She raised her hips to invite him in, and he thrust into her. If she could only keep him within her, like this, she would know him, all of him.

He grasped her face. "Maggie, you have given me my life here within you, where I have found peace for a time. I long to be inside of you, like this, always." He swelled within her again and thrust with agonizing slowness.

"I do not deserve you, but I love you, do you hear?" He kissed her, his lips bruising hers.

"Don't say that. You have given me life, Ian." She responded in kind, anger and bewilderment bruising his lips as well. She searched his eyes, tightened around him, to keep him to her, to keep him safe, so she might always feel those waves of pleasure and his essence pulsing within. She lay within the shelter of his chest, arms on his to hold him there.

Long before dawn, she awoke to an empty bed and thought she heard the soft plucking of a lute and Ian's rusty voice trailing alongside it. But he was gone.

Chapter Twenty-Three

Hours later, Maggie set her shoulders back, determined to go about the day as if Ian had never left. Her mind approved of this strategy, but the body had other ideas. It still hummed with the memory of their coupling. She had felt his desperation, and her body had responded. Why then had he left? Had he already tired of her? No, she would not spend the day in doubt. There was much to be done and she would do it, as always. But how could he leave when they needed him so?

As she drank her tea, she received a summons to the Siren Inn by a young lad she didn't recognize. He said there was something wrong with the foreign girl.

She did not see Lena upon her arrival and went straight upstairs. "Sabine, good afternoon, my dear. It's Miss Maggie. I have..."

She opened the door. A fist smashed into her face, and she fell backward into the hallway. Edward Carter grabbed her by the shoulders and dragged her into the room, shutting the door.

"You stupid bitch," he said. "You could not keep that ugly yap of yours shut." He let go suddenly, and she staggered, blinking her eyes to clear the red mist. Sabine cowered in the bed, a bloody knife in her hand, and Jonas was doubled over, his hand covering his side, blood seeping from beneath it. Another man Maggie had not seen before, rough-looking, big, grabbed hold of Jonas so Carter could hit him in the stomach.

"You imbecile! Henson here said he had overheard you talking to her husband about me, about that night. You're coming along."

"No," Jonas screamed.

Carter put a hand over his mouth. "Quiet or I will gut you like a fish, right here."

He grabbed Maggie by the arm. "We are going on a journey. Come along with me, or I will hurt the little slut." He motioned to Henson, and the man yanked Sabine out of the bed, wresting the dripping knife from her hand. Thank God Lena had the babe.

"You cannot move her," she screamed. "She is not well, thanks to you. It will kill her."

"Then you had better prevent that, midwife." Carter laughed, slapping her face.

Where were they going? Carter would not be able to get them downstairs without discovery. She could call for help but not when he pointed a knife at Sabine.

Carter went over to the other side of the room and felt for something in the paneling. There was a click, and a panel opened up, wide enough to admit one person at a time. She had forgotten the stories told about the secret staircase, where many men had escaped the wrath of the Reformation. Carter held a knife to her throat and a candle dangerously close to her head and commanded she begin her descent. She made her way carefully down the narrow stairway, holding onto the cold stone walls for balance.

Sabine's moans echoed in the cold darkness. They stopped at a narrow landing, and she felt the heat from the fireplace on the other side of the stone wall. They climbed down another passage, into a network of underground caves used by smugglers for centuries. The stories were true then, she thought hazily.

Henson muttered an epithet as Sabine whimpered and slid to the floor.

Carter said, "What are waiting for, you big oaf? Pick her up then."

Sabine had fainted or God forbid, worse.

"If you have killed her, you monster, it will be on your head," Maggie yelled, white hot pain igniting in her jaw where Carter had hit her.

The monster must have big hands, she thought absently, for her entire face felt swollen. No matter. How to keep them alive? She had given her knife to Sabine, the one she normally kept on her person, and the other one was in her bag, dropped in the room. She could only pray and try to keep her wits about her.

By the time her bad foot became so stiff with cold she could barely move it, they came to a heavy iron door. Edward Carter strode ahead, leaving her for a moment to knock upon the door. Sabine's keeper answered it, his head heavily bandaged.

"I have the other," he said.

Who else had been taken? Her heart beat in her throat as they walked down a long passage. Was Sabine still alive? Torches ensconced in the stones revealed water seeping down the walls. They turned the corner into a corridor of barred cells. In the darkness a man screamed, guttural and primal.

Edward Carter opened a cell at the end of the row and shoved her in, followed by Sabine and Jonas.

"No," Jonas screamed. "I helped you, didn't I?"

Carter ignored him and instructed the man carrying

Sabine to put her on the ground.

Without another word, the three men left the cell and locked it.

As her eyes adjusted to the darkness, she saw her, in the corner.

"Sarah."

She lay slumped and shaking against the wall, opening her eyes when Maggie touched her.

"Maggie," she croaked. "I'm sorry. I could not stop their voices, telling me I must seek vengeance. Ruthie returned to take the baby over to Joannie's so I might sleep uninterrupted, and I ventured out. That man with the bandaged head grabbed me and brought me here."

"Are you hurt?" She rubbed Sarah's hands with her own to warm them.

"No," she whispered. "Just bleeding and so tired, Maggie."

"We are going to be fine," she said, not believing it. "I must tend to Sabine now."

She lay sprawled on the floor, unconscious. Straining her eyes in the dim, flickering light of the sconces in the passageway, she lifted Sabine's skirts and felt the blood seeping out in a slow steady stream. She would not live if left like this. There was little she could do for the girl, except for one thing, but it was too risky and it might kill her. She had none of her midwife materials, no medicines, nothing. Would she watch the poor girl die, and Sarah as well? No.

She could not think clearly with Jonas' caterwauling. "Jonas, stop your noise and help me take Sabine over to Sarah. They must keep each other warm. And give me your coat. Jonas!"

He obeyed, and they put the two women together

so they might share body heat. Between her cloak and Jonas' ragged one, they were at least covered. Sarah had rallied enough to wrap her arms around Sabine. The girl stirred, and Sarah crooned to her.

All she could do, Maggie determined, was to keep moving, tend to Sarah and Sabine. And pray.

They had disappeared without a trace, and no one but those monsters knew where they had gone. Had they left them there to die? Where was Ian?

Chapter Twenty-Four

Ian cursed himself for he could not control the memories that crashed in his head like cymbals, and the rest of the music within him could not help but join in the cacophony. He staggered out of town through the Landgate; it towered over him; ancient and judgmental and shadowed him to the outskirts of town. He had a bottle and a hope it might serve to silence that which plagued his mind, those melodies ever present, growing in volume and intensity, their piercing harmonies on the edge of darkness. The bottle was the last chance of stilling them so he could return to Maggie. But in his current state he could help no one.

Damn Phillip White, for he had once seen him at his very worst, and reminded him he could not hide his wreckage from her any longer. He must leave. He wandered along the shore, hoping the water lapping and the sea birds crying would calm him, but how could they when not even the heart and soul of Maggie could do so? He had so hoped she would be his savior, but he was wrong. He threw the bottle into the river. It would not serve him. And he had felt the remedy within his grasp, if only he had more time.

Eventually, Ian walked amongst the salt flats toward the Channel and watched a ship head to sea. There had he escaped before and could remain forever anonymous, moving from sea to province to sea again, always moving, and the music trailed him, padding behind like a predator in the soft marshland and sinking a claw into him with a song of sorrow and stark need, and he gave himself up to it.

He looked out at the water and glimpsed the mermaids, their shining heads and coy eyes enticing him further on as they bobbed in the whitecaps so he could hear their song. He felt it, the rise and fall of his soul as their keening harmony buoyed him up, as he joined them in the whitecaps. The music so exceedingly sweet, his head swirling with it, his soul rising and falling with it as the piercing melody resounded within him.

He had heard music all over the world, music haunting and joyful, celebrating life and honoring death, music so strange its melodies lingered within him still, and he had made them his own, but this! If he could but remember their song, their secrets carried on the waves and lifting him in a swell of sound and harmony, beckoning, inviting him to know their secrets.

The mermaids had shared their songs with him, they were the soul of the sea, and he must write them down while they coursed through his body, making every nerve pulse with their urgings. He would not let them vanish like sea mist, he must write them down on the parchment he always carried in his cloak, but he had not his cloak. He must return to town and write them down, for if he did, if he could but write them down, he could play them, and they would be songs of such beauty that the town would build a statue of Ian Pierce with lute in hand, because he knew the secrets, the song of the mermaid, soul of the sea.

He hastened to town, melodies and words crashing

within him had so taken over his senses that he could only feel his way back. He entered the Shipwreck Hotel, demanding parchment, demanding pen, grabbing at lapels as the melodies drowned him with their demands. He must write them down so they might flow out of him before the rush of their urgency did drown him.

His desperation and demands were unmet, for they had no parchment, the crash of glass, his own laughter and insults like shards of glass, glinting in his eye and fist meeting flesh. Harsh words and a vise-like grip on his arms, a trip across the cobblestones and cursing. The clang of a cell door and he with no parchment and the melodies, the sweet piercing melodies leaving him ebb by ebb and he would never know the secret of his soul and neither would his good neighbors. And instead of those melodies, inside his head clamored the melodies of every song he had ever heard.

He gave himself up to his infirmity.

Chapter Twenty-Five

She had petitioned her God in the dark cell but could not merely stand and pray, helpless. Who knew how long they would be there, or what plans Edward Carter had? She must do whatever possible to comfort and care for Sarah and Sabine.

Terror raced through her. She could do nothing except watch them all die. The two women would die first, and then her. And she would never again see the sea change in Ian's eyes. Her very being railed against that possibility. She must do something.

She heard water dripping and the muffled rustling of rodents. The metallic scent of old blood rose from the packed dirt floor and dank cold seeped into her bones. Rocks lay scattered about the cave, nothing else. Through the dim light of the torches, she saw the outline of Sarah and Sabine huddled together, Sarah sheltering the younger girl. Jonas held a hand to his stomach. She would treat his wound and solicit his assistance.

She lifted her skirts and using a sharp stone, scored her shift and tore as much fabric from it as possible. She wrapped his torso, and then folded a square of cloth, instructing the man to put pressure on his wound. She placed the rock in her apron pocket.

"Jonas," Maggie urged. "You must rally round and help me. If we are to live, all of us, you must help me."

He trembled, the whites of his eyes glistened in the shadowy light. "For God's sake," she groaned and grabbed him by the shoulders. "You must help keep the women warm if you can do nothing else."

She pulled him over to the women and set him down next to Sarah. Fear glinted in her eyes, her forehead covered in sweat, tremors racked her. And it came to Maggie that in Sarah's mind, she was once again underground. Her arms encircling Sabine stiffened, and Sabine's head lolled to the side.

"Sarah."

No response. She would not let her sister slip into terror again.

"Sarah, we will get out of here, I promise you."

She stared blankly.

"Look at me!"

She started. Her eyes struggled to focus. And Maggie remembered the words, the words that had soothed her that night she lay in bed and on her wedding day.

"Sarah. All is well. All will be well."

"The darkness," she panted. "Heavy weight, I cannot breathe, the shroud."

"All is well," Maggie repeated, and gently wiped her face. "Breathe, Sarah. All will be well."

Her tremors stopped and indeed, as Maggie said the words, a feeling of peace came over her as well. Out of the corner of her eye, she saw Jonas forage in his coat and pull out a flask.

"Why did you not tell me you had that?" She grabbed it from him. He screamed and reached for it. She held it up to Sarah's lips and implored her to have a sip. Sarah sputtered at the putrid taste of the gin but swallowed a few mouthfuls. Maggie gave Jonas a few swallows and put it back in her apron.

She was just preparing to examine Sabine again when footsteps echoed down the passageway, and Edward Carter appeared with Sabine's keeper. He slammed the cell door open.

"Are you dead yet, then?" He looked around, the lantern swaying in his hand and revealing Sabine and Sarah heaped together in the corner. "You look dead. What a waste of coin you are, damn you."

His lantern light revealed Sabine's blood flowing on the dirt floor. She must do something for Sabine quickly, or she would most certainly die. Carter gestured to the keeper, who carried a small parcel.

"Food. I want some meat on your bones when we sell you." He shot Maggie a look of unbridled contempt. "Except for you, crippled slut. You I'll just kill, when I get around to it."

She backed away from him, feeling for the rock in her apron. He grabbed her by the ears and twisted them, then turned her around to wrench her arms behind her back, up and up and she felt her shoulder tear.

"I guess you haven't heard what your new husband is doing." He shoved her so she careened into the wall. He ground his hardened member against her. "He's spent the day carousing at the Shipwreck. He was quite popular with the ladies. He must have tired of you already, then. Made such a nuisance of himself they threw him in gaol."

No. She would not think about that. Not here. Not now. She straightened, fighting dizziness. "We need water or ale."

"You need whatever I desire to get you. And I'm

not inclined at this time."

He spat at her feet and turned around. The two of them went out the door.

She parceled out the food and urged Jonas and Sarah to eat. Her wrath had at least warmed her, and she forced herself to think what she must do. Her eyes adjusted once again to the dark. She grabbed the torn piece of chemise and lay Sabine out to be examined. The bleeding had worsened. As she kneeled her knees sank into the slurry of blood and dirt. She must stop the flow of blood, no matter the risk.

The light in the passageway flickered out and darkness enveloped them. Jonas screamed, Sarah moaned. Maggie could not see her own hand in front of her, let alone Sabine. Down the passageway a guttural scream pierced the silence. Ian? Pray God it was not.

The darkness wrapped around her like a shroud. Panic overtook her, and she yearned to join her voice with that of Jonas and Sarah. Only Sabine was silent; perhaps she had already died. No.

Maggie felt the ground beneath her, and her hand dripped with blood. She knew what must be done; it was the only way to stop the bleeding. Her right arm hung limp at her side, her shoulder throbbed with pain. She tasted blood, metallic in her mouth. The screams from the next cell continued, and the acrid odor of urine filled the air as Jonas gave in to his fear.

Maggie took a deep breath and prayed for strength, for the easing of pain, only long enough, please God, for her to help Sabine. She lifted up her skirt, and did the only thing possible. She thrust her fist up her birthing passage, at the same time pushing on her womb, to stop the bleeding.

For what seemed like hours, she held herself still, feeling her own consciousness waver as the pain in her shoulder worsened. Sabine stiffened and went limp. She must have fainted. Maggie dared not remove her hand, for she had no way of knowing if her bleeding had lessened. Her ears rang, and she began to crumple with a tingling weakness. "Sabine, I am sorry," she whispered.

Suddenly, Maggie felt upon her arms cool hands like her mother's, like God, lifting her, murmuring, "All is well, all will be well, and all manner of things will be well."

Hands laid a blessing upon her head as she continued to stanch Sabine's bleeding and felt the nun's strength flow into her. And then the woman was gone, but her power remained.

Eventually, Maggie began to feel the pulsing of blood in Sabine's womb slow. When she gently removed her hand, the bleeding had all but stopped. But for how long? Poor Sabine. Out of necessity, Maggie had caused more suffering for her, and her whimpers stabbed like a knife in her side. She felt the absence of the holy woman as acutely as a babe yearns for its mother.

Chapter Twenty-Six

The echo of chants and words and melodies slammed against Ian's head. The back of his eyes blistered fire. Every pore shrieked in agony, for the sirens' songs had shattered into shards and cut him. If he moved his eyes at all, the fragments exploded in the darkness, blinding, breaking him, piece by piece. And he knew not how he came here, in this place of shadows. Where was Maggie's steady grey gaze, her calm regard? He bore the lava flow of blood in his veins, as he had seen, from the cone-shaped mountain on those Islands, the breath, the ragged fragments of fire seething through his lungs. He closed his eyes, but could not mend the shattered pieces. He was a shard and not human anymore.

"Is he dead?" A voice in splinters reached his ears.

"No, I saw the poor bastard breathe."

He lifted his head, impaled upon himself and could only scream.

"Easy now, chap."

With great effort. "Where am I?"

A laugh. "Where do you think you are, you poor sot?"

No answer from him.

"You're in King's Harbour gaol."

He lay for hours in fragments of shame and madness and opened his soul to it, when from the depths appeared his Maggie's face, grey eyes wide with shock. He smelled the fear on her. He must find her.

A sepia-colored light filled the room. Rough, gnarled hands soothed his brow. At first, excruciating, tormenting touch, sending splinters slicing into his body.

Then, soothing words, a sip of liquid, another sip, the low, ancient voice, hissing, "Drink, you are needed. We must go." She spoke in foreign words, but he understood them somehow.

After a while, the shards came together as one, and though the pounding still lingered, he came to conscious thought, seeing the old, bent woman kneeling before him, offering her cup, the snake upon her head with yellow eyes, mesmerizing and comforting him, earthy smell of clay dust in his nose. She straightened, bones creaking, held the cup to his lips again and said, rheumy eyes searing, "*Recuerdas*, remember. *Litio. Litio.*"

"We must go." She led him out of the gaol without speaking. He did not know where he was going, only that he must. The drink she gave him, this *litio* mended the fragments, for rational thought had returned. Maggie. Where was she? There was something wrong. The gnarled woman nodded and faded from view. He would find his Maggie.

Lena met him at the door of the Siren Inn. "Where have you been? They have disappeared."

"Who?"

"Lena, Sabine, Sarah. Thank God I have the baby."

"Where is Samuel?"

"He's searching for her now. Ruthie and Sarah's baby are with Joannie."

He climbed the stairs two at a time, ignoring the pounding of his head and the remnants of disharmony and found the room in shambles, and Maggie's midwife bag on the floor. She would never have left it willingly.

"Edward Carter. He has made good on his threat."

She nodded. "I have not seen him, and by now he is usually here with one of his doxies."

"Have you called the constable? Is there any other way out of the inn without being seen?"

"*Ach*, I don't know. I don't think so. It was quiet when Maggie came in, and after she went upstairs to see Sabine, I lay down for a nap with the baby. I did not hear a thing. When I got up, I assumed she had left. It became crowded in here, so I did not check on Sabine, and the baby slept so I did not bring her up to feed. But my husband was about. Would he not have heard?"

Ian scanned the room. There was a scuff mark and blood on the wood near the paneling. The stairway! There was a latch in the grooves of the wood. He lifted it, and a rush of cold air met him.

"Lena, alert the constable."

He descended the secret stairway. He had not been able to keep her safe but would do his best to deliver her.

Chapter Twenty-Seven

Edward Carter kicked Maggie's boot. "Wake up, bitch. I'm bored."

The lantern cast spectral shadows upon his face. He had not bothered to shut the door.

She felt Sabine and was relieved to find her breathing regular. The cold had seeped through her bones; she did not know how much longer the two women could withstand it.

"Did you hear me, whore?" He kicked her again and jerked her to her feet, causing Sabine to slump onto the cold floor.

Maggie held the sharp rock in her closed fist as he put her arm behind her back again, sparks of pain turning her vision red.

"It is exceedingly dull down here. So I thought I might chat with you a while." He grabbed her chin and squeezed the swollen part of her jaw, laughing as she winced, then kissed her roughly, thrusting his tongue so far into her she could not breathe.

He dragged her across the cell by her chin and slammed her up against the wall. "You could not keep your mouth closed, could you? You had to ask questions. I warned you, did I not?"

"Why," she croaked through his fingers. "Why would you kill helpless women when all they try to do is bring forth life?"

"I do it because it is easy and lucrative, and I am providing a service, to the betterment of medical science. So easy, easy in London and easy here: deliver a few babies without incidence with my wonder herbs, then keep an eye out for the weak ones, be solicitous and caring."

He released her arms and ground his groin into her, hands rough on her breasts. "Then when they deliver, perhaps they were ill, or bleeding, or stricken with a disease like brain fever, for instance. Women die in childbirth all the time. You ought to know that, midwife." He sneered. "What's one more? Mind you, you're not the least bit attractive, but you have the right parts and like I said, I'm bored."

When he bent to lift her skirts, she stabbed him with all her might in the neck with the rock. It drew blood, and he knocked her to the floor. The blood from his neck dripped on her cheek.

He slapped her face. "If you struggle, I'll kill her."

"Who?"

He laughed. "Does it really matter? One whore is the same as another, and I might as well enjoy the blonde's charms before I kill you."

Her vision burst red. Without thought, she rammed her head into his, fire exploding behind her eyes. He swayed, held his head, tugged his breeches down, and slapped her again.

He yanked up her skirts, straddled her. His cock pulsed against her stomach.

He will kill me, after.

She struggled. He thrust his tongue into her mouth again, grunting, until she gagged.

Suddenly, his body was lifted off her.

"Maggie!" Ian had his knees on Carter's stomach, his hands on his neck. "Are you hurt?"

She ran over to Sarah and Sabine and gathered them to her, as the two men rolled on the dirt floor. In the dim light, a flash of silver glinted, and Carter broke away from Ian's grasp and crouched to his feet, wielding a knife and jabbing it toward Ian's stomach. The lantern cast their struggling shadows on the wall, spectral and towering.

In a sudden rush of movement, Ian kicked his leg out and knocked the knife out of Carter's hand and with the sides of his hand jabbed him in the neck. Carter moaned and dropped to the floor. Ian held him down, pounding his fists into his face until he was still and then tied him up with a length of rope from his pocket.

He rushed over and gathered Maggie in his arms. "You are safe now. Maggie, did he abuse you?" He took inventory of her face and ran his hands over her, grimacing at the injured arm.

She clung to him, the fingers of her good arm digging into his skin. "Where have you been, Ian?" She forced herself to relax her grip. "Never mind, not now. And I am fine, but cold. We must take care of Sabine and Sarah."

Just then, footsteps approached. Samuel and Henry the night soil man burst into the cell.

"The magistrate and his men are coming," Samuel said.

Samuel stood over Edward Carter. He lay on the floor in a fetal position, nose bleeding, one eye already swollen shut. Samuel kicked him once, hard, and gathered Sarah into his arms. She put her arms around him and reassured him she was fine.

"Can you walk?" Ian helped her rise.

"Yes, of course," she said. "Help Sabine."

He scooped her unconscious body into his arms.

"What about Jonas?" Maggie said.

"Leave him here for the magistrate," Samuel said gruffly. "It is all he deserves."

Sarah, her voice muffled against Samuel's neck, said, "Jonas buried me. But...he dug me up, as well."

With the hysterics borne of the cold, shock and exhaustion, Maggie began to laugh.

"Maggie."

One word uttered by Ian and an assurance of comfort swept over her like an island zephyr. She came to herself.

Henry stood over Carter. "Get them out of here. I will wait for the magistrate and his men." He grinned savagely. "He may be missing some teeth when he returns."

They made haste down the passageway and stepped over the keeper's body. He was bound with rope and unconscious. She could not help a shiver of satisfaction at the sight. Progress was slow as the men climbed the narrow staircase sideways, Sabine and Sarah in their arms.

Ian and Maggie made it back to the Siren Inn and soon had Sabine tucked into bed. Maggie was relieved to find her bleeding had abated completely and knew it was not from her ministrations alone. As she and Ian made their way home, she heard the holy nun's words, and with thankfulness and joy, leaned against him as the words warmed her chilled skin.

"All is well, and all manner of things will be well."

Chapter Twenty-Eight

Once home, Ian sat Maggie upon the settee and gently removed her clothes. She could not control her shivering, and he soon had her drinking a strong cup of tea laced with brandy while he brought the bathtub in. The warm liquid soothed her throat and washed the horrid taste of Edward Carter from her mouth.

She shivered less from cold and more from shock as the realization hit her full force. She would have died if not for Ian and Samuel. Ian moved quickly to and from the tub with hot water from the fire, but his eyes never left her for long.

"We will bind up your arm after your bath. I will not lie to you, Maggie. It will swell and you will be in pain for a few weeks."

He held her head in his hands, kissed her forehead, hands and gazed at her. He helped her into the tub; she felt stiff and sore in every muscle and very weak.

He rubbed a linen handkerchief with rose-perfumed soap. "Close your eyes and I will wash you, sweeting. I will put you to bed, and then I will tell you what happened to me, so you might know what you are up against, so you can make a choice."

Too tired to speak, she laid her head back and let Ian minister to her with profound gentleness. The hot water worked to soak the grime, fear, and the stench of Edward Carter's hatred from her. Ian placed a lavender-scented cloth upon her swollen and battered face and washed her body with care, paying special attention to her legs and feet, massaging them gently. He dried her and bandaged her shoulder, put a nightgown on her.

He helped her upstairs to bed and settled her with another cup of tea and some potato soup. Warm at last, she could not keep her eyes open. He lay down as well and gathered her in his arms, laid her head upon his chest. With the dawn light seeping in through the window, they slept.

****

Maggie awoke much later, her heart beating heavily like Samuel's hammer, and looked around, disoriented. Then she felt Ian's arm around her, and at her movement he said, "How are you feeling?"

She moaned upon shifting positions. "Oh, I am sore. I can only imagine how Sabine and Sarah must feel, weak as they were to begin with."

"Here, sit up and I will bring us some breakfast, with a bit of whisky in our tea." He kissed her hand and went downstairs.

They ate thick slices of bread and potato soup, and as she sipped the tea, he began. "Maggie, I am damaged."

There were hollows below his eyes as dark as the caves; his eyes were red and seemed old beyond the grave.

"I am sorry I was not there to keep you safe. I was trying to protect you, Maggie, by leaving. For I would not willingly cause you pain and knew that I would, if I stayed."

"Ian." She reached out a hand to touch him.

He rose and paced across the room. "You must

hear it all, so you can decide if this is the life you want. I would not want you to suffer, not for a moment, and look at what has already happened! It is because of my association with Edward Carter—Phillip White—that you were captured."

"Ian, I am fine."

"I would have you know, Maggie, how bad my affliction is." He sat upon the bed and took her hands.

She would give anything to take the anguish from his face. "It doesn't matter. We will face your infirmity together. I want you here, to live with me and love me, to have your children." To have his children, yes! The realization brought warmth to her face but was soon cooled by the agonized look on his.

He sat beside her again. "Listen to me, Maggie. I am flawed, and I cannot control it. I have tried." He put his head in his hands. "Oh God, I have tried."

"We are all flawed, Ian."

"No. My sleeplessness is only the beginning. I feel the change in my blood, the pulse of music beating through me that can't be stilled. Every pore is alive, I feel...everything. My skin tingles with awareness; I see colors so bright, so acute. And I hear the music of life around me. When these...fits are upon me, the music comes crashing like a storm, and it is frightening. And so beautiful. I burn with the passion to write it down, record it, catch it and if only I can do that, the answer to life's mysteries would be mine, and I feel a sense of wonder and desire so profound. If only I can capture it, everything would be as it should be."

He paused, squeezed her fingers, and exhaled shakily. "But then, I break inside, and the music becomes shards, broken pieces that pierce and destroy me, and I cannot control it, Maggie. Eventually, and I never know when, I come to myself again, with a sadness so profound, as if I am in a pit and cannot climb out."

"Oh, Ian." She longed to touch him.

"No treatments or potions, nor drink have helped me."

"Ian, it is all right. I am strong."

He lowered his head, and she strained to hear the rest.

He then took her face in his hands, eyes searching hers. "Yesterday, when I knew my affliction was upon me, I thought I would go, so I would not subject you to it and cause you shame."

He told her of his unraveling and the time in gaol yesterday. She kissed him, to show the tenderness that hammered in her heart, with her eyes willed him to believe her. "You are mine, Ian. What you are...is. We will do what we must do to be together. I will care for you, you will care for me, and sometimes it will not be good. But I cannot live without you now, now that I know what it is to be alive. For you are life to me, you are my respite and my escape. I am not afraid of you or your affliction. For I love you and I will take the pain with the joy, whenever it comes."

His body loosened with relief, but he warned, "You do not realize. It will not be easy."

"When has life ever been easy?"

He laid his forehead upon hers and caressed her hair. "Oh Maggie, I love you so."

Their bodies met in tenderness and passion, her fingers trailed over his face as if she could take from him every pain. She looked into his eyes and with her body urged him to know her acceptance of him. With her fingers she traced his pain and his strength. With labored breath and skin on fire, she begged him sink into her softness.

Maggie kissed the hard plane of his chest and rubbed her breasts against his rough-haired chest, tasting him, settling herself upon his member and sighing as she took him in, feeling his hard strength and his fierceness and her tenderness turned fierce too and their cries blended with the power of possession. They lay entwined, his member throbbing within her, and drifted off into a dreamless sleep.

Later, he examined the swelling in her arm and administered a draught for pain. He told her of the old woman, this Ixchel, that she had taken him out and led him to her. He jumped from the bed.

"What is wrong?"

"She gave me something to drink, and it calmed me. I came to my senses, Maggie! And then I was able to save you. Oh merciful Jesus."

"I don't understand," she cried.

He closed his eyes. "I was still so shattered then. I remember that she said, '*recuerdo*,' which means, 'remember' in the language of New Spain. And she said, '*litio*.'"

He clattered downstairs, two steps at a time. Moments later, he ran back up the stairs. "It is the chemical element, lithium. It can be found in mineral springs. We can find it. We will figure out a way to make this, Maggie."

She nodded, heart throbbing in her throat. Ixchel had given them a gift. They would find this lithium.

"Mayhap," he said, "I can take this, to alleviate my

symptoms. Oh Maggie. She as much as told me it was possible. I know it. She said, '*recuerdas*'—'remember.'"

They touched each other again, in joy and hope for a future together.

****

Later that afternoon, after a bit more sleep, they walked over to the Siren Inn to check on Sabine and found her sitting up in bed, spooning in soup with a shaky hand. Her eyes grew big. Maggie remembered her face looked quite a sight, despite Ian's tender ministrations.

Ian questioned Sabine. She nodded, blushed, and spoke.

He interpreted. "She is feeling better and has not bled more than is normal after a birth. She said Lena has invited her to live with them, and she is moving into their quarters downstairs today. She will work for them when she is recovered."

Maggie smiled at her. "Someone is going to have to teach her the King's English."

"Maybe Ruthie," Ian said. "She seems to have a knack for it."

Lena brought the baby up for her to feed just then, and embraced Maggie. "*Mein Gott*! Your face looks horrible. I made strudel. Come down and have a slice and coffee, too." She patted Ian's cheek before she left.

Maggie quickly examined the girl and was relieved to find the rather brutal treatment of her did not have lasting effects, although she would be sore for some time to come. She bent to kiss her forehead.

A short time later they sat around the table with Lena and her husband, Josef. The hot coffee felt heavenly on her injured throat, and the apple pastry tasted delicious. Lena told them about the constable's questioning of Edward Carter.

"I heard it took a while to hear Carter's full confession," she said. "They could not understand him well, for his teeth had been pulled, every last one."

Maggie nodded. Henry. "No less than what he deserved."

"Someone rode to Hastings to question people. It is expected more evidence will have been gathered. He and the other bastard will be taken to London tomorrow, to await their sentences, probably hanging."

"What of Jonas?"

"He is off to London as well. He could not confess fast enough," Josef said.

"God have mercy on their souls," Ian said.

Lena looked between Maggie and Ian, smiling and nodding. "It is as it should be, with the two of you."

Maggie nodded. "And it will be, no matter what befalls us."

She rose and wrapped a huge piece of strudel into a linen napkin. "Enjoy your strudel." She laughed and winked. "And your knockwurst, too."

Shortly thereafter, she and Ian found Sarah and Samuel sitting at the table, his arm around her, and Ruthie rocking with the baby.

Ruthie cried, "Aunt Maggie, your face! Does it hurt? I was so frightened when you and Mama disappeared."

Maggie kneeled stiffly and embraced her. "Ruthie, all is well. They have caught and will punish those men. We will always keep you safe, you and your sister."

"She's right, my dear," Sarah said.

Maggie took a good look at Sarah now. She seemed herself again. They gazed at one another with understanding and awareness of what they had shared. She had her sister back in earnest.

Samuel cleared his throat. "I trust that you are well, Maggie?"

She nodded. "You have no cause for fear or doubt, Samuel."

Nevertheless, he gave Ian the gimlet eye.

A bit later, Ian and Maggie left them to their peaceful reverie and fought the Channel wind to their home. The cold, moist air felt good on her sore face, and Ian's arm around her shoulders shielded her against the night.

They stood at their doorway and gazed at the moon over the tide.

She laid her hand on the side of his face. "I was empty without you. You have delivered me into life, my Ian, as surely as I deliver life to the babes."

He smiled. "We will give each other life."

She pressed against him to feel his bright pulse beating and gave herself up to the pull of the moon and her heart's desire.

A word about the author...

Jennifer Taylor spent her childhood running wild on an Idaho mountainside. Although she's lived across the U.S., she's still an Idahoan at heart and a notorious potato pusher. She has a degree in Human Services and has been a roofer, a hoofer, a computer data entry operator, and a stay-at-home mom.

She's dreamt of writing historical romances since reading *Wuthering Heights* at the tender age of twelve, and is now living her dream of writing love stories set in eighteenth-century England. She feverishly lobbies for the return of breeches and would love to see her husband of thirty-four years in a pair.

Jennifer lives in rural Florida with her husband and enjoys the comings and goings of their three grown children and three grandchildren.

She can be reached at:

jenntaylor888@gmail.com

Visit her website:

www.jennifertaylorwrites.com

www.ingramcontent.com/pod-product-compliance
Lightning Source LLC
Chambersburg PA
CBHW060526260626
47161CB00003B/779